Dangerous Secrets

Jenna Gunn

About This Book

The former SEAL's new mission has a serious perk—a fake date with a beautiful stranger. Unraveling the lies surrounding her life? That's where things get lethally dangerous.

Justin 'Dozer' Roark didn't expect to need a fake date for his first civilian security mission. He would quickly flip you off if you told him he'd fall for the cocktail waitress he paid to help him.

He wasn't in the market for love. Ever. His heart was locked down behind a shield of dark emotional scars from his past.

When McKenzie Rush's father died in an accident, her life was shattered. Desperation landed her far from Alaska and thrust her into an abuser's hands.

Climbing out of his cruel web and getting back to life as a homesteader seemed impossible.

The second Dozer realizes the dire situation McKenzie's in, his mission focus shifts to doing anything he can to keep her safe. That means uncovering the dangerous secrets that surround her, and if he gets his way, showing her that love isn't always based on lies.

Cover Photo Model: Derek Newborn
Instagram: @dnewborn
FB: Derek Newborn

Photographer: Wilfredo Ramos
IG: @abovebeyondimaging
FB:Above & Beyond Imaging

Cover Designer : Book Sense Designs
FB: @BookSenseDesigns

Chapter One

DOZER

This is one of those moments where you realize life is never going to be the same.

Welcome to Civilian Life 101 where shit gets weird fast and I'm about to pay a woman to take off her clothes for me.

With a grin, I brace myself as the line rings through my truck's stereo. This is a helluva way to reconnect with a friend from the past.

Please let this work. If Beth says yes, then at least I won't be hiring a stranger. Not that I give a fuck about getting naked in front of a stranger, but I'm zero percent keen on taking someone that I don't know on a sensitive mission.

Call me Type-Fucking-A. But in the SEALs we knew who we were working with and could rely on them to have our back.

After a few rings, a cheery voice answers, "Hello there, frogman."

Whew. Got an answer. This is a good start. My grin gets wider when I reply, "Beth, it's damned good to hear your voice."

"You in town?"

"Sort of. Not for long. Look, I need a favor."

"Oh yeah?" she asks, but I can tell she's distracted. Something is clacking in the background.

"You free to help me with a civilian security job? I need a date to go with me to a resort for a few hours, maybe a day or two tops."

There's a heavy sigh. "Dozer, you know I can't just up and go wherever. I've got a business now."

"Right."

Did I know that? It's been a *long* time since we talked.

Beth was the girl next door a while ago, the one I never hooked up with because we decided it would ruin a perfectly good friendship. She told me she liked me and I always liked her. She was funny and laid back and we had plenty of fun without having sex in the mix.

"This pays." I dangle a carrot and hope she bites.

"A date that pays? That doesn't sound sketchy at all," she says with a laugh.

"It could pay a lot."

"Look, *shug,* as much as money would be nice, I can't just go along with whatever plot you're hatching. I've got customers." Her voice fades, "Chop those strawberries too, please."

"Holy shit, badass. You did it, didn't you?"

"Yeah. I did. I opened my own café," she replies with pride in her voice. Even though I can't see her, that smile hits me through the airwaves.

"Damn. I'm proud of you. I know you always wanted that."

"Thanks, I appreciate you saying that."

After a beat, she says, "Sorry I can't help. Maybe you can use an escort service."

I snort. Even though it has crossed my mind as a last resort.

She laughs. "Okay, since that's off the table, I have an idea. Would you be close to Bay street by the way?"

"Ten minutes out."

"Good, I'll try to keep her here. She's having a latte right now."

My brows go up and hope springs up inside of my chest. "Her?"

"I don't know her name, but I can tell she's... struggling. She's got ghosts in her eyes."

Sighing, Beth's voice drops lower so only I can hear. "I think she needs the money. She works across the road at this horrid strip club. It can't pay well. I've been giving her free meal coupons when I can, which truthfully, I can't believe she accepted. But she has a few times, and she came in this morning for breakfast. So, maybe you can help her."

Key words jump out from Beth's comments.

Money. Check, got it covered.

Ghosts. Check, I can relate. Mine are scary as shit, but not going there now.

Strip club. Maybe the nudist thing won't be a problem.

I knew Beth was a free spirit after catching her nude sunbathing at the apartment complex more than once, so I know she probably wouldn't have much of an issue with accompanying me to a nudist resort.

But other women? Yeah, that could be a dealbreaker. Maybe this chick was the answer to my dilemma.

3

"Don't let her leave. This could work."

Beth grumbles at me, "Okay, bossy. I said I'd try to keep her here, but if she does leave, I'm sure she's just going across the street. She doesn't have a car."

Beth finishes with, "And try not to look too scary when you get here, okay?"

"*Me?*"

"Yes, you big, grump-faced SEAL."

"I'm never grump-faced." Probably a lie, since people tend to scatter when they see me coming.

Beth thinks that's hilarious, apparently. Her laugh is loud. "Right, keep telling yourself that."

"We need to have a conversation about this," I reply sternly before I add, "But not right now, I'm on a tight ass deadline for work."

More banging and clanging in the background, then a machine fires up. Sounds like a lawnmower. Over the noise, she yells, "Copy that. I was hoping you're doing okay. All those crazy missions and all."

"Doing fine. I'm out of the teams now. Working for a private firm."

The lawnmower noise dies and the line goes quiet for a beat. "Hey Doz, just so you know, I've got a guy in my life now. A nice guy."

"Happy for you."

What she's really saying is she met a guy that's not living behind a wall of armor made of regret and pain. When we agreed we'd never hook up, I was sure part of that was because she saw me for who I really am. Fated for barbed-wire fences, not white picket fences. Broken. Damaged goods.

Lightly, she says, "Maybe sometime you'll meet him."

"Yeah, maybe. Take care of yourself, Beth. No more

asshole boyfriends. Any red flags and you kick his carcass to the curb. Call me if you need help."

She laughs. "Right. Thanks again for saving me all those years ago. Ron was such a jerk."

"It was my pleasure. I hated that fucker's smirky grin. I'm hanging up now because I'm about three minutes out."

Café Sunshine is decked out in bright-colored flags, has a huge outdoor dining patio and a vintage Volkswagen Bus that's been turned into a walk-up takeout window. Damn. She went all out.

Eager, I kill the truck engine, jump out, and stride toward the small crowd that's waiting for food.

Beth waves and beams a bright smile in my direction. She holds up one finger, *not the middle one,* before she goes back to helping the next customer.

I lean against the wall, checking out the people, searching for—

Oh, damn. My spine snaps tight.

Fuck. Hello, beautiful.

If that's her...

Beth appears at my elbow and pokes a finger into my ribs. "Stop staring," she hisses violently. "You're definitely going to scare her. Heck, you might scare everyone off and I need the customers."

She grabs my arm and spins me around, but I crane my neck and get a good look at one beautiful blond. "Christ, how old do you think she is?"

"Twenty-one, maybe twenty-two."

My voice sounds ten shades deeper. "How are we doing this?"

"*We?*" screeches Beth.

"Yeah, how are you going to introduce me?"

That earns me a scowl. I chuckle in return. Damn, it's

5

been a long time since the woman looked at me like that. It was usually for keeping her up at night when I'd come in late from some kind of SEAL training and I'd be banging around in the kitchen that backed up to her bedroom in the apartment next door. Course she'd soften up when I invited her in for bacon and eggs.

"I have an idea," she grumbles. "But this is on you, big guy. I'm not responsible for whatever you're up to."

"Lay it on me."

"Come on." She grabs my wrist and pulls me toward the smoothie bar. Less than five minutes later, I'm holding two tall cups. They've got something bright pink inside. "Pink, of course you'd make my drink pink. Aren't there green smoothies?"

Beth's grin is wickedly pleased. "You'll love it. Bursting with flavor. Besides, this is the one she always picks. More importantly, the pink softens that steely exoskeleton you wear around all the time, frogman."

Shaking my head, I turn toward the outdoor dining tables. "We're gonna have a talk. But thanks, seriously, and wish me luck."

She blows me a little kiss, then hustles off to help the line of people ordering from one of her helpers.

I draw a breath. A familiar determination roots in my chest.

I've found my target.

And I never miss.

Go time.

Chapter Two

Candy

How am I getting out of this mess?

The coffee that felt so satisfying in my stomach a moment ago feels like sloshing acid. Ack.

The sun is nice. I should be thankful to have a latte provided by the café owner. But that only reminds me more of the disaster that's now my life.

People are laughing, the smoothie machine is humming, orders being called out, but that all fades around me, and I slip into the sightless stare that I find myself in often.

I was so stupid. I never should have come to California.

When I spin to look for the clock that hangs over the smoothie bar, I nearly tumble backward off the little stool.

I save it at the last second by shooting a hand out and grabbing...

A very muscular thigh.

Of a giant.

Ohmyfreakinggod.

I blurt, "I'm so sorry."

"I'm the one that should be apologizing," a gruff male voice booms from way above me. "Didn't mean to startle you."

I lurch up and find myself standing face-to-chest with a beast-man in a black T-shirt and a pair of nicely worn jeans. Before I look sky high at his face, I find a smoothie under my nose.

"Beth sent this."

"Sorry, what?" I'm still mortified from grabbing his THIGH.

When I finally look up at his eyes, I lurch backward. Lot of lurching going on today. Holy smokes. Talk about penetrating gazes. This guy's got that on a lock. "Uh, Beth, right."

He carefully pushes the cup toward me. "She made too much when she made mine and said to bring it to you."

"Oh." My startled expression softens, I feel my face resuming its normal position, even though my cheeks are burning. "Thanks."

"Can I sit?" he rumbles, and I freeze up. God, who has a voice like that?

"I was just leaving. I can't be late." I might hate my job, but it puts a roof over my head, and I can't afford to be homeless.

The hard brackets around the giant's mouth soften and his mouth transforms from brutal to eye-catching. "Shame, can't you stay for a little longer?"

"I need to get to work."

"Where's that?" he says as he kicks out one of the stools and lowers his body onto it.

Oh. Lord. I always thought the little rainbow-colored stools that Café Sunshine has are cute, but now I find them hilarious.

A laugh bubbles up in my chest. "Maybe you need two of those seats."

"I'm gonna have a talk with Beth, about this and some other stuff," he says with a shake of his head.

The smile he flashes is downright dangerous. Disarming-dangerous. Men like him scare me. Not that I've ever seen one of this particular species.

The tall, dangerous-eyed, ripped species. My hand won't forget for a verrrrry long time what his thigh felt like.

I'm weirdly breathless when I say, "I should go."

"Sit and enjoy your smoothie."

I open my mouth to protest, but he gently grips my wrist in a very warm, very large hand, and pulls me toward one tiny, blue and yellow stool. My brain officially shuts off.

Such a bad idea. Somehow, I manage to eke out, "Five minutes."

Before I realize what's happening, I'm sitting. With him.

Baffled, I ask, "Are you always so persuasive?"

He chuckles, and his eyes glint as they catch the California sunlight. "They call me Dozer."

"I'm not sure I understand."

He laughs this time, it's warm, earthy, and a disastrous combination with his smile. "That's alright, sweetheart."

His luminous dark gray eyes flash toward the serving counter. "We'll see how persuasive I am when I tell Beth she's gotta put some man-sized furniture on her patio."

That's when I realize I'm sipping my smoothie and I'm

actually talking to a perfect stranger beyond asking for their beer order. What the heck?

I should go.

"Those your shoes?" He nods toward the stupid pink and silver platform heels on the ground. They—in all their ridiculous glory—are standard issue for employees at The Pink Palace. They're laying on their sides on the concrete next to the table—I wish they were laying in the trash can.

"Unfortunately."

"Can you walk in those?"

It's my turn to laugh. Then my smile falls off my face. "Barely."

Before last month I'd never even put on heels, much less seven-inch-platform shoes. That kind of sums up how bad of a fish-out-of-water I am working in a club.

He studies me and a shiver races down my spine. I flick my eyes away and stare into my cup, mortified that I've got on my work uniform—a tiny white tank top and a barely butt-covering skirt. I wasn't planning on being at the café long before I went in and started prepping for the lunch rush. If you call five people a rush.

I try to deflect his attention. "Aren't you drinking your drink?"

"Forgot about it."

When I look up, he's not just looking at me, he's leaning an elbow on the table and has practically got me under a microscope. Those eyes burn right into me.

A cold shudder squeezes my lungs. With an inspection like that, people see too much. Things that shouldn't be stirred up.

Dark, painful things.

I must be losing my touch because I'm an expert at

hiding my heartache in plain sight. Watching his face, I ask, "Do you always look at people like that?"

He shifts and picks up his drink, drawing my eyes to the scars on his knuckles. Those aren't the only ones. More are on his corded forearm, and even on his neck.

"My job requires figuring out how people tick and knowing how to respond."

"Well, I get paid to serve drinks. I try not to look at people too closely. I don't really want to engage."

He leans back, takes another drink of his smoothie. "Not bad. What's in this?"

"Strawberries, peaches, coconut—"

"Fuck." He tugs off his black baseball cap and smacks his forehead.

"What's wrong?" I look around because I have no clue what's got him growling out a curse word.

"I'm allergic to coconut."

My eyes nearly fall out of my head. "Didn't you know?"

He shakes his head. "Beth didn't say what she was making, I thought she'd remember."

I scramble off my stool, sending my work shoes skittering. "Do I need to call an ambulance?"

He looks down at himself with a frown. "Why?"

"Because you said you're allergic."

"I just need a Benadryl. Otherwise I'll be sneezing like a wild goat in about twenty minutes. Got any?"

I gather up my things. "Come on. Hurry, there's some at work."

He rises to stand next to me, nearly knocking me over with his sheer size. "You can have the rest of mine."

"I guess so."

Chapter Three

DOZER

I somehow convince the woman—still nameless and barefoot—that it's safer to drive across the four-lane, than to play frogger.

That's when I see something that makes my blood fucking boil.

"Are those handprints on your arm?"

She flinches and turns to look out the side window.

My voice dips low, to that place where it goes when I'm really working up a fucking rage. "Are they?"

Holding the two smoothies keeps her from being able to cover the purple marks that I know she wants to hide.

"Who did that?"

"It's nothing."

I slam my truck into Park in the lot in front of The Pink Palace. "Bullshit. No man should be hurting you."

She pushes a cup my way. "Let's get you that allergy medicine."

"Wait a minute. We're not done."

She flicks her eyes toward me. Fucking, fuck. The woman's got the prettiest eyes I've ever seen and that vulnerable look that just flashed through them sends me into a feeding frenzy.

"Who?"

"Some nobody."

As I clench my jaws, I watch the micro-movements around her eyes. She's holding back. That's not the whole story.

"Let's go. I don't want you sneezing all over me."

"I'm fine," I snap. "But you're not."

"They're bruises, Dozer," she retorts, using my nickname, the one I only mentioned once, but she remembered. "They'll go away."

I take the cup before she dumps it on me, but when she reaches for the door, I growl, "I'm coming around to help you out."

That gets me a weird scrunch of her brows.

Before she can ask, I say, "Because that's what gentlemen do. They don't fucking grab women by the arm."

Her expression is so surprised I wonder if anyone has ever opened a door for her.

When I stride around and offer her my hand, she accepts it warily.

"I need to put my shoes on. I would never walk around in there barefoot."

It takes a minute, but she latches on those ankle-breakers while I watch her legs. Holy fuck. Talk about some stems.

And the thirst trap doesn't stop there. This woman has miles of curvy, strong legs that draw up into narrow hips, that kick out into a full, round ass. Big creamy tits are tucked into a tiny white tank top. That with her pale skin, ethereal shimmering hair, and eyes like some mystical creature—the total package looks like a sexed-up woodland fairy.

When she's done, she's seven inches taller and the top of her head now comes close to the bottom of my chin.

"Okay." She takes one of the smoothie cups from my hand.

Not okay. Very not okay. I'm not sure I can go to a nudist resort with her for a mission because I'm gonna have a rocket in my pocket. Only, there won't be any pockets.

She heads off, more like teeters, toward a run-down building that's got a giant pink shoe on the roof.

Beth is right, this place looks like it's one breath away from the morgue. But hopefully this lead will get me what I need.

A faded pink door marks the entrance. A threshold to me doing something that's got me shaking my head. While I knew this week was bringing a lot of firsts, new job and all, I didn't think it would be *this*.

The pepto-colored door creaks when it swings inward. Cool air rushes outward. With a loud thunk it closes behind us and cuts off the daylight.

The odor of knockoff perfume and some kind of oil hangs like a noxious cloud as I walk further inside. It's been an eon since I stepped foot in this kind of place, but the smell is the same.

The woman heads off to the bar, presumably to get some allergy medicine for me.

With a quick sweep, I take in the cheap titty bar. Poles. Cages. A floor that's sticky with who knows what. Sagging drop ceiling tiles make my skin crawl.

Probably full of rat's nests up there. I shudder and scratch at my neck. *Christ.*

My mind goes to one of my missions.

I'm doing a raid in some-fucking-stan, enemies are hiding in a condemned building. As we breach the location, I notice the rotten on the floor and the ceiling sagging, but we need to find our targets. As I enter a dark room, the ceiling gives out and a dozen screeching, furry nightmares fall on my shoulders. I shake and do a weird dance to get the fuckers off me.

Thank the good lord I have on body armor and none of those wiggling bastards get down my shirt.

I shake my head and come back to the here and now. Flashbacks are a bitch.

I fight the urge to wretch, and finish my visual sweep of the barroom. A sleaziness hovers in the space that no exhaust fan on Earth could ever get rid of.

This armpit has to be on the bottom of the list of San Diego's strip clubs. But that suits the assignment. Where there's desperation you find people who will do weird shit for money.

Inhaling deeply, I catalog the odors of civie life. The cacophony of odors coats my tongue like rancid toothpaste.

The only thing missing right now in this place is the stench of sweaty, overweight men and beer breath.

"Welcome to the Palace."

As I pull up to one of the tall tables near the bar, I find the source of the voice through the flashing lights. A bacon-colored woman is on the stage. She gives me a teasing wave —a flick of her two-inch glow-in-the-dark fingernails.

Fake from the tip of her head down. She's spray-tanned, has fire-engine red hair, not the kind that comes from genetics, and looks way too excited to see me.

A pair of acid green pasties covers her nips and a matching green string runs between her muscular butt cheeks. Everything about the dancer is sinew and corded muscles—beef jerky on a human skeleton.

I'm not the least bit interested in her. Plain and simple —I don't like fake anything on my women.

Give me curves—the real kind that are soft beneath my hands and pliant under me in the dark, hot hours of the night.

Like a small blond with crystalline eyes and a rack built for sin.

Not that my mission involves sex. I never mix work and pleasure. *Nothing* fucks up your head faster.

Seen it. Never going there.

The dancer circles the pole and swings her eyes my way again, trying to squeeze a few bucks out of me with a come-hither pout of her glossed up bottom lip.

She's high. Stoned. Or something. The last thing I need for this operation is a tweaker or a stoner.

As if on cue, a flicker of movement draws my attention to the end of the bar. And... there's my girl.

Interestingly, she's assessing me back now. Pale jade eyes study me. For a beat, I almost grin because I feel like she's in predator mode too.

Or wary as fuck, at least.

But not scared-rabbit wary. This is a cunning fox kind of wary. But her inspection of me isn't what I'd call savvy.

It's clunky and unpracticed.

For a beat, we check each other out, and I consider how I'm going to convey that she's not prey. I'm not here to eat the girl. I just need her to come with me and ditch her clothes for a few hours.

As if I've telegraphed that thought right into her brain, her body tenses. She jerks those gut-punching eyes off of my face.

An unsteady motion in her hand makes my attention focus more, sharpening in a way that I only do when I'm in the field with my team.

It's time to get down to business.

Chapter Four

Candy

"Candy! Don't take any damned orders for fries. We're out. Bosshole gets a big, fat F. That moron left all kinds of things off the resupply, gonna be a fucking nightmare."

I barely hear Alec, the chef, because my marrow is still quaking from the K.O. punch I just took.

The fact that a stranger got me to talk to him, to get in his truck, and to let him follow me to work. It's a gigantic freaking mystery to me.

Now, I've got the most intense eyes I've ever seen locked on me like two rifle scopes.

"Sure," I call back, not bothering to turn my head toward Alec, but I barely get the word out because my breath feels lacking as I shift on my heels, trying to get my balance.

Who does this guy think he is, staring at me like that?

Too bad Miranda isn't working. She thrives on the intense ones. Not me.

But I'm the fool that talked to him.

Now I need to shake him because it feels like his big frame is taking up too much space. That was before he turned his eyes on me again. Now it feels like he IS the space.

Yikes. My throat aches from holding onto the little oxygen I can find. But he's breathing just fine—a steady, deep rhythm—so I know this place didn't turn into a vacuum.

Nope, that's on me alone. Knocked back by a flick of those dark gray hammers.

Forcing my ribs to work, I straighten my spine.

He's totally out of place. Bob's clients are the shady, the saggy, and the rotten-mouthed kind that forget to leave tips. On purpose.

Dozer's got clean clothes and clean hair, and a body that's hard all over.

I kick myself for noticing.

Stupid hormones.

With the allergy medicine from the first-aid box clutched in my hand, I start toward him. As I go, I grab a cup of water and the plastic serving tray which I've renamed the 'surviving tray.'

The other girls taught me to use it as a shield-slash-weapon when I started at the club, so I balance it in front of me and start to close the distance between us. But every step I take makes my spine tingle.

A shiver grates down my back. I try to settle my nerves. *Not like he's going to do anything bad here.*

But he could...

"Take one of these. Can I get you anything else?"

A look crosses his face that has me taking a precarious step back on my break-neck heels.

You—he practically roars without even opening his mouth.

My body is suddenly a deadly mixture of fire and ice.

You. His eyes repeat as they scorch me. Who knew gray eyes could be so incinerating?

I swear I'd turn and run if I wasn't in danger of breaking my legs on these stupid shoes. That is if I could get a single cell in my body to respond to my command.

Oh, god.

I should have stayed in bed this morning, because no 'training' by the other girls has prepared me for this moment.

The moment when I know life has gone from utter chaos to something much more dangerous.

Chapter Five

DOZER

"Can I get you anything else?"

You.

In my bed. Right. Fucking. Now.

My brain's firing on half its cylinders, but it's capable of flashing a warning. *Shut the fuck up, Doz.*

My voice sounds rough as a washboard road when I finally speak again. "Something from the tap."

The woman's slender blond eyebrows rise, changing the shape of her doe eyes for a second. "You don't want to pick?"

Fuck yeah, I want to pick.

I pick you.

I shake my head. Her gaze jumps to my arm as I lean back and hook my elbow over the stool's back. She swallows quickly and meets my gaze again with that wary, straight on assessment.

My gut tightens against that weird falling sensation again. Man. Not good. You're not bedding this woman. *You're working. You're working...*

Yet, I can't pull my eyes away. It's like the sun has never touched this woman's pale skin. The veins will show through at all her pulse points. I suppress a grin as I think about licking her like she's an ice cream.

Her lack of knowledge makes me want to smile. Her nerves are so tight she's about to shatter into a million slivers of ice.

Almost criminal that I'm going to take advantage of her nerves, but I am.

I tip my chin toward the bar. "Just pull one of those levers, sweetheart. Whatever comes out is fine. I promise."

I add, "I trust you. You look like you can handle it."

She blinks, then looks over her shoulder as if someone else would be able to do the job better. "O-okay, but I'm new. Plus, I don't drink, although maybe I should start. Anyway, I'm definitely the wrong person to pick your beer."

Her voice sets loose a lightning bolt of excitement across my skin.

"I'm not picky."

About beer that is. My guns and women, that's a whole different story.

"Maybe you should be," she murmurs, as she pushes back her hair, and if I wasn't trained in body language, I'd have missed the tremor. Only, she rallies and looks me right in the eyes and says, "You'll still have to pay, even if you don't like it."

I take out a twenty. "You can hold this if it makes you feel better."

Her eyes flash to the money, then she takes the bill, careful not to touch me, and folds it into her palm, but she doesn't leave, even when she says, "You shouldn't drink with that medicine."

"I'm fine. No sneezing. I don't think I drank enough to affect me. I'll just have a beer to wash it down and dilute it."

She blinks at me with disbelief. "I'll be back." But she doesn't budge.

Christ, I'm working, I scold myself. As I clear my throat, and sound a lot like I've inhaled a boulder. Not because I drank coconut. Because of her. She's got my briefs twisted in a damned knot.

For a second, we just stare at each other.

Up close, the woman is not just pretty, she's devastating. From the curves, the muscles in her legs, to the nutmeg lashes that rim those big, otherworldly eyes.

I could write a whole fucking story about those eyes. The green color is streaked with darker shades of ink and obsidian that are only visible when you're right next to her. But her irises are translucent in a way that catches light and mesmerizes me.

I get a distinct falling feeling, like I've stepped out of an airplane.

Man overboard.

Wait. That's when you're on ship, idiot.

Man without a parachute. Yeah, that's more what this feels like.

The cool air from a vent above me crackles over my skin, fighting the heat that's growing in my veins.

I'm a second away from reaching out to touch her to see if she's real.

After a beat of looking at me through narrowed lashes,

23

she turns and walks away, clinging to that tray and teetering to find her balance.

Whoever this woman is, she's not only new at working at The Pink Palace. This girl is as clumsy as a new fawn in her silver and pink stilettos.

I find that oddly endearing.

Beth was right. She's gotta get out of this fucking place.

As she moves between the tables, the waterfall of pale blond hair slides over her shoulder. It reflects the pink and blue lights like some mystical substance, creating a mesmerizing display. I've never seen anyone like her and I've seen a helluva lot.

Something about the combination of wary, innocent, and confident captivates me. With that unreal beauty, this woman whips my brain to predatory froth.

To say I'm fixated is a stupid and pathetic explanation for how I feel. I'm locked on.

This might be one of those missions that's doomed from the start.

Fucking fuck.

Chapter Six

DOZER

Elbow on the table, I plot how to move from chatting over a smoothie, to ordering a beer, to laying out the real ask.

Not *the* ask I'd like to ask—come home with me—but the ask that's for WORK. Because this girl is not at all what you expect to find when you come to a place like this.

She's got the habit of contracting in on herself to hide her tits, when I expected her to shove those babies high and saunter over to me and talk me out of a shitload of money for drinks.

That little movement adds another layer to the woman's story. That's the way it is when you watch someone for the hallmark body cues that are a window to their emotions.

They add together, one by one, to paint a picture that no one can lie their way out of.

In the SEALs, my unofficial specialty was gathering intel by observing human behavior. Amongst other things— mainly blowing shit up and getting out of dicey situations. But my fascination for the human mind should make picking apart the little blond a cakewalk.

Within five seconds I knew that her nervous tell is pushing her hair back and touching the tiny star-shaped charm laying at the base of her slender throat.

Her body language is laced with unease. She's strong, but there's an undercurrent of fear. Like a dark, cold current running in the bottom of a river. It's there, undeniably changing her behavior.

Something fucked up is going on here.

Whoever this young woman is, she doesn't want to be here. Her body language is glaring, even though she's got a stiff backbone. Plowing through. Doing something she hates.

But that doesn't stop my mouth from getting dryer. She's spectacular.

Innocent-but-not hot.

I-see-you-and-return-the-inspection hot.

Gonna-cause-a-big-headache hot.

Okay, so maybe I won't kill Mako after all for hooking me up with this job.

She's the one.

Everything lines up for my needs. The cash I'm going to offer her will be enough to get her out of this shitty fucking bar until she can do something she wants to be doing.

So she doesn't even think about working her way up to dancing. I cast my eyes toward the stage. The pole girl shows me her goods, and I mean *all* of her goods—with an upside down split. I get a straight on view of the light sparking off her pasties and the green sting running through her labia.

My libido yawns.

I've got eyes for one woman right now, though I force myself not to watch her draw the beer.

It's hard. I want to know more about her.

She's on her way back to me two minutes later. And this time her approach is faster. She swoops in, clipping quickly on her heels. I find my eyes locked again on her mouth. Next to eyes, lips are the most telling feature on a face.

Christ. Those babies look soft as fucking pillows and make me want to smash my own against them. But I get hung up on the contour of her pout, the pale peach color, and almost miss that she's pinching the bottom one with her teeth.

There's a tall glass of burlap-colored beer on the serving tray this time. Keeping her distance, she quickly places the sweating glass on the table and pushes it toward me.

"Here's your drink. It's a Snowdrift Ale, whatever that means. I can say however that it's cold and wet at least."

My mind goes to a place that I'd gladly make wet, only there would be nothing cold about it. We'd make fire.

Burn beds.

Scorch the sheets.

Set off smoke alarms.

"Well, some say that being wet is what matters the most," I reply with a wink.

It goes over her head for a beat, then she goes for a full eye roll. "Points for originality. I haven't heard that one yet. I might argue that size matters more."

Then I'm your man, sweetheart.

I burst out laughing. "Touché."

She grins, but won't look me in the eye, another fact I find interesting. So, she can sling the shit, but she's embarrassed about what she said.

"You hear a lot of barbarian crap, I'm sure."

She chuckles softly and the humor from a moment ago disappears off her face. "You have no idea. Let's just say the vocabulary of the patrons is a few thousand watts shy of bright and interesting."

I'm leaning on my elbow, taking her in. No wonder she gets caveman comments. She should be registered as a WMD with the primary target being male brain cells.

"Sure that gets old."

"I haven't worked here long, and it's as old as a scratched up forty-five."

"You like music?" I ask quickly, before I even think about it.

She glances at my eyes, then looks back at the stage. "Some kinds. Mostly older stuff. Rock and heavy metal, believe it or not."

Well. Fuck.

Ever had sex to heavy metal? I can vouch for it.

"Ditto." I take a drink off the beer. It's not half bad, or maybe it's the company.

"Not this kind of music, truthfully," I add as the song changes to something pop-40ish, and the beat vibrates the floor. Together, we watch the woman on the pole, and I wonder what she's thinking as Rowdy Red shakes her ass in my direction. But I get my answer when her cheeks start to burn pink and she mutters, "Gotta go."

This girl is so far out of her element in The Pink Palace that she might as well be walking around on Mars. This is the last place she wants to be.

A major point in my favor.

Expecting a hasty retreat, I speak before she can leave. "Food any good?"

With a little tip of her chin, she replies, "People tell me the BLT is good."

"Haven't tried it?"

A quick negative sends her hair falling around her shoulder like shimmering strands of the finest silk. "Nope. I am not allowed to eat while I'm working."

I skim her frame again. She's got curves, but she's not eating enough. I've seen that look on my little sister when she's too damned stressed to take care of herself. The little hollows under the eyes are the first giveaway.

"I'll take two."

Her brows go up for a second time, then back down. "Sure. They're kind of big, but—"

"So am I," I finish for her. "Size appropriate."

That makes her brows go up lightning fast.

Again, she teeters off with her short, black skirt hugging the curves of her ass and the fall of her hair skimming along her waist.

The vision is seared into my brain. Wow. But she's laughing as she walks away this time.

Only I'm not. Wasn't expecting to be hit in the gut like that. And just like that, I'm pissed.

I return to staring sightlessly at the stage as the dancer swings around the pole, contemplating what brought the blond girl to The Pink Palace. And what the hell is this pull she has on me. Because it feels like a fucking siren song. Alluring. Irresistible.

But I never, ever, fucking ever, mix sex and business.

Chapter Seven

Candy

I hide out by the kitchen window while Alec makes the double BLT order. The scents from the kitchen are annoyingly tantalizing. But not as much as the man at table twenty-one.

Making myself busy, I wipe down the bar and the work table behind me for the second time this morning, just to have something to do. My nerves are shot and the day hasn't even begun.

It shocked me to share some laughs with the dark-eyed stranger. He's disarming. A fact that sets off more alarms, truthfully.

My unease about Dozer is growing by leaps and bounds. He's all I can think about. Not in a good way. It's an overwhelming sensation, like a building storm is coming.

Without letting him know, I check him out. He's ripped, and it doesn't look like gym-guy ripped. Not that I know any gym-guys, but I've seen enough magazines to recognize that pumping iron and doing work make different kinds of bodies.

This guy looks like he could hurl people. Not just lift dumbbells.

But as much as his exterior paints a picture, it's the things his eyes are saying that his mouth isn't.

Beyond lust.

He's got some other agenda. That's the one that worries me.

Lust is becoming old hat, sadly. Easy to rebuff after some practice. Not that I like it, or am comfortable, but a few well-placed words and most of the jerks leave me alone to do my job.

I'm stocking the beer cooler when Alec shouts, "Order up!"

Good, the sooner I can feed him, hopefully the quicker Mr. Big Stuff moves on.

As I head to the window to retrieve the sandwiches, I startle. A man is standing by the bar.

Christ. When did he come in?

He holds out a package. Warily, I glance down at the brown envelope. "This is for Bob."

"He's not in right now."

Bob's a scumbag and it's not a far stretch to think he'd be dealing drugs. I don't want my prints on anything. "Just leave it on the bar, I'll put it in his office."

Hopefully, Bob shows up and I don't have to move the brown envelope. If not, I'll put on some of the gloves I use for cleaning and relocate it to his desk.

When the man tosses it on the bar, he sways and looks at me like I'm about to be a meal.

Ick. I grimace before I can hold my face stiff.

With bulging bloodshot eyes, he tracks my movements. I try to push my rising unease away.

Nothing new, I mutter internally.

How wrong I am. If only I knew my day was about to go all sideways.

Chapter Eight

DOZER

A slash of daylight suddenly cuts across the stage. The front door swings closed as a six-foot-tall beer gut on legs waddles through the entryway.

Red-faced and panting, the man shuffles to the bar in beatdown flip flops. Looks like a real winner. I expect him to order something to soothe his obvious alcohol addiction, but he throws a brown package on the bar. Words slurring, he says, "Got a delivery for Bob."

Over the music, I barely hear the woman's reply, but I can read her lips as she says, "Just leave it on the bar, I'll put it in his office."

The man's eyes narrow. His mouth slowly opens. One hand falls down to adjust his junk. Dumbstruck by lust. I know that look. My sister makes hordes of men do the exact same thing. Every damned time, I want to throat punch them.

Hell, I have a few times, if truth be told. Nothing like having a hot sister when all the ranch boys start to feel their oats. Testosterone makes guys do stupid shit. Good thing my brothers and I were there to deal with most of them.

But if you asked she'd say she was pissed that we handled things for her. Nothing makes her angrier than people making it look like she can't manage her own trouble.

So, I've seen plenty of barflies looking at her like the man's looking at the waitress.

Fucking predictable.

His rheumy eyes are glued on her ass as she reaches up to the pass-through window to retrieve my order. It's a stretch. The window's high, so she reaches up, leaning into the counter behind the bar. Her skirt inches higher, revealing the pale, perfect curve of her ass.

My gut clenches again and burn sizzles down to my dick. Fuck. I'm not better than dickhead is.

As soon as the waitress realizes what's happening, she grabs the fabric and cinches it down.

But it's too late. Fuckface is leering at her like she's a piece of cake and he's about to smash his face into it.

Hell. No. Not on my watch. Half a second later, I'm on my feet. Just in time for fuckface to grab her ass when she passes by with the BLTs.

My temper pegs red in a half second flat.

"*Hey!* Jerk!" With a startled cry, the woman lurches away, haphazardly managing the tray with the sandwiches and the heels she's obviously not used to wearing. For a second, it looks like shit's about to really go all to hell.

I snake a hand out, grab her arm and steady her. With

my other hand, I shove the bastard so hard he teeters and falls backward like a rotten tree. A horrendous crash shatters the stank air and rattles the neon light behind the bar. Two barstools tangle with the guy, making a heap of wood, limbs, and curse words.

The music screeches to a stop and the green-pasty girl leaps off the stage, disappearing behind a black curtain like she's expecting gunfire.

"You okay, Miss?" I ask without taking my eyes off the drunk who's trying and failing to sit up in the midst of the barstools.

"Yeah. *Yes.*"

Tipping my chin, I say, "Go ahead to my table while I deal with this."

She takes off with her heels clicking rapidly on the floor. Once she's cleared out, I get back to dealing with this fuck. My fists twist into the front of his sweat-stained polo shirt and I yank the handsy bastard off the ground.

He's still quivering and sputtering as I shove his face into a sign that's nailed to a wooden post next to the bar. "Read it."

His bloodshot eyes pinwheel in his head. Between the alcohol and the shock of getting knocked on his ass, he's totally screwed.

I'm about two seconds from introducing him to the bar top. Face first. "*Read.* It."

"*No touching unless invited.*" He screws up his ugly face and slurs, "That's horseshit. *Everyone* knows it."

Oh yeah? Well, not on my fucking watch. The man gasps when I wrench his right hand behind his back until something crackles in my hold. "The lady didn't invite you to touch her."

He huffs and puffs so fast he sounds like an ancient

steam engine that's double timing up a mountain. Between his rancid exhales, he says, "Aww, come on. They all like it. That's why they're here."

My vision short circuits, coloring the air around his head hazy red. I detest men like him. Entitled pieces of shit with the morals of a rat's asshole.

I have to unclench my locked jaw. Over my shoulder, I shout, "Sweetheart, did you like this man groping you?"

Lips pressed into a hard line, she shakes her head, causing her hair to dance again. But her color's paler than it should be, which makes the protector in me rage.

Turning my fury back on the man, I hiss, "If I catch you touching her or any of the other girls again, I'll cut your hand off with a wire."

He gulps, and I slowly grin a feral, evil smile. "Do you have any idea how bad that fucking hurts?"

He meeps. Probably pissing his pants too. I lean closer. "Takes a while too. Bloody as fuck."

He's wheezing now. The breath rattling in and out of his pickled body as terror grips him by the balls. Somehow he manages to speak. "Who the *fuck* are you?"

I lean into his ear, drop my voice. "A very angry SEAL."

He goes still. "Oh, fuck," he hoarsely whispers with a tremor in his voice. "SEALs. Crazy bastards."

"Get the fuck out." I shove him toward the door. Another stool tumbles to the concrete floor as he scrambles away, nearly breaking his neck as he hightails it out muttering something about those SEAL guys being lunatics.

I shake out my hands, straighten my hat and right the stools, setting them precisely back where they were.

The little pixie is watching me warily, her teeth now pinching her bottom lip until it's colorless. She's still holding the tray, the sandwiches forgotten.

I step in front of her, close enough to keep our conversation private. "You okay?"

Jutting her chin out, she replies, "I could've handled it."

"You're pale."

Her hand rises to her throat and dances over the tiny star necklace. "J-just shocked. I didn't know if someone was going to get killed."

"No need to kill anyone. I hate unnecessary violence. Especially when a few choice words had him nearly pissing in his pants." I nod toward the table where I had been sitting. "Seems I've really worked up an appetite now."

After a beat, she laughs and shakes her head in disbelief. "I guess you did. I've never seen anyone move so fast."

I might be fast, but fast is not what she makes me think of. No, I wanna go slow with this woman. Long, slow exploration. Inch by inch. Tongue. Teeth. Fingers. Cock.

The rhythmic thrum in my veins intensifies, resonating like a primal tribal drumbeat.

I'm acutely aware of everything about her. Long fingers. Short, clean nails. Strong hands. That's what my eyes catch on as she places a plate laden with two sandwiches and a pile of chips. She places a napkin and silverware next to it. The smell of crisp bacon and fresh sliced tomato makes my gut growl.

Silently, the girl hovers as I take my seat again. After I'm settled, she asks, "Need anything else, sir?"

"For you to sit down and talk with me."

Shifting, she toys with the plastic serving tray as she watches me. All the while dancing her sexy fingers over the edge of the plastic as it goes round and round in her hands.

But those crisp eyes are taking in details. Pixie girl is smart, you can see the intelligence in her gaze.

"What's your name?" I ask casually.

The hair push. The necklace touch. Her eyes fall down in a jerky motion, so I know she's about to tell a lie. "Candy."

It could be her stage name. I study her while she looks around the room, avoiding my eyes. When she faces me again, she seems embarrassed. "You can probably guess that's not my real name... and I'm not one of the performers. Yet." She adds the last word with a grimace.

"All right. I can call you Candy. Doesn't matter to me." But it does. For some reason, I want her to confide in me.

I ask, "How about taking your fifteen minutes and getting a load off?"

Her mouth opens and closes as she glances at the back of the building.

"There's no one else here. Might as well take the stress off your feet. Those heels look like they hurt like a mother-fucker. I know mine do."

She steals a glance at my feet, which are tucked inside a pair of black cowboy boots. A small grin flickers over the contours of her pretty, make-up-free face when I say, "Gotcha."

I slide off my stool, towering over her five-foot-seven frame (in heels), and pull out the seat next to mine. "I'm guessing your boss isn't here since there were only two cars in the parking lot. One belongs to the redhead because of the pole dancer sticker on it, and the other to the cook in the kitchen because there's a greasy handprint on the window."

She blinks slowly, then presses her lips together to hide her expression. "What are you?"

"Observant. It pays in my business." I nod toward the empty stool. "Besides, bossman would be happy if you kept me around and sold me some more beer. Take a break before the afternoon crowd starts to show up."

With a little huff, she accepts and climbs onto the stool. "Ahh, you're right, that feels incredible." A little sigh follows.

Again, we stare at each other. She breaks the silence this time. "Thanks for saving me, not just scaring the heck out of that guy, but for catching me when I was about to fall."

"Nothing to it," I say as I lift my beer and fight the urge to inhale her sweet scent like I'm an animal hunting a mate.

She watches with an innocent kind of curiosity now as I take a few long pulls. The defenses are falling, little by little. She's tough. Strong. Determined, but she's not worldly. Curiosity and something else keep her at my table.

My throat is tight. My blood hums harder. That fucking innocence. It gets me.

After swallowing and telling my nuts to chill the fuck out, I ask, "Now why don't you tell me the truth about why you're working in this shithole?"

A movie of emotions plays in her expression before she hardens her jade eyes. There's a roughness to her voice when she says, "Look, Dozer. I'm here because I have to be. This is not my dream job, trust me, but when you're out of options, you'll do anything."

That's when I know we are the perfect fit. For the job.

Chapter Nine

Candy

He doesn't fit the profile of the men that usually drift in and out of The Pink Palace. Men like him go to the classier clubs. Not this crappy, out of the way, pathetic excuse for a business.

I'm positive he wouldn't be here if he hadn't followed me in.

Which baffles me. Something tells me to be alert with this one. It's hard to put my finger on, but an edge of danger surrounds this man, wrapping all that muscle and power in an energy that practically screams 'run while you can.'

Reminds me of coming across a bear in the woods. They might amble off and leave you, or they might rear up and turn your regular day into your last.

A shudder runs through me.

The way he threw that man down with just the shove of his palm. And whatever he said to the guy was enough to make the man shake in fear.

I'm still rattled. The disquiet of adrenaline clings to my insides as I sit on the hard seat of an ice-cold barstool. *I wish I had a sweatshirt.*

Not that Bob would let us wear a sweatshirt. His idea of a uniform consists of the smallest amount of fabric possible.

I cross my arms to ward off the chill that's rooted somewhere in my marrow. It doesn't help in the least.

Or maybe it does when those gray eyes drop to my chest and send a flush of warmth through me.

I clear my throat and turn my head. However, it's not before I realize that the way he looks at me might be appreciative, but it's not creepy.

Shifting, I make myself refocus on the man who is more muscle than any other man I've met, as I try to figure out exactly what that look in his eyes is.

He smiles. One of those sucker-punch smiles that knocks the wind right out of you.

Ooof. It rattles through me like an earthquake. Wasn't expecting that. Man of contradictions. All scowls and violence one minute and the smile of a movie star the next.

"What you thinking, darlin?"

"That you confuse me," I blurt and instantly regret the words. "Look, I'm sorry, but I've had a lot of weird interactions since I started working here, but no one has stood up for me when guys got aggressive."

His smile pivots one eighty. In a flash, he's back to cold and hard. "That's a crime. Because no man with honor should let that happen to a woman."

I stare at him, and he looks at me like I'm made of something other than flesh, which is what those men think of women that work in places like this. That we don't have souls, or feelings, or deserve respect. "Thank you for saying that."

He lifts his chin. "God's honest truth. My father didn't raise any pieces of shit like that. And lord, if my mother found out one of my brothers or I acted like that, she'd have us castrated by the local veterinarian."

My eyes go wide. "Ouch, but I have to admit, I've met a few guys that I'd gladly submit to that."

His scowl softens, and he asks, "You taken any self-defense classes?"

"No. I've never had a chance."

"I could teach you some things."

God, I bet he could. Dirty, delicious things.

Now I'm definitely not cold. Heat's burning its way up from some place in my low belly. I'm pretty sure I've never felt anything there before, but for some reason sitting at this table, within touching distance of the tall stranger, is causing an effect.

The damp panty effect.

Crap. I almost laugh out loud. That's just ridiculous, I can't be aroused by a man I just met. My hand goes to the table edge to steady myself.

"I'm not being a creep," my rescuer adds with a grin. "I'm serious, I've taught defense classes before. I could meet you at the gym."

"Thanks, but—"

"Think about it, you don't have to answer right now."

He must see my wariness. I used to be a mostly trusting person. Didn't have any reason not to be. Not that I was out gallivanting in the world, but that's all screwed up now. After getting burned by Bob, I'm not sure how I feel about this guy's intense inspection.

I shouldn't have agreed to sit down. Clearly, I've lost the last remaining threads of my sanity. But the fact that I'm here at all in The Pink Palace is testament to the fact that I am losing my freaking marbles.

Like I have a choice.

There's got to be another way. I just need a little more time to figure it out.

Since I can't solve that puzzle right now. I turn my attention back to the stranger. He's built rugged. With corded arms, a sharp, square jaw, eyes that drill out the answers he wants.

When I told him I had to work here, his intensity changed so quickly, I sucked in a little breath. That shiver I've been holding back finally races down my spine.

I'm not sure exactly what his reaction says, but the dark-eyed giant doesn't need to hear my story. It's sad enough to have to live with it. No use telling it to anyone.

A wave of bleak, cold despair washes over me, chased by another nervous shiver, causing his attention to focus more.

What am I doing sitting down with him? I should go.

Besides, Bob Claymore will lose his freaking mind if he ever finds out I'm sitting down while working. I'm sure he's got cameras. *Ick.* That thought turns my stomach. He's probably watching the bathroom, knowing the creep.

"How long you been around here?"

"Not that long," I reply vaguely even though I've counted and loathed every minute.

A rumbling sound comes from his throat. Then he puts his attention on the food instead of me, giving me a break from his eyes. His thick, corded forearms flex, and big, capable-looking hands lift up one of his sandwiches.

Scratch what I said about the BLT being big. The thing

is dwarfed by his massive paws even though it's made with Texas toast, stacked triple decker high.

Before I can get up and back to my duties, he nudges the plate toward me. "That one's for you."

"The sandwich? Oh, *no*. I couldn't."

"Why? You need it."

Frowning at the sandwich, I reply, "I told you, I'm not supposed to eat when I'm on the clock."

His piercing gaze sweeps the inside of the building. The cockroaches are probably scurrying.

He says, "No one is looking. Besides, if they have a problem, I'll speak to them about labor laws."

"That would only—"

I stop myself from saying that any such action on his part would bring the wrath of the boss down like a lightning strike. *Yeah, no way, not going there.* Not something I want to experience. I've seen the way he deals with the other girls when they make a mistake. Verging on violence.

Voice dropping lower, the man pushes for me to continue. "Would *what*, sweetheart?"

Swallowing a little too hard, I look down at my clenched hands. Why does this guy make me feel like my skin is dissolving right under his assessment? I sigh. "That would only make things worse."

I'm glad Bob's not here, because I don't think this conversation would end well for him. That expression is fierce.

Even if my boss claims to have 'saved me,' I still despise him. He uses the women that work here like livestock. Bob doesn't really care if the patrons grab the girls. He's too much of a lowlife to give a damn about anything but money.

This guy seems a few dozen steps above Bob, already.

The fact that he stood up for me gave him major brownie points.

He softens his expression again as he nudges the plate again. "Eat. You're too thin."

What? I laugh, and stare at him like he's sprouted a unicorn's horn. "Well, that's the first time I think those words have ever been said in this building."

He glowers, completely pissed, and I wonder if he's going to punch a hole in the wall or something to let off his steam. "Someone said otherwise to you?"

His expression amuses and warms me even though I quickly remember that the subject is nothing warm or amusing. I tug the plate a little closer. "The girls get hassled about their weight sometimes."

He chomps a rough bite out of his sandwich, simmering. After he angrily chews, he mutters, "Real fucking nice boss you've got."

"You have no clue." The man's right again—about the fact that I'm hungry too. I haven't been taking care of myself. And I'm not used to the kind of food I've been eating, so I'm feeling the effects.

My stomach turns itself inside out as I look down at the tantalizing sandwich. Bacon has always been a rare treat for me growing up, but my mouth waters at the memories.

A very unladylike growl comes from my belly, sneaking out from the place where my tiny tank top hovers above my belly button. I press my hand flat over the spot and shoot the man an apologetic look. "Maybe I will eat a little of this."

"When's the last time you had real food?"

Scoffing, I reply, "I eat all the time." Just not what I want. But hey, we can't always have what we want. I'm learning that in the school of hard knocks right now.

He grunts and looks down at my body again, obviously not believing me.

I lift a shoulder in a shrug as I peek under the bread on the top layer of the BLT. "Money's a little tight. I eat food, just nothing so decadent." As if a cheap strip club BLT is decadent. But everything is relevant.

Now he's staring right at me. The intensity scorches my skin. "Eat the sandwich while I tell you about a proposition I have."

Screech. My pulse leaps. *A proposition.* Instantly my mind goes to the worst places. No. I'm not that kind of girl. Nervous adrenaline fires up again making my cells jittery. I almost quake myself right off the barstool.

God, please do not let him see me looking like a nervous bunny rabbit staring down a hungry wolf.

But he does, taking my distress in, and quickly saying, "It's not illegal. It's not prostitution. I promise. You're safe with me."

I'm so shaken and confused I pick up the sandwich, squishing the corner down so it will fit in my mouth, and take a bite just to have something to do.

He finishes his sandwich in crackling silence as I nibble and chew. The whole time my mind races a million miles an hour. *Proposition.*

I'm still eating when he fishes around in his pocket for his wallet. After opening the plain black leather, he produces a card. My curiosity grows. Do pimps carry business cards?

Stop. Just stop it. Your freaking imagination is going crazy.

But my eyes laser in on his hand. His index finger is thick and calloused. I noticed a few of his scars at the café already, but I have the time to study them now. Some dot-like scars from stitches cross one of the knuckles. Other scars zig this way and that in various shades of white and tan. Using the tip of his finger he pushes the rectangle of paper across the table toward me.

It sits there between us for a beat. My nerves jangle a warning. I don't want to listen to his proposition, do I?

Using extreme caution, as if the thing could explode, I lift it off the table. Hoping my hand doesn't shake as I angle it so I can read it in the dim interior.

Bold black font marks the paper, proclaiming, Agile Security & Rescue—*Elite protection, high-stakes security, and hostage recovery services.*

After reading it again, it hits me that there's no name on the card, it's just generic. A card he could have picked up anywhere, like the ones on the bulletin board at my grocery store back home. A fact that makes me frown. "Is this your job?"

"Yes, and that's what I'm here about." He reaches for his beer and takes another deep drink without saying more. Hm. What does this have to do with me? But I'm also still hung up on the fact that this is a card for a business, not a person.

"Why isn't your name on here?"

"Just started. Boss said my cards are on the way."

"Considering the name of the business, I'm wondering if you're a bodyguard."

"So to speak. We do offer security. That and we conduct other types of rescue missions."

When I look at him this time, I see him in a totally different light. The protector. I can picture him throwing himself in front of some important person to protect them from the paparazzi... or even an attacker, like he did me.

He'd be amazing. All Herculean. Tossing people left and right like ragdolls.

He interrupts my imagination by saying, "Starting this afternoon, I'm working on a case. I'll be backup for my boss who's doing personal security and recon detail at a local resort."

"Sounds interesting, I guess. Not that I know much about personal security other than what I read in suspense romance books."

"Never read one."

"I can give you some good titles."

He grins. "Think I'd like to read a romance book?"

I fight to hide my own grin. "Depends on how comfortable you are with your masculinity."

Chapter Ten

DOZER

I laugh at her cute expression, which surprises me. Been a while since I laughed. Too much real life shit going on.

Pointing at my chest, I raise my brows. "So, you think I would have a problem with my masculinity?"

She looks down my body and makes a little shrug. "Well, the authors of that kind of book are very descriptive about the male characters, and of course they write the men as exceptional lovers for their heroine. So, if you aren't very comfortable with your masculinity, it could make you feel... inadequate."

Good thing I don't have any beer in my mouth because I would be spitting that shit out.

"Sweetheart, I'm more than comfortable with my virility. They call me Dozer for a reason."

She purses her lips for a second. "Women call you that or your male friends?"

I chuckle as her eyes sparkle, reflecting the club's strobe lights. "Both."

She makes a little eye-roll and I'm surprised how much that little sass brings me pleasure.

"Dozer. I wondered if your parents didn't like you or if it was kind of like you calling me Candy."

I laugh. "Yep. Kind of like that."

I'm struck by how normal it feels to be sitting here with her in the middle of the day, in a rundown strip club no less. Having a beer, and shooting the breeze.

Weird.

Maybe spending a few hours... or even the weekend with her will be a whole lot less work that I was thinking it could be.

That is, if she says yes to my ridiculous request.

Chapter Eleven

Candy

So, Mr. Bodyguard is on some kind of mission that's had him following me into a strip club. This sounds like the beginning of a book.

I grin, and before I realize what I'm doing, I'm studying him again, against better judgment. Looking at a man too long is bad for the retinas.

Surely hotness has to be a cause of eye-strain. But I can't seem to stop myself. Everything about the man is so foreign to me. The way his throat moves. The shadows in his eyes. The dusky tanned skin that's stretched across all those mountains of muscles.

Then I see it. My body jolts. My breath hitches. The tattoo on his left biceps entraps me from where it peeks from beneath his black T-shirt sleeve.

A bone frog.

I know the tattoo. My father had one too, only his was faded from years of sun.

For a few seconds my pulse pounds. If this man is a SEAL, then he probably knows my boss. He might have even known my father.

The special forces community is a small world. Even though Bob the Terrible has been out of the service for more than a decade, these two could know each other.

My heart stutters and speeds. Fear starts to trickle through me, stealing any amusement I might have had moments ago.

This could be a set up. Some cruel trick by Bob or his son.

The nerves in my scalp go electric and the part of the sandwich that I ate feels like a grenade sitting down below in my stomach.

Forcefully, I straighten my spine and try to seem casual. "You're a SEAL."

I'm not sure if my intent was to ask a question or make a statement. But it comes out strained.

For a beat he looks at me quizzically with his head tilting, then he pushes up his sleeve. "You know this tattoo?"

I nod as I bite my lip while nerves flutter under my skin.

The black ink is fresh, stretched taut over his muscles, and clean-lined. It's well done. Since working at the Palace, I've seen some really crap tattoos. Lots of naked women tattoos, which I'll never stop being shocked by.

Finally, I say, "My father had one."

I can literally feel his energy darken and wonder if I've offended him somehow.

"If you're on hard times, where's your father?"

I lick my lips as my throat dries. I hate saying the words. It takes work for me to force them out. "He died."

"Did you come to San Diego because of him?"

He obviously knows I'm not local. That's easy for anyone to tell. If it's not the accent, it's the lack of sun on my skin. A fact that made me an anomaly in the club, which attracted even more attention. I nod once. Which I seem to do a lot with this man. I was never really talkative, but now I'm all nods and stares.

He continues, "Did he live here?"

"Not in a long time. He moved away right after his years in the service. His friend lives here now. He and his son own this... place."

Is he sneering?

The cords in his neck definitely tighten, and his voice is an octave lower. "About that proposition, how'd you like to make some money, maybe enough to help you get on your feet or go somewhere else?"

Huh? That's my first thought. Then a warning bell starts clanging in my head.

I'm not sure what's happening here, but given that I know he's a SEAL, the offer now feels dangerously like it could be a ploy. "Don't most west coast SEALs all know one another?"

"I know a lot of guys. Who is your boss?" The question sounds genuine, but I might not be a good judge. I've had my failures in that department. Big fat failures.

"Bob Claymore."

He shakes his head sharply. "No. Don't know the name. But I will know everything about him in a few hours, after I reach out to some contacts."

The alarm in my head sounds louder. "Don't say

anything about me talking to you. *Please.* I know it's not a big deal to you, but this job is critical for me right now."

Talk about bad timing. The back door of the bar slams open, crashing against the wall. I jolt and whip my head toward the noise.

Instantly, my stomach tanks.

Oh. Hell. This is going to get ugly.

Bob strides in, his fists clenched, his sunglasses shoved on top of his balding head. He bellows across the room and his voice is so loud it's like a crack of thunder. "Candy, what the fuck are you doing?"

I sway as he strides toward me with barely restrained fury. "You know the rules," he bites out through clenched teeth.

The next second, he realizes that there's no music and the stage is empty. Bob's voice gets louder with his growing outrage. "Where the fuck is the dancer?"

I almost fall as I try to scramble off the stool, but a big hand wraps around my wrist to steady me, and I glance at the bodyguard quickly before I focus on the impending tornado. Next to me, the man growls. In a low voice meant for me, he says, "I got this." Then he pulls me behind him.

Bob makes a disgusted sound. "Girls are always slacking on the fucking job. Bunch of thieves. Think they can get paid for nothing."

An eerie calm settles over the bodyguard as he tilts his head, slowly looking over Bob's paunchy body. "Candy was talking with me at my request."

Bob snorts out his displeasure. "Well, I'm paying the fucking bills around here."

"Since I'm your only customer, *I* am actually paying the bills around here. Now, unless you want to see me really mad, you need to rethink the attitude you bring to my front door."

There's a very weighted pause. Then the man continues. "Because when I get real mad, I tend to break a lot of shit. Barstools over people's heads, you know, things like that. So, I suggest you go back to pushing papers or some other boring bullshit, and leave me to talk to Miss Candy here."

The laugh that follows is full of disbelief. "Who do *you* think you are?"

Oh. So not good. The hair on the back of my neck stands up like I'm a Halloween cat.

"I'm a SEAL brother that's calling you on your asshole attitude."

The room falls quiet. I brace for impact. I don't know what's going to happen, but you could at any second hear one of the many rats in the building scurrying for safety.

A nuclear bomb is hovering in the air. Anything with half a brain is going to flee.

It's a standoff that lasts long enough for my heart to try to escape my chest. The bodyguard's still holding my arm, keeping me tucked behind his back.

"I saved this woman from sexual assault by one of your customers. The lack of security and your fucked up attitude won't set well with the teams. You know that. Someone might pay you a late night visit."

Bob sputters something, and perversely I'm dying to see his face, but I stay hidden between two gigantic shoulder blades.

My protector says, "I'd think long and hard about your next words."

"Fuck you, asshole." Muttered words that are distant and accompanied by the sound of shoes on sticky concrete.

The hand around my wrist falls away and I look up to find the hero of the day looking loose-limbed and relaxed. Just like he was during the whole confrontation.

I peek toward the back door. "I can't believe he just left like that."

"He knows how to read a dangerous situation."

"Will someone really be paying him a late night visit?"

A slight grin tugs at his lips. His handsomeness ratchets up. "It's going to be fun as fuck."

Okay, so my admiration of him also goes up. Is it bad I'm thrilled at the idea of Bob shaking in his pajamas?

I can't hide my own grin, even though it's fleeting. "I'd like to see his face when that happens."

But there's a sinking feeling in my gut. Somehow Bob will continue to take it out on me and the other women here. Men like him don't change.

I must look worried because the man says, "He knows he's fucked up. I wouldn't be surprised if things changed around here."

He shifts, crosses his arms and resumes a scowling expression. "Even if things get better around here, there's something going on in your life. I don't know what that is, but I know enough to tell you that you need to get the fuck out of here."

He picks up the napkin on the floor that fell from my lap, wads it up, and tosses it on the table. "You don't belong here."

For a beat I stare at his muscular chest, unable to take the intensity in his eyes. Every painful emotion inside of me wells up. No, I don't belong here. Not in California. Not in The Pink Palace.

But I don't know where I belong.

I blink a dozen times to try to get my composure, but I'm sure I look like I'm about to lose my grip.

I hate knowing that someone can see the chaos inside of me. I thought I was better at hiding, but not with this man. He's been in my life for twenty minutes tops, but in those scant minutes he's looked too deeply. And I have no defense system that will fight it.

My voice comes out sounding ancient. Maybe because I feel like I am, and not like a twenty-four year old. "I need out of here. But I can't just leave right now. He provides the housing I'm using. I can't get out without help."

With a decisive motion he jerks his wallet out of his back pocket again, this time he tosses some cash on the table next to the plate and extends his hand. "Let's go."

Chapter Twelve

DOZER

Candy looks at my hand with her pulse hammering, her fingers twisted in her necklace.

"Just like that? Just walk out?"

"Yep," I reply as I hold my hand out, palm up.

After chewing the corner of her lips, she asks, "What do I have to do?"

"Act like you like me for a few hours. Maybe forty-eight hours tops."

I'm sure it sounds like it's too good to be true. Who gets paid to act like they like someone?

Her voice catches and fills with disbelief. "That's it?"

"Yeah. I need someone to go on this low-key surveillance mission with me. So yeah, in a manner of speaking all you have to do is act like you like me, that you

58

want to be with me. All inclusive. Meals, lodging, you know… drinks with fruit and all that."

Creasing her brow, she steps back. "I don't have to have sex with you?"

I chuckle and lean close, taking a few seconds to enjoy the proximity. Her small size, and the sweet, soft smell of her. *Fuck. Me. I'm pulled by her magnetic draw.*

I growl next to her ear, "Sweetheart, I know I'm an ugly motherfucker, but I don't have to pay to get laid. So no, you don't have to have sex with me, or anyone else."

Relief and shock fight for the win in her expression. It amuses me that I've rattled her in a good way. "No sex required. This is a job for Agile. I have to have a date to make this mission happen."

"You're not ugly," she says flatly and crosses her arms. Her tits bunch up even higher than before, making my eyes fall to them. *Ungh.* Caveman brain tries to take over.

Gruffly, I reply, "I'm sure not pretty. You in or out?"

Tightly, she demands, "How much money?"

"Ten thousand dollars."

She straightens her spine. If I could see cogs in her head, they would be snapping into place. Decision made. I've seen plenty of people come to that kind of realization before. Where going forward sure as fuck beats standing still.

Candy picks up the sandwich, wraps it in a clean napkin and faces me with her shoulders squared. "I'm in." Under her breath, she mumbles, "I hope I'm not walking out of here with a serial killer." Then her voice grows louder again. "I can't stay in this situation. As you can tell, it's not safe."

I almost smile because I've won the first battle. "Not a serial killer."

Far from it. Little does she know I wouldn't stop until I know she's safe, whatever that takes. Call me overprotective, but that's what growing up with a little sister made me. Add to that, all the bad shit I've seen happening to females at the hand of very bad men. Candy stirs something in me, something I don't want to look too closely at. I'd like to tell myself I'd do it for anyone, but I'm not sure I'd be willing to go as far as I think I'd go to help her.

Which is why I act like a total caveman and pick her up, sweeping one arm below her knees, the other around her back, causing her to shriek, "Oh *my* god! *What are you doing*!?"

"You're safe, babe, and the second thing I'm saving you from today is breaking your fucking leg in those shoes."

Chapter Thirteen

DOZER

She's in shock, but she waves her hand toward the bar. "Wait! I have to get my bag."

I round the bar, dip her down so she can grab her bag, then stride out the door. Enjoying carrying a very warm, incredibly soft, woman against my chest.

The velvet skin of her bare thighs is against my arm and makes the crotch of my jeans feel a hell of a lot tighter.

Fool. You're just torturing yourself.

Apparently I like torture.

There's no one around to stare as I cross to my truck, open the passenger door with one hand and ease her into the leather seat. Not that I particularly care about someone seeing me carrying a woman, but I'd rather not have any more confrontations this morning, especially the kind involving a cook and a meat cleaver.

I've had my share of knife fights, my least favorite kind of fight, but one I still have yet to lose. And right now, I'm not in a hurry to put Candy down.

However, by the time I get her settled in the truck, the air in my lungs is searing hot from me holding it in. The last thing I need right now with her in my arms is to smell her baby powder scent.

Yes, *baby powder*.

Where is this girl from?

She's as innocent as a dogwood blossom. But I have no doubt she's got a backbone as tough as a Detroit steel worker.

I'm familiar with women like that. My mother and sister are the same. They might bend, but they will never, ever fucking break.

Whatever's been going on with Candy is bending her hard, but she's strong and she saw my offer for what it is—the opportunity she needs to take care of herself.

Fucking dickhead club owner. I hate the way men use women, take advantage of hard times. I'm determined not to let Candy suffer any because of her ex-SEAL boss. Yep, he's going to be getting a visit from me once this mission is all said and done. He knew better than to challenge me, because not only will I kick his ever-loving ass, I'll bring the wrath of the brotherhood down on him. SEALs don't let other SEALs act like fuckheads.

I close the truck door—a mighty act of restraint to set her down and pull my hands off of those sexy curves when I really just wanted to lean down and take a bite of her creamy inner thigh.

Inch by inch, my body grows tight. I'm a banjo string. A

guywire, a fucking loaded weapon with a hair trigger. My cock is ready to get down to business.

God. Sometimes it sucks to be a fucking dude. I seriously doubt, no matter how bothered a woman is by a guy, that she's driven around by her clit.

It hits me all of a sudden that my brothers would think this was gut-splitting hilarious.

Nothing affects me. Nothing. Ever.

Until. Her.

Maybe it is a good thing I got out of the teams. I'm losing it. That razor edge of cool that made me so fucking good.

Right now, my testosterone is pumping triple-time. My brain, on the other hand, has gone into limp mode, and not as in limp dick, but as in the helm of the vessel has been taken over by a singular need.

Fuckity.

You're working, asshole.

Grumbling, I stomp around the front of the truck. At least the first task was accomplished—find a willing accomplice.

Now for the part I didn't mention. The landmine. One not so fucking teeny detail.

Cursing myself, I stare out the front window of the truck. I should have told her everything.

Asshole move. But I got so fucking caught up in saving a woman in distress, that the only important thing was getting her out of there. And in here. Where now I'm paying in spades and testosterone. But thanks to not revealing the whole scope of said mission, I'm gonna come off as a fucking pervert that tricked her.

Just what she fucking needs right now, after dealing with Bob-the-douche.

How will she look at me when I spill the fucking beans?
Deceived. Angry. Hurt.

Yeah, that last one will be the knife in my rib cage. Maybe I'm about to lose my first knife fight and there won't even be any steel involved.

I don't want to hurt her. For a boatload of reasons. Including that deceit is a terrible way to start an important working relationship.

For a good thirty seconds I contemplate banging my head against the steering wheel. Hard.

Maybe seeing stars will help clear this clusterfuck up.

This mission is already giving me gray hair. I've survived everything the SEALs threw at me, but one slight blond with jade green eyes, dewy lips, and that air of innocence may cut me down and leave me in shreds.

Okay, fuckhead. Get your ass in the game. I draw some controlled breaths. *In. Hold. Out. In. Hold. Out.*

Before long, I'm dizzy from the sweet, clean scent of her and the heavenly smell of bacon from the sandwich sitting on the console.

What fucking guy can resist something like that?

I groan, clenching my jaw and refusing to look at her.

"You're tense," she says in a concerned voice.

"I'm working. This is how I am when I'm on a mission."

Total bullshit. I'm usually fully in charge of what's inside my head and what my body is doing. I've taken biofeedback to the next level. But not now. Not as she sits next to me looking like she belongs over there in my passenger seat.

Slowly unbuckling one shoe, then the other, she watches me. When she's clear of the shoes, she tucks her feet under her, causing the leather to creak. With her slender fingers, she tugs her tiny ass skirt as long as it will go.

When she's done arranging herself in the seat, she twists her hair into a little rope that hangs over her shoulder.

If it weren't for the made-for-sin rack spilling out of her tank top, she'd look as innocent as a virgin.

Yeah. Not.

No way a woman that looks like her is a virgin. She's been getting chased by boys since she hit puberty. I'm sure she's had a boyfriend or two. *Christ on a cracker.* That is a highly irritating thought.

My skin tightens and pricks as she looks me over.

Does she like what she sees over here? I'm pretty sure I've never wondered if I was a woman's type before. But here I am. Wondering just that.

Women like me for my body. The size. The ruggedness. One look, and they know I'm not some pansy-ass lame lover.

I'm big, which they assume means I'm BIG. Which is true. But all that means is that I'm nothing more than a muscled-up jungle gym for them.

I'm not a pretty package. Scars range over my body, puckered, angry, indentations or raised cords. My jaw is like a steel beam, not some elegant thing. I haven't shaved since yesterday. My hair is too fucking long, curling out the bottom of my baseball cap and itching the fuck out of my neck.

People say my expressions are terrifying. The ranch dog even knows my moods and scurries when she sees me coming when I've got a thundercloud trailing my six.

Yeah. Not the kind of face women fall on because it's beautiful.

Fuck.

I did not go there.

Why did I think about *that?*

Now all I can do is fantasize about two lovely, very pale

thighs lowering until I've got a mouth full of sweet, dripping-wet pussy and two hands full of those heavy tits.

I almost bite my tongue clean off. But what a damned tragedy that would be. If Candy... sweet fucking Candy does ever let me between her porcelain spindles, I want my tongue to be in prime shape.

Groaning, I scrub my hand over my eyes. When did I turn into a teenage boy again?

Chapter Fourteen

Candy

My new friend... *is he a friend?* No. That's the wrong word. But I don't know what he should be called. Anyway, he's as prickly as a big bear now.

Which makes me feel prickly too. Like the inside of the truck is too small for all his bad energy.

But I'm not a wilting flower.

Determination filling my veins, I cross my arms. I'm not going to let the weirdness of this situation steal my opportunity.

However, it's undeniable that this is one of the oddest days of my life. And I've had some weird ones. In very fast succession at that.

I blow out a breath and wiggle my toes, letting my eyes take in the man's spotless truck.

So, he's also a neat freak. Makes sense. Military order and all that. My father was anal about his belongings, so I'm not surprised. Only, he seems barely in control of his emotions right now. Nothing like the cool, calm man-in-charge he was inside the club.

Maybe he's regretting the offer...

"If you've changed your mind, I could—"

He stops me with a raised hand. "Haven't changed my mind."

"What now?"

"We get the fuck away from here."

A realization hits me. "Then I should get my things. I don't have much, but I don't want Bob to burn them."

"Where do you live?"

"A room behind the bar. Kind of an apartment... Drive into the back alley and we can go up the stairs."

He grunts and wheels the truck in a U-turn that would have a cop's eyeballs falling out.

Three minutes later I'm opening the door with the key that was stashed in my bra. Like a bull, he crowds me out of the way before I can step inside. "I need to clear the space."

I step aside as a wall of heat rolling off of him hits me. My heart does a little thump behind my ribs.

Ooof. This guy takes protection to a whole new level. It feels good.

Like a-girl-could-get-used-to-it good. *Stupid thought.* I chastise myself. He's a one-way ticket to money. That's it.

Before I can react, Dozer's already inside, sweeping his gaze over everything, even pulling back the curtain to the small shower in the corner.

Oh, lord. He's super thorough. Heat infuses my face because my hand-washed panties and bras are on the line, drying in there.

He turns toward me, and something flashes across his expression. Those damned eyes of his drill me. I nearly incinerate on the spot. Especially when his rough voice says, "It's safe. Come on in."

I don't care what he said, it could have been a complaint about the fact that the shower is the size of a cracker box, and I would have felt it all the way down to the tips of my toes. It's the timbre, the warm resonant sound that his words deliver.

I'm fast realizing that this man has another super power. Not just that he sees right into me, but his words are hypnotic, lulling me and stirring me at the same time in ways that I can't even understand.

My hand comes up and I flutter it over my neck when I really want to smack myself.

Maybe I can knock some sense into my poor brain. Only I don't, and I move further into the space, unable to deny that my little room feels tiny with him in here.

I glance around, letting out a slow breath, hoping some of the heat dissipates as I take in the fact that the room is just like I left it a few hours ago.

Not that I expected Bob to slash my things, but you never know with a man like him. Especially after the confrontation. His unpredictability has always made me wary.

But what bothers me most in this moment is the crap apartment. Yeah, *not* proud for this man to see where I 'live.' Not that I come from fancy, but this is a real piss-poor place to hang your hat at night. I scrubbed it clean, but nothing would make this place look like anything but what it is...depressing.

His expression isn't much better than mine the first time I saw the place. Barely hidden disgust. But he also looks almost sympathetic, which is quickly replaced with a barely bottled-up anger that tightens his shoulders as he looks around.

A bare bulb hangs from the ceiling. The cot that stands in for a bed is rusted. There's one tattered blanket and only one dingy sheet.

Yep. Living in style.

The rest of the room is no better. Maybe even worse. The makeshift table is made out of an oversized cardboard box with water stains all over it. There's a saggy, scuffed up set of shelves that serve as a dresser of sorts. At least that's how I used it—to hold my meager stack of clothes.

Other than that, there's a small cube-shaped black fridge that was disgusting when I moved in, a microwave—also equally ick when I opened it for the first time, and a stack of a few mismatched, chipped dishes.

Ducking my head, I move around the room, picking up my belongings. "As you can see, this won't take me long."

He crosses his arms and assumes a position by the door like a big guard dog—a very pissed guard dog.

That visit to Bob is gonna be hell on wheels. Oh, how I'd like to be a fly on the wall for that.

Gruffly, Dozer says, "It's okay, do what you need to do."

I throw the few things that I have into the plain Navy-issued duffel bag with J. RUSH painted on the side of it. My dad's first initial and last name.

My very basic clothes go in first. Jeans and T-shirts. A pair of practical hiking boots, my heavy coat, and a small stack of paperbacks. Silly, I know, but my books save me during long, sleepless nights.

I leave the Pink Palace tank tops and the stupid skirts that the other girls gave me laying in a pile on the floor, and slip on a pair of flip flops that I bought when I arrived in

California because my leather hiking boots were not going to cut it in the heat.

"I don't have much." Especially not what I need to go to a resort. Not that I know what it's like to go to a resort beyond what you see in travel magazines at the library. So, the only thing I have in my mind are flowy, bright colored beach dresses, fancy black bathing suits with little gold adornments, and big floppy sun hats. Those things and fancy cocktails by the pool.

I'm going to stick out like a sore thumb. Which makes me feel kind of green, as in pukey green. But nothing is keeping me here if I can make ten thousand dollars. That will give me room to breathe.

"Don't worry about the clothes," he replies from his station by the door.

Knowing I'm going to be burning with embarrassment, I save packing the lingerie for the last task. Finally, I snatch the pieces off the makeshift clothesline and shove them in my case with coals flaming below my skin.

Not like my stuff is sexy.

Calling what I own lingerie is a huge exaggeration. Lingerie should be reserved for pretty things. There's nothing fancy about what I've got. Plain. Simple. Black. Boy shorts and hip hugging briefs. My bras aren't even lace. I shouldn't feel embarrassed by something so utilitarian, but I do.

And *god*, do I feel his eyes all over me. Like he's picturing me in those pieces of black fabric.

I have no idea how to deal with that realization. A shiver races across my skin. Turning my back to him does nothing to relieve my distress. Or the tremor that's in my hands as I fold my under things.

I thank god when that's done and getting back to busi-

71

ness, I give myself a jolt and look through the shelves and the small bathroom area to make sure I didn't leave anything there and remind myself not to forget my cash.

When I drag over the only chair in the room to the cabinets in the tiny kitchen, I feel him beside me. The man dwarfs me and it makes me momentarily jealous and also keenly aware of his... everything.

He's just so big. Energy and body. He doesn't even have to stretch to reach the top cabinet. "Here, I'll get whatever you need."

"That soda can in the back corner." It was a nightmare to cut the lid off so I could put stuff inside it and still have it look like a normal can.

He doesn't say anything as he moves aside the cans of beans and corn. Then he hands the makeshift safe that's holding the only money I have. But he doesn't need words to show he understands.

"Took forever to cut the lid off of that thing," I muse to escape lingering on whatever he's thinking as I pivot and I slip the stash in my bag, tucking it deep inside. He's watching me too intently with worry in his eyes as I zip the bag closed.

I've never had anyone look at me like that and I don't know if I like it or if it makes me uncomfortable.

Dozer finally drops his eyes from me and glances at the pair of jeans and T-shirt I left on the cot. Voice deep and rumbly, he says, "I'll just step outside while you change."

Chapter Fifteen

DOZER

I nearly bit my tongue off when I stumbled upon her bras and panties in the shower.

Again, my team would laugh their damned heads off if they saw me fighting to keep it together.

But it's not just the innocent underthings—that would look not the least fucking bit innocent on her—that have me pulverizing my molars, it's the fact that she's living in a shithole in the back of a titty bar because of some tragic fucked up thing that's led her to this level of desperation.

Call me a caveman, but I want to drag her out of this damned place and make her forget the nights she spent on that rusty ass cot. To cleanse her mind of the time she spent staring at that fucking disgusting ceiling, because I know what being at your limit, at the point of desperation does to a human.

If she says she was sleeping like an angel with this fucking situation playing out, she's lying. Straight up. She's fucking lying to herself if she thinks this is okay.

Because it's so far from okay that she's been manipulated into this that it should be criminal. Hell, it might be. And I'm one hundred percent sure that Bob—god, that name makes me want to break shit—was using Candy and somehow capitalizing on the fact that her father was a man he'd served in the Navy with.

I shudder to think what might have happened to her in the future. Sex trafficking? Worse?

Unclenching my fists, I stalk out of the room, pretending to give her space while she changes, while the truth of the fucking matter is that I need a minute before I throw that damned mini-fridge through the wall.

My veins are filled with pure fire.

But when the door closes between us, my blood pressure goes up. Not down. This time it's because I know she's stripping out of that stupid fucking costume and putting on her civies.

My mind latches onto the vision of her tugging off that little tank top, and my hands itch to help.

I want to do it.

Fuck helping.

I want to shank it over her head and dive my face between those big ass tits while she knocks my baseball cap off so she can fist my hair.

It's a good goddamn thing the door is between us, because if she saw my face right now, she'd run.

With good reason.

What. The. Literal. Fuck?

A growl grows in my chest.

I'm pinwheeling here, one minute furious, one minute so lust-fogged I'm losing my focus on the mission.

Scrubbing my hand over my face, I curse long and low into my palm.

When my phone rings in my pocket, I thank the distraction. A text from Mako.

My former SEAL teammate is one of Agile's intel guys. A good transition for Mako after getting out. He slid right into the protection and security work. Balls deep. Spent fourteen months hunting for one woman. Chased her around the globe... before he claimed her as his own.

How'z it?

I stare at the words on my phone screen as a lightning bolt hits my brain. A mission for Agile is how Mako met *his* match. A sinking feeling hits my gut. Lead pulling my organs to my toes.

No. That shit is not happening to me.

I've got no time for... dalliances.

How the hell do I even know that word?

Then I glance at the door, which is thankfully still closed. Chuckling darkly, I respond. *Brother, it's real. I didn't know civilian missions were so...*

He sends back a laughing with tears emoji.

I thumb out a response. *You fuck.*

The dots blink. Then his reply appears. *Find your assistant?*

I chuckle.

Maybe. TBD. She seems down. OTW soon.

The door swings open and I reconsider what I sent. 'Maybe' is the wrong word. *Hope* would have fit better.

I'm not ready to walk away. Whatever the hell that means.

Chapter Sixteen

Candy

When Dozer steps outside, I realize I've been vibrating with nervous energy.

Wow. Okay. Being alone with him is intense.

I pant for a few seconds as my skin does some kind of hot-cold-hot thing.

"It's too early for menopause," I mutter. Then, I jerk off my tank top and the stupid excuse for a skirt, and throw them in the trash can in the corner. Rushing, I pull on the plain black T-shirt and jeans that I left out of the duffle bag.

Why do I feel a blush of embarrassment as I dress?

Because he's standing right outside the door.

I can feel him as if he's still playing guard inside the door. The man has some kind of invisible power. Magnetic.

Electric. Chemical. I don't know what it is, but I'm being sucked up in the wake.

I wiggle my shoulders and shake out my hands to move the stuck energy out of my body. When I catch sight of myself in the mirror, the reflection staring back is flushed with color that I'm pretty sure I've never seen. But beneath that is a kind of traumatized sadness in her eyes. Damn, that woman looks like she's been through a tornado.

You have, girl. You have. *You're doing the right thing,* I coach myself.

Ten thousand dollars will change everything. I think.

Whipping my hair into a tight ponytail, I use the band off my wrist to secure it. *Alright, McKenzie, this is it.* You've got no one and nothing. This is a chance to at least have some cash in your pocket, enough to maybe put down a deposit and rent a place, somewhere I can look for a real job.

I yank the door to find two piercing steel-gray eyes on me. They hit me so hard I almost stumble back.

I'll admit, my breath feels a little tight every time I look at the man. The intensity opens something vulnerable. For a second my feet feel glued to the floor.

You can do this. Move. Just go. *Do it.*

With a little grimace, I say, "I hope this is okay."

A slow grin forms on his face. It's devastating. If he was handsome when scowling, he's gorgeous with that cocky tilt of his lips. "Better than okay."

Self-consciously, I glance down and tug at the hem of my cotton shirt. Boring, plain, old cotton. Like my panties, also boring and plain. The color in my shirt is starting to fade, but it's soft. That's the one thing my ragged clothes have going for them. They feel like home.

Home.

Christ, that word makes me flinch.

For the first time ever, I feel embarrassed about the lack of girly things in my wardrobe. "I don't own anything nice."

There's a subtle shift in his expression. A warming to his gaze. Quietly, he replies, "Jeans and a T-shirt are nice."

A fizzle works its way down my arms and hits my fingertips. Oof. Why does his saying my clothes are nice feel like he's saying something wayyy different.

While it would be nice if my casual clothing was nice enough for him to say that, I know it's not true. "You don't have to say that."

"Truth."

That hits me too. A single word that means so much to me.

Truth, isn't that what we're all after?

Someone who will show you the real side of themselves. A person that you can let your guard down with because you know that there's no manipulation behind their words. Someone that's got your back.

I might not know a lot of people and I may have been sheltered in a cocoon for my twenty-four years, but I can already tell that truth is rare.

I did get it from my dad, who took truth to the harshest sense of the word. The man minced nothing. He was brutally truthful. But since I got to California I've learned a few hard lessons. Truth isn't universal.

Hearing the word nice about my clothing is not an honest compliment. But maybe I'll take the white lie that this man just told me and let it slide.

I'm not really ready to have him tell me I look like I got my clothes at the hardware store ten years ago. Even though that's pretty much the truth.

My introspection turns to fidgeting, so I spin and head

back into the little apartment. Just to get away from *those* eyes.

He calls after me, "You ready?"

"Just going to make one last check." That's when I realize I've almost left my journal. It's hidden behind the shelving. The last thing I wanted was for Bob to find something so personal. It was violating enough to have him leering at me.

After pushing the shelf back into place, I tuck the notebook under my arm and glance around at the pathetic space that I've occupied for the last month.

This *almost* feels like a moment of celebration. Maybe if I were moving into some nice place, it would. Or even going home to our—a pain lances through my chest—*my* cabin in the woods. There is no such thing as *our* anymore.

But this is neither of those things. This is me taking flight into the dark night sky without an anchor. Only now, I'll have a cushion at least without having to work for Bob the Terrible.

Feeling swamped with the melancholy moment, I say, "I think that's all of it. I didn't bring much when I came to California."

Dozer steps toward me, enveloping me in his clean woodsy scent. For a beat, I wonder what he's doing, then he lifts my dad's old duffel bag with one hand. The move is so unexpected I stare.

It would have been heavy for me, but he makes it look like a feather. Then he holds the door open for me, all gentlemanly.

Some little voice inside of my head says, "Hang on, McKenzie Rush. You're in for a helluva ride."

Chapter Seventeen

DOZER

Command, we have a situation.

Damn it to hell.

I thought her getting into street-clothes would douse some of the burning flames in my groin.

But, fuck me. *Wrong!*

I fire up my F-350 and whip out of the alley. We bounce through a dip and I gun it to slip between two cars. Basically driving like a dick.

Candy grabs the oh-shit handle but doesn't say a thing. She just lets me be a dumbass.

I loved her long legs being bare, but *shit,* she looks just as hot in those ass-hugging jeans.

Better really. Not that I minded the tank top, but the whole get-up cheapened her natural beauty.

I'd take her strutting around in my house in a tiny little tank top like that and a pair of lace panties, sipping a cup of hot coffee on a cold morning. Now, that's a damned vision.

I grumble and grip the steering wheel like I've got vices instead of hands. With the hounds of hell on my heels.

Working. *Wor. King.*

Not thinking about morning-afters.

It takes all my focus to look at the road because the woman is the definition of temptation. So many things about her yank my chain. She's bea-fucking-utiful. Those layers I see behind her pale green eyes demand that I learn more. Her vibe stirs the primal part of me that protects others. I want to get to the bottom of whatever the hell is going on and win a chance to have her share her sweet smile and that soul-rocking laughter with me.

Beside me, Candy shifts. Something's bugging her, which means it's also bugging me. I don't like when crap wraps people around the axle. I'm a fixer. I solve shit. Whether with guns, fists, wrenches, an ear to listen, or a shoulder to lean on. So, her apprehension bugs me.

I'm about to ask when she says, "I appreciate you saying my clothes are fine, but I'm concerned about going somewhere important with what I have."

Not what I expected, but a valid concern. Women worry about that kind of crap. *Me* on the other hand? I could give a fuck what someone thinks I am supposed to be wearing.

Once I bounced into civilian life, my staple is a T, a pair of jeans that feels like an old friend, and a pair of shit-kicking boots. So, her casual clothing is fine with me.

"It's not a prob...lem." The word kind of sticks in my throat. I clear the lump there and try again. "Not a problem."

Because she won't be wearing any clothes if I can pull this assignment off. And not because I'm a sex-starved asshole. No, because it's work. Fucking work without clothes.

I give my head a shake and concentrate on getting us to the resort without getting killed in San Diego afternoon traffic. Damned if there isn't always some hundred-thousand-dollar luxury car cutting you off as they hurry their ass to get their next burrito or hit their Barre class or whatever the fuck they do that makes them drive ninety in a sixty-five zone. So, it pays for me to look at the road and not her, even though it's hard as hell.

But with her silence, the worry in my gut is growing by the mile as the road passes beneath my tires. The clock is ticking, Marshall needs my ass on duty, but I can't get there if Candy doesn't agree to go all the way.

I grimace.

Oh. No. She eyes me as I scrub my hand over my mouth.

NOT *all the way*.

All the way as in hanging out with me at the resort.

Next thing I know, I'm spouting off like a bottle that's ejected its cork. I blurt, "We're sharing a room."

She freezes and frowns.

"No sex," I mutter as I try to regain my composure. "The op requires us to be a couple, as in cohabitating."

Jesus, what is happening to me? I'm never jumpy under pressure. I like shit smooth. Jumpy as a teenage boy at his first school dance is in no way cool. It's like a whole other zip code.

Candy makes a little sound in her throat. "Okay, I guess. But I admit, your weirdness is starting to worry me."

Yeah, me fucking too. *Mission*, Doz, you're on a goddamned mission.

Quit beating around the fucking bush. I internally grimace and agree with her remark and shift subjects, sort of, because I'm lame as hell. God, the guys on my team would have a fucking field day with this patheticness.

"You think I'm weird?" I ask.

"You *are* weird. You hire a strip club server to help you with some super-secret mission—reconnaissance—like some kind of spy thing. Then you knock a guy down for grabbing my butt, you tell my boss off and threaten him like a boogey-man. So, yeah. Weird. It fits."

I'm grinning. I like her. "Maybe I've been called weird a few times before. My sister actually says that, but she's just horsing around."

After a beat, I sigh and admit, "I'm rambling, but the point is, I probably am a little weird. I've never been a conformist and that's worked just fine."

She looks at me hard, and I expect her to continue the dialog about my odd as shit mood, but instead she frowns and says, "Must be nice to have a sister that cares enough to horse around."

Another fact about the woman goes into my mental file cabinet. No siblings or a bad relationship with them.

"You have any?"

She gives a tight shake of her head. "No. Just me."

"You said your dad died, what about your mother?"

"Gone," she replies succinctly. Almost like she's said the word a million times. Saying her father died, that was harder for her. But telling me her mother's gone was a zero on the scale of emotional reactions.

I change the subject again. "Anyway, I guess it does seem pretty weird. Honestly, I admit, when I found out I needed a date for this mission, I was a little puzzled. But I knew money would take care of the problem. That and some charm."

She blinks at me, then laughs out loud, sounding disbelieving. "Charm? When did you apply this charm?"

"When I got you to sit down and talk to me."

"Maybe I still had five minutes before my shift and was really in the mood for that smoothie."

Damn. I like her playfulness. Hanging out with her is starting to feel easy when it doesn't feel like I have pins being jammed under my nails.

Only, things are about to lean toward pins right now. I need to tell her the rest of the facts. But I'm grinning when I reply, "Maybe. Or maybe it was my animal magnetism."

That leaves her laughing for a solid minute. Which makes me like her even more. Craptastic.

That laugh. Wiggles its way inside of me and says, *Hey Dozer, guess what? This girl is fucking cute and fun.*

I find myself laughing with her, but it's not just a random haha. It's an *oh, shit,* I'm on a slippery slope laugh that rumbles out of me.

My team would definitely know that sound. They'd be on it within seconds of it coming from my chest.

Command, the situation is getting worse over here. Send back up, STAT.

Afterwards, we ride in silence for a few minutes, with guilt starting to eat at me, more and more, stealing bites out of my gut like a piranha. No laughing now.

"Candy, I need to tell you something."

She stops fidgeting with the journal on her lap. The lingering smile falls from her face making my gut turn cold. With a wary glance, she says, "This sounds serious."

"It's complicated."

"What exactly do we have to do for this mission?"

Trying to unclench my jaw, I weave in and out of San Diego traffic. Now I'm being the dick that's going too fast and making questionable lane changes.

The tension in the truck rises to boiling. At least in my seat it is. That's when I decide that I need to look at her for this conversation. One wrong move she could want to bail on the mission, so I start looking for an exit ramp.

While I hope she'll agree for many reasons, I've already decided I'll give her the money anyway. Fuck it. I've got 10K to spare, and obviously she doesn't.

Chapter Eighteen

Candy

Dozer takes the exit ramp and pulls into a dusty patch on the side of the pavement. I've got that grenade in the pit of my stomach again.

Nervously, I blurt, "You're making me uneasy."

He shifts the truck in park, grumbles, "I'm making myself nervous."

I'm acutely aware that when he looks at me this time, there's something different in his expression.

Is that guilt?

Would a serial killer feel guilty before he choked you and threw you in the bushes?

McKenzie! That's awful.

Regardless, guilt just doesn't add up. The man has yet to give me any scary vibes. Other people, yes, they should be scared of him, but he's been nothing but gentle and helpful to me.

After drawing a breath, tightening his jaw, Dozer says, "About this resort..." He scrunches his nose and silently curses. "They're having a nudist event."

I stare at him. If I wasn't puzzling over his words, I'd think seeing this big man so uncomfortable was cute. But... Nude. *Nudist.* "As in, people without clothing will be there?"

The scrunched face turns to a grimace. "I'll be nude."

I start to chuckle and I'm not sure why. "Okay... this is really weird."

His discomfort grows. Which I find oddly amusing and also alarming. Dozer doesn't seem like the kind of guy that is easily made so uneasy. I decide to tease him,

"I thought you said you were comfortable with your masculinity."

His whole body tightens in a snap. He pivots his face forward again and stares out the windshield as his hands clench into fists on his thighs.

That's when it hits me. *The scars.* Dozer has scars. In that moment I've never felt lower for teasing someone in my life. After a really awkward silence I can't stop myself from asking, "Are you worried about your scars?"

He swivels his neck. For a beat he looks at me with his head tilted and his brows tucked together, "My what?"

"I saw that you have scars on your arms and your neck, and it only makes sense that you have more..."

Softening his voice, he says, "No. I'm not worried about my scars. What I'm worried about is the fact that I need you to be naked also."

Oh. Ooooh. Now I get it. Why he looks like he's about to have to eat a lemon.

He's been deceiving me.

That news hangs in the air between us and he watches for my reaction. Which has to be somewhere between shock and hell no.

He goes on with that worried look in his eyes. "You see, no one is allowed in the resort's entertainment areas right now with clothing. Once they've checked into their rooms, it's a nude event."

My face starts to flame, and I know I'm as red as a tomato. "Uh. Wow. That is a complication. Did I miss something when you told me about the offer?"

He shakes his head grimly. "No. I didn't tell you everything."

My brows draw down. That sinking in my gut returns. So, he didn't tell me the truth. Or maybe he did, but not all of it. That feels like a sucker punch to my stomach. "I feel like I need to ask why."

"Because I was honestly just caught up in all that bullshit back there and the only thing I had in mind was getting you out of there safe and making sure you get whatever money you need to get on your way to somewhere better."

I let out a long held breath. "I need some air."

Chapter Nineteen

DOZER

Well, fuck. I check the mirrors. "This isn't a good place to get out."

Candy tries the handle on the door, but it's locked because we were in motion.

The flare of fight or flight sparks in her eyes. Quickly, I hit the unlock button, freeing her. I'm not holding her against her will, and won't ever do that.

But I still curse her choice of moment to get some air.

I'm out a second after her, hustling around the front of the truck, wishing we weren't on the side of a highway exit ramp. It feels exposed as all hell.

She paces, then stops near the rear tire of my truck. Arms crossed, toe tapping in her flip flop. She looks cute but as happy as a baby rattlesnake.

"I owe you a big ass apology."

"Yeah. You do." She stares up into my face with her chin jutted and eyes alight.

"I don't like that you kept that very important piece of information until now."

Fuming, she jams a finger toward the highway. "Conveniently until you have me stranded. If that's not a jerk thing to do, I don't know what is."

I reach for her arm and she glares, but doesn't pull away when I wrap my hand around her elbow. "I'll give you the money anyway. You don't even have to go to the resort."

Her mouth opens and I expect her to tell me I'm a dick but she halts, her breath stutters.

"I'll transfer the money to your bank account now, just give me your ACH details."

Her shoulders sag and her anger morphs into something else. "I don't have an account."

"How old are you?"

"Twenty-four."

I draw in a breath and look off for a second. When I look back down at her pretty gaze, I'm more troubled than I was before. "You've never had a bank account or you currently don't have one?"

She flinches, but holds her chin higher. "I've never had one. I don't have an account. I don't have a phone or a car either, in case you didn't notice."

I shift my weight around as I process. "Where exactly are you from?"

Biting her lip, she watches me like she's trying to figure out exactly how much she should reveal. "Alaska, a tiny little place."

A held breath leaves my lungs in a rush. "I'm glad you

didn't say a cult. Wait, you didn't escape some cult in Alaska, did you?"

"No," she replies with a little shudder. "No cult. Just a very remote place where I lived with my father. He's gone now."

"I'm sorry. I know that has to be hard. Is that where you want to go? I can buy you a plane ticket."

She pulls out of my hold and opens the truck door. Turning to look back at me, she eyes me with sadness written all over her face. "Yes. I want that. I just know it won't solve my problems. But I wouldn't feel right just taking your money when you needed help."

Chapter Twenty

Candy

He drives a few more miles and turns into a big resort. Inglewood Retreat.

The place is like something out of a magazine. I'm wowed. But it's brief because the reality of my situation is riding me like a big storm cloud.

Dozer's not letting it go either. "Tell me what's going on."

"It's nothing. I'm fine."

Fudge. I hate lying. Why did I say that?

I'm not fine. I'm devastated and scared and don't have the first clue how to make my way in the world alone.

A car blares its horn accidentally as someone tries to park their car. Dozer throws them a glare before looking back down at me. "I'll give you the money. Cash if I need to, but I will have to withdraw it after I finish this assignment. That's going to require a trip to the bank."

My shoulders sag a little deeper. While having money will help, I don't have the first idea how to go about starting a new life.

He reaches for me and rubs the back of his knuckles over my thigh. "You okay, sweetheart?"

"Just... tired. Tired of this whole nightmare." More of the fight leaks out of me.

That's when he tugs me forward and wraps me up in his big, strong arms. God. It feels so good to be held.

I've never had arms around me like that before. My father wasn't the hugging type. Sure, he had the man-hug, back slap down. I always wondered why he did that, but once I started working at The Palace, I'd see other men doing it. Never women, only men giving that half-hug with the thunderous back smacks.

This is a whole different world. I burrow deeper without thinking. This is what it feels like to be falling and be caught before you hit the ground.

Relief.

For a long time, we don't say anything. I just lean on him and let him hold me. *God,* it feels good. I want to bury my face in his shirt and just let go for a while. So, I do.

His breathing is steady. The beat of his heart is slow and strong, but I know his brain has to be firing on all kinds of questions right now.

What is he thinking?

That he's gotten hooked up with some kind of nutcase? But his touch is gentle, and I can't think of anything that I need more right now.

After a few minutes, he brushes my hair aside. "You don't have to talk if you don't want to. But I have to get going. Sucks because I'd like to stay here all day and hold you until you feel safe."

Ouch. Good ouch. That unfurls a pain in my heart that I'm not familiar with.

He strokes a very large and warm hand down my back. "I have an idea. We can check in—wearing clothes, and then you can stay in the room while I do the other recon work. I'll just say you're feeling sick. I doubt they will kick me out."

He tips me back so he can see my face. "That way you can take a bath, relax, decompress from everything that's been going on. I'll order room service for you."

Pensively, I look into his eyes. Not an ounce of deceit there. "You'd do that?"

He smiles slowly. "I'd be glad to."

I glance around. Not like I can take off walking from here. I don't even know where I am.

"I could use both the money and the time to figure out what the hell I'm doing."

He slides out of the truck, strides around the front with purpose and helps me down. He hoists both our bags over his shoulder and loops an arm around my neck. "You've got yourself a deal, sweetheart. When I'm done here, I'll help you figure out next steps."

And before I know it, I'm standing in a hotel lobby, being checked in as his wife, under the names Candy and D.C. Smith.

Chapter Twenty-One

DOZER

Second hurdle taken care of. I got into the hotel. We're settled in our room. Now it's time for me to get on with surveilling the targets. A few minutes ago Candy disappeared into the bathroom. Water has been running since, so I suspect she's taking that bath.

Keeping my distance from the door—because getting close to a naked woman in a tub full of bubbles is just stupidly tempting—I call out, "I'm heading downstairs now."

But I get a knock-you-on-your-ass surprise. The ornate bathroom door swings open and I almost fall smack on my face.

For a solid fifteen seconds nothing in my brain works. I

finally squeeze out a jumble of words. "Are you naked under that towel?"

Cinching the fabric tighter, Candy says, "I'm going with you. I don't like the idea of taking your money and not helping you out."

Her eyes flit down my chest, to the towel that's wrapped around my waist, and back up. Pensive but curious. Then determined. "Let's do this," she says with a conviction that I question.

"You're sure?"

Her little chin juts out as she slides on her flip flops. "One hundred percent."

I stare at her in shock as she flutters around. An awkward pause for damned sure, but seeing her standing there in a cotton-candy pink towel, knowing she's got *nothing* on, has frozen me in place.

The first thing I want to do is tell her fuck *NO*. She's not going.

I don't want any other man seeing her.

The second thing I think about is calling in sick. Screw this mission.

Yeah, I'd never do that, but she's the kind of temptation that makes a man go AWOL.

"Dozer, aren't you supposed to be downstairs in two minutes?"

I clear my throat but still sound like I'm chewing gravel. "Right."

Christ. What the hell am I going to do now?

"I'm in," she says resolutely, and there's a new kind of fire in her eyes. "I'm going to do whatever you need for this mission. I'm *gung-ho*, or whatever they say."

I'm not.

Abort mission.

Walking toward the door causes her hips to sway mysteriously below the hem of the towel. My mouth starts to water. My brain contracts and sputters, threatening to shut down the logical side that keeps you from doing impulsive shit.

Dude. You're a fucking jerk. Here she is, trying to help you out and you're one damned breath away from yanking that towel down and taking a bite out of that perky, round, little butt cheek.

"You're up for it?" I croak and I wonder if I'm asking myself or her.

I know I am up. I'm fucking *up*. All nine and a half inches up.

Rock hard.

She nods curtly and clings to a small handbag as if it's a lifeline.

Holy mother fucking fuck. I'm about to spend the next few hours with her naked and on my arm without being able to do any of the things I want to do.

"We should go," I say abruptly because I need to get the hell away from anything that resembles a bed.

Casually, Candy asks, "So, we're meeting your boss, Marshall, and this woman, Dannee, for dinner?"

"And some people that Marshall is investigating with Danee."

"Do I have to do anything?"

"Just act like you like me." And for god sake do not rub your breasts on me. I'm tough and good at my job, but I'm not that tough. Not by a mile.

A little grin tightens her pretty lips. "I'll try."

"Fuck, I'll try not to like you too much."

That makes her chuckle softly. "Just do your job. I'll play along."

Would Candy like to play the games I really want to play with her?

"It could be dangerous," I warn, and I'm not sure if I'm talking about the situation with the suspects we're investigating or the fact that I'm a hungry wolf right now.

She squares her shoulders, looking cute as hell, and says, "Let's do it."

I hold out my arm like I'm going to the prom, not to gather intel on a suspect, and she slides her delicate hand into the corner of my arm. I whisk her out the door so I don't look at her again, because fuck if I can do that right now.

I've got a job to do.

Chapter Twenty-Two

Candy

I guess he was right, I didn't have to worry about clothes. I'm also really grateful that I'm not wearing those heels, because my legs are so shaky I'd take a header for sure.

But I'm determined. I won't take the money without doing my part.

Besides, I'll admit it, I'm more than a little curious about what Dozer and his boss do. The sensation of being in a spy book, one with the world's hottest hero, returns.

Now if I can just keep my cool. Not freak out about being naked. All while not drooling on the tablecloth, I'll be good.

I think.

I hope.

Heavens. When I agreed to his proposition, I never

Jenna Gunn

imagined it would be this. Then when he said it involved nudity, I never imagined I'd be standing in an elevator, about to drop my towel for the world.

Him included.

That thought sends a sunbeam of heat right into the place between my legs. If he looks at me like a hungry wolf when I've got a skirt and tank top on, what's going to happen now?

I almost laugh out loud, but his scowly expression stops me. The man looks like he's one step away from exploding or chewing someone's head off.

"You think this is funny, don't you?"

My brows shoot up. "Mildly."

He chuckles and glances down at the protrusion at the front of his towel. "I wouldn't describe this as mild."

"I don't really understand how erections—"

"Don't breathe that word near me right now."

I press my lips into a grin. "Sorry."

"I'm serious, Candy. I'm a good man, but you strutting around in that towel is about to make me turn into an uncontrollable beast."

What if I want you to?

I swear he can read minds. He growls. "You do not want that."

"Not right now," I say lightly. When did I start enjoying playing with fire?

His hand shoots out and tags me around the back of the neck. With a quick jerk, he pulls me to him and buries his face in the top of my hair.

"I'm one second away from kissing you."

"One second too long," I whisper as I press my palm onto his bare chest.

He curses, fists my hair and tips my face up. God, he's fierce looking.

But the kiss he drops on me is gentle. It's a closed mouth kiss, a slide of his lips across mine. The shadow of his beard grazes my chin.

Until I whimper.

My embarrassment bursts into heat along my throat.

Then Dozer goes all dozer, and plows his way into my mouth with a growl. Our teeth bump, but it's instantly forgotten. Taken place by a decadent glide of his tongue.

I know he's stepped closer because my nipples brush his chest. Lightning shoots from the peaks to my womb. I jolt and fight the moan that's building in my throat.

He doesn't hold his back though. A heavy vibration rattles his chest, rises into his throat and pours into me. Slipping along our tongues. Tightening my body from tip to toe.

His mouth is hot. The feel of his chest against me is overwhelming. The thrust of his tongue is rough as he explores every twist and turn we can try. It's so hot. So dirty that I almost vaporize.

Never be fooled. Dozer knows what he's doing.

His aim is true.

When he pulls the trigger on a kiss, you're gonna be toast.

Chapter Twenty-Three

DOZER

The elevator drops slowly. The symbolism of going lower doesn't escape me.

I'm going to hell.

The thoughts I'm having right now are a one-way ticket.

Fifth floor, fourth, third. Each floor brings a ding.

As we near the second floor, I tear my mouth off hers, wipe my thumb across her glossy-wet lip, and curse myself.

Shit. I've done it now. This mission is officially sideways in the birth-canal.

She's starry-eyed, and I love the way she's looking up at me, like I'm the bomb. Which means she truly is crazy.

My voice is hoarse, and admittedly I'm puffed up with pride when I lean into her ear, and tell her, "I'm not done."

The elevator dings signaling this ride is one floor from

our destination. What a freaking elevator ride it's been. Best one yet. Only, I can think of one that would best it. Me and that stop button might be getting acquainted on the return trip.

"Here goes nothing," Candy says as she reaches for the fold of her towel. Then she's naked and on full display for me in the shiny elevator door.

Color brightens her cheeks, but that's as far as I can see because I AM NOT looking at her tits... or her pussy.

I am not.

Fuck. I am.

The little tank top didn't do her any justice. She's perfection with her dusky pink nipples and heavy breasts. My mouth starts to water like I'm a rabid wolf.

Christ. I can't help but look at her banging body. I adjust the towel that's around my waist, which is now officially a circus tent. What the fuck do I do about that?

The bell dings one last time. The fuck-me-this-is-happening lobby level. The door slides open and she steps out into the warm lighting of a hallway with walls of mirrors.

I'm admittedly in disbelief for a few seconds. But Candy's shoulders are square, her head is high, but her towel and purse are in a grip that says she's not nearly as confident as she'd like for the world to think.

Our little secret. She's a tough chick, and damn, I love that about her.

With a chuckle, I stride after her. "Hold on there, hotshot." With a pivot, she lifts her brows and gives me a pointed look, one that falls to my towel. Which is still firmly fastened around my waist. "Uh, hum."

Nothing's awkward about this.

How about what the *FUCK* isn't awkward about this.

Right. Naked, now.

Dropping the towel, I stand up straight. And when I say stand up, I mean all fucking six-four of me and my nine-and-a-half-inch cock which is proudly erect from sharing a very small space, and the best damned kiss I've ever had. With. Her.

The look she gives me says more than words. Wide eyes, and her teeth pinching at her lip.

I laugh at her furious blush, her unblinking gaze, and the hand that goes to her mouth. I say, "You agreed."

As she whirls on her heel, she's not only got that fire in her cheeks, she's got a mischievous grin on her face. "I didn't know what I was getting into."

"Well, now you do."

Chapter Twenty-Four

DOZER

We meet the boss and his client Danee in the lobby. Danee, also naked, looks as if she's about to faint. Beside me, Candy is vibrating with energy, but she's got a stiff spine and a determined expression on her face.

Damn. I sure do like her grit.

Not to mention that I love the way she tastes. My grin probably looks like I just won the lottery. Not to be disrespectful of the situation, but I can't get my face to comply.

Thankfully, we don't stand around inside the hotel lobby long and start our walk to the on-site restaurant.

As we turn right on the sidewalk, we pass a few other guests, and I notice Candy stiffens suddenly.

I pull her to a stop and nod toward Marshall, letting him know we'll be right in. "Hey, are you okay?"

"I just need a second."

"What happened?"

She shudders, pinches her lips in, and looks away.

"I don't know. It sort of hit me. I'm naked in front of about a hundred men. It's a LOT." Her voice goes up. "And they're looking at me."

"Well. Fuck them."

"Shhh. Those people might hear you cursing."

I glance over my shoulder and scowl at everyone that's passing by.

When I face her again, she's watching my face.

"So what? All I care about right now is that you feel like that."

"It's okay. I promise. I just needed a second."

"Well, I can give you more than a second. But we are really exposed here," I growl and squint my eyes at a guy that's looking a little too damned hard in our direction.

"There are beautiful naked women everywhere." A fact that has not escaped me, but I've got eyes for one. Only one.

She goes on. "I'm not sure why they'd want to look at me, but I just felt like all those eyes pivoted to me and stuck."

"Sweetheart, men are gonna look at you. How can they not? Shit, you're like some woodland fairy crossed with a Playboy pin-up."

She makes a face. "You think that?"

I grin and nod. "But I'm not making light of this. I don't want you to feel like you are a part of some exhibit."

"It's okay. I just don't know how to process this now that I'm in it."

That makes two of us.

"Just pretend they are wearing a bozo wig or something."

Her eyes flash to mine and she almost smiles. "You're right. I have to think about something else. I just need to catch my breath. It's just that I've never been naked in front of a man before... So, it's a little crazy to be in front of a bunch of them."

Screech.

Everything halts. I crowd her to the side of the sidewalk. Processing what she said. "Can you repeat that?"

Her head tilts to the side. "What part?"

"The part where you said you've never been naked in front of a man before..."

"Right. I've..." she daintily clears her throat. "I've never been naked in front of a man before."

I'm trying really hard, but that information does not compute. "What do you mean?"

She blinks and color starts to creep up her neck again, but this time it's deep red and darkened with something different than her playful embarrassment before. Her next word comes out reluctantly. "Nothing."

"Candy..." I growl.

"It's *nothing*."

"No. This is something. You just told me, twice, that you've never been unclothed in front of a man. That's a big fucking deal." My hand goes through my hair. I want to tear it all out. I feel like I'm pushing her past her breaking point and that is not fucking right. "We don't have much time, but I want you to tell me exactly what you meant because right now I'm feeling pretty fucking shitty about you being so uncomfortable."

"I'm fine."

I growl and lean close. "Don't lie to me, Candy, or whatever your name is."

"McKenzie."

I rear back and look down into those pale, cool eyes. Only they're not cool now. They're brimming with some kind of emotional storm.

Vulnerability.

That's what it is.

A layer has peeled back, and this tough, mysterious woman has just opened a new door for me.

Softly, just for my ears, she says, "It's McKenzie. Rush is my last name. You probably saw that on the Navy-issued duffel."

"McKenzie Rush," I murmur, letting the name slide over my tongue for the first time. It tastes right there. "Justin Roark."

"That's your real name?"

I nod as I look down at her, feeling like we're crossing bridges here.

For some unexplained reason, I imagine I'll be crossing a lot of bridges with McKenzie Rush.

"There's a lot we need to talk about," I say with finality. Even though I'm not sure what that encompasses. I just know I'm off keel right now. "If you want to go back upstairs right now, I'll walk you there."

She touches that little star necklace at the base of her throat and looks up at me. Resolve replacing the vulnerability. "No. I'm going to help you do this because your money will help me in ways you'll never understand."

Damn.

"It doesn't have to be like that. I'll still give you—"

She rests a hand on my bare chest, the coolness of her delicate fingertips instantly triggering a landslide of want.

"Dozer, take what I'm offering. I don't want to be a charity case. I'll be fine. I've done hard things before."

My hand moves up and presses over hers, caging it to my sternum. "I don't see you as a charity case."

"What, then?" she asks as she stands taller.

I glance up at the people passing us, entering the restaurant. I wish I knew. Fuck, how I wish I knew. "Something I can't explain right now."

Her fingers spread wider against my chest. "Let's do this, Dozer. I'm ready."

Christ. I'm not. I want to stay here with her cocooned against the wall and kiss her until she runs that hand up and loops it around my neck. I want to protect her. I want to keep her safe from the eyes of other men. The last damned thing I want is for her to be uncomfortable because of my job.

She pushes me gently and swings her hair over her shoulder revealing the swell of her breast. "Come on. I'm hungry. That BLT was just a tease, now I want something really good."

So. Do. I.

So damned bad.

My throat constricts as she ducks under my arm and takes a step toward the restaurant door. I'm hungry, and it's not for anything a damned restaurant will serve.

With a little come-hither wave, she smiles softly. And that's when I know I'm a goner.

McKenzie Rush is so damned beautiful with her pale skin, her long shimmering hair, and eyes that twist a man's brain to shreds.

All the years I've resisted getting involved with a woman have come to an end. Even if this doesn't go any farther, I'm involved in a way that I never thought I would be.

I just pray that I can do right by her. Because McKenzie Rush deserves a better man than me, of that I'm sure.

Too bad I might not be enough of a man to let her walk away.

Shaking my head, I step toward her, take her offered hand, and refocus on the mission. I'm good at compartmentalization. One of my super-skills, also one that every single counselor I've had detests. But right now, while I'm working this case with Marshall Lake and his client, I'm not a man that's got a gorgeous probable *virgin* accompanying him to dinner, and sharing a room with him at a nude resort.

I'm here to dig out evidence that they need to take down a threat.

A risk that I've now dragged Candy, AKA McKenzie into.

Chapter Twenty-Five

Candy

Dinner is fascinating and stressful. But the beautiful women at the table—Danee and Vanessa— and the man with Vanessa, are obviously the objects of interest at the table. With the focus on them, I actually get to relax.

Mostly, I watch Dozer as he slips into his element. The observer and the interrogator, silkily asking questions that seem to drag out information that he and Marshall need.

I have no idea what the case is about, but little pieces filter into place, however, not enough for me to understand the overall picture.

Many of the books I've read were suspense stories, with little bits dribbled to the reader as the story unfolds. Tonight is like being inside of one of those stories, with all the players at the table, secrets being held tight.

It's exciting. The food is delicious, but almost forgotten. Not completely, though. The courses set before me are so beautiful and so elaborate that it feels like I'm not only inside a mystery novel, but also inside a fairytale.

Danee and Marshall leave quickly, but Dozer hangs in there, casting me a glance to make sure I'm okay. That's when the man across the table, the man who said he was Vanessa's boyfriend, begins to share openly.

Maybe it's the alcohol. More likely it's Dozer doing what he does. Unraveling your protective layers and slipping behind your armor.

Fascinated, I lean on the table and follow the conversation, only the man and woman might think I'm just enjoying the company when I'm actually enamored with the man who's resting his hand beneath mine under the table.

For a little while I forget my troubles and fall into the moment. Another hour passes, and the man gets drunk. *Straight up sloshed*, as my father would say.

Barely able to talk, Vanessa escorts his leaning body out of the restaurant, with the man practically hanging on her supermodel body.

Dozer offers me a hand. "That went well," he says quietly. "Now I need to go have a chat with Marshall."

We hurry through the lobby, our towels draped over our arms. Weirdly, it doesn't even feel like we're naked now, or maybe it's the mission-mode that Dozer is in. His brain is whirring with something as he rests a hand on my lower back and ushers me into the quiet of the elevator.

When the door closes, his eyes skate to mine. "You did great."

"No, you did." I smile at his reflection. "You're a master at that."

His eyes soften. A little roughness enters his voice. "I've got lots of experience."

For a beat, I consider the comment. Not only is Dozer good at his job, he's probably very experienced at *other* things. The kinds of things I have no experience with.

That's when I remember where I saw a man like him. A body like his. At the library, on the front of a men's magazine. A boxer... no, wait, an MMA fighter. Whatever that is. I didn't stop to read the magazine, but that man was stuck in my head. All that honed muscle and restrained aggression. That photo was a moment of stillness in a life defined by motion. That is Dozer.

His eyes hold mine, but the awareness of my body is there in his eyes again, as if the job is fading for a moment at least.

"I wish I didn't have to follow up with Marshall right now."

I nod, but I don't know what I'm nodding to. He turns to face me, carefully reaches out and loops a strand of my hair around his fingers. "I'd rather come back to the room with you so we could finish—"

The bell dings and the door whooshes open. Two naked people are standing there, expectantly waiting for us to exit.

"Finish what?" I ask as Dozer drags me out of the door by my hand.

A few seconds later the door slams behind us. Dozer throws his towel on the ground. We breathe at each other.

It feels like I've been running. My chest is pumping. My heart skipping. Everything tingles. Everywhere he looks with those commanding eyes heats like he's touching me.

God. I'm ready. So darned ready to feel his hands on me.

Dozer was careful not to touch my body in the elevator.

113

He had one hand fisted in my hair, the other around the base of my throat, but he didn't even skim my body below that.

"What are we finishing," I needle. Because if he doesn't touch me soon, I'm going to go all crazy and throw myself on him. Forget what I don't know... Who cares if I'm awkward.

Now, I need to know.

Bing. Bing.

Dozer glares furiously at the phone lying on the dresser. "Fuck," he bites out. "Fuck. This has to be the world's worst timing."

He takes a step closer to me, close enough that I have to look up into those burning eyes. "I'm not going to touch you, even though it's the single hardest thing I've ever done in my life. But if I touch you right now, I'm going to start something I can't finish. Leaving a mission unfinished isn't in my ethics. When I do something I do it right."

My throat dries totally. I lick across my lips. I can't wait to be the focus of that mission. My body's vibrating for him. For him.

The words echo inside of my brain. Making me feel tipsy and unsteady.

Dozer's done something to me. And I don't know whether I should lean in or hide. But if I follow my body's intuition, I want it all. Everything he has to give when he gives his all.

He draws in a breath, slow and long through his nose. "You smell so fucking good. I'm gonna devour you. Every single fucking inch of you."

My eyes drift closed as I sway. "I want that."

He makes a rough sound. Steps toward me. Even

though his phone dings again, he slides his fingers into my hair. Dropping his head, he trails his lips along my neck. Nipping. Pressing the heat of his mouth against me. "I have to go meet with Marshall right now, but when I get back, we're going to talk about boundaries. Because I need to know if you're ready for what I need."

"What do you need?" I whisper hoarsely.

"More than you can ever imagine."

His lips slide to mine. His tongue drives in again and he drags me against his chest. We're locked together thigh to shoulder with his engorged cock pressed against my stomach.

That contact is the single most beautiful feeling I've ever felt. Like coming home.

Crazy things are happening in my body. Heat. Flutters. Wetness between my folds.

When he pulls away, he curses. Drags my hand between my legs. I shudder as he presses my fingertips to my clit, holding my hand firmly beneath his own. "Do you know how to get yourself off?"

"Yes..." I reply hesitantly. I've masturbated enough to know my way around my body. But having him touch me, makes me realize that giving myself an orgasm is a freaking poor substitute.

"I want to think about you in here touching yourself, waiting on me to come back."

When he pulls his hand away, he licks his fingers as he looks me right in the eye. "Be ready for me," he murmurs.

Oh. Heavens. Yes. I'm already there. This ferocious ache he's started isn't going away until I get the antidote —him.

He breaks away. I'm left standing. Weak. Touching

myself with shaking fingers. He dresses and walks out without looking back.

My god. What just happened?

Chapter Twenty-Six

DOZER

"Brother," Marshall says when he opens the door. I'm dressed in jeans and a T-shirt again because fuck the resort rules, I have shit to do. Marshall has his pants on too. "That was weird as hell," he adds as he motions me inside.

Shaking my head, I have to laugh. "I've done a lot, but let's say that's the weirdest. After actually going to a strip club to recruit my companion."

"No shit?" Marshall half-snorts as he halts. "She's a *stripper*? I thought she seemed embarrassed about being naked."

"A cocktail waitress... sort of." I add the last bit, but we don't have time to get into the story. But I do think it is time I test the waters on the 10K I'd promised Candy. He said the budget was open-ended, but...

"By the way, I promised her ten thousand to be here for the weekend."

He shrugs, "Whatever you need. Like I said, when you work for Agile, you have whatever you need, whenever."

I watch his face for micro expressions that would reveal that he's joking. None.

"Copy, I just wanted to give you a heads up." I hold his gaze as I let his reassurance sink in. This job is gonna be hella-interesting. And I thought I enjoyed the SEALs, this could be a fucking awesome new career.

Marshall offers me a drink from the wet bar. I accept a bottle of water instead of anything alcoholic because I'm sure this conversation is going to end with me on a flight. "So. What else did you find?"

"I think I've got the lead you're looking for."

Relief washes over Marshall's face. "Fucking-A, that is the best fucking news I've heard in a month." He grabs me and slaps my back in a man hug. "Well done, brother."

I stand. "Mind if I bring Candy over?" Because I don't want to be more than ten feet from her, which puzzles the hell out of me.

Marshall pushes up off the couch, "That works. Time to return the watch."

"Watch your six, man."

Marshall nods. "I won't be gone long. Besides, he's twelve sheets to the wind, according to how much you said he drank at dinner. He probably won't even remember me dropping the thing off."

When I return to Marshall's room from getting Candy, things have gone all to shit. And I'm not talking about my control. Even though she was ready and willing, I kissed her. Helped her get dressed and dragged her off to Marshall and Danee's room. Because work isn't going away tonight.

But the all to shit I'm talking about is that the case took a nosedive. Fuck, that happened fast, but that's how missions tend to go. One minute you're cruising, the next you're in a firestorm.

The woman from dinner named Vanessa is now in Marshall and Danee's hotel room and Danee is comforting her.

Marshall wastes no time getting down to business. He launches into a plan that fits right into my skill set—a stealth water approach of the suspect's sailboat.

Which means, I'm leaving. Without Candy.

That hits like a punch in the gut. My mind starts to spin ways to keep her from taking off. But there's nothing to tie her to me... except ten thousand dollars.

I'd be a bastard for using that.

But I might just be willing to stoop that low to figure out why I get such a visceral reaction from the woman.

Chapter Twenty-Seven

Candy

When I thought the evening... heck, the whole day couldn't get any weirder, Dozer hustles me to his boss's hotel room.

My self-given orgasm did nothing to quell the burn the man started. But my attention swings abruptly from him to the madness inside his boss's hotel room.

When the door opens, the inside is total chaos.

Vanessa, the woman from dinner, is crying.

Danee's comforting her and Marshall looks like he's gonna break something. Maybe the whole building if someone doesn't intervene.

I shrink back and let Dozer deal, because I have no idea what to say or do given that I've just met these people.

Obviously, something heavy is happening and I'm not able to see the puzzle pieces. All I know is that Marshall refuses to leave Danee alone for more than a few minutes. Smart call. Danee had been in danger from a recent attack.

Which means Dozer's going to be doing the dangerous work of chasing down the bad guy. Thank god, Marshall says he's getting a team together and making preparations for Dozer to do something they're calling a stealth water entry.

A shiver tightens my chest. The image of an inky black ocean swallowing Dozer makes my stomach twist and turn acidic.

He's a SEAL. Of course he's going to do dangerous things in the ocean. But an image of him climbing aboard a sailboat in the middle of the night with a knife clenched in his teeth is too much to stand.

"You okay, babe?" he asks, when I visibly flinch next to him.

"Sorry, just rattled."

He strokes a warm hand over my thigh, pressing against the butter-soft silk pajama pants I have on. Reminding me that he had room service deliver the pair of beautiful pajamas to the room for me.

For me.

McKenzie Rush got a pair of silk pajamas as a gift from a man.

Hell might be freezing over right now.

When room service arrived, I couldn't hold back the mist that formed on my lashes. So, I did what any embarrassed woman does—flee to the bathroom.

Silly. A little gift. Only, that little gift meant *everything*.

Especially when he said, "I wanted you to have something comfortable, something beautiful."

I almost lost it. Came a fraction of a breath away from bursting into tears. But thankfully he hugged me and I could hide my face in his shirt. I just hope he didn't see the tear marks on his cotton T-shirt.

Turns out Dozer is more than observant. He'd seen the delicate pink silk pajamas in the window of the hotel boutique on one of his passes through the lobby. But that wasn't what made my throat tight. It was that he thought of me.

With his warm, strong hand on my leg, I am starting to believe that he really is interested in me.

Ridiculous. But hope is alive, I guess. Only things are about to get rough. Another bracing thought hits me. Dozer's going away on a dangerous mission.

This could be it.

The end of something precious that hasn't even had a chance to grow.

I turn to stone inch by inch as I sit here on the couch in Marshall and Danee's suite. No one knows that on the inside, I'm erecting my armor, bit by bit. I can't take another slice to my heart. It's suffered too many blows in my short lifetime. I know that I won't survive another.

Once I'm officially encased in ice, I clear my throat and catch Dozer's attention. "Does this mean we're done now?"

Danee instantly jumps in. "I'm sorry you got caught up in this, I'm not sure how you got here, but I'm sure this has been a weird evening. I hope your dinner was good at least."

I like the woman. Too bad I'll never see her again. "It was, but I was so nervous I could barely talk. I apologize if I seemed rude."

"Well, I'm thankful that you came and helped Dozer get into the resort."

Marshall studies her like she's the most fascinating book he's ever held. Like he's reading between every line and nuance. He's so much like Dozer but so different. Marshall says, "I'm sure that was an interesting ask. Hey, want to go to a nudist resort with me?"

I laugh, even though it feels wooden. "He made me an offer I couldn't refuse."

Marshall tips his chin at Dozer. "I hope you made it worth her while."

Dozer looks at me then with a clear, open expression. It startles me, then he adds to the effect by saying, "I'm going to do my best."

The room falls silent. I'm not sure how long we look at each other, but my breath is locked in my throat, and my body is crackling with awareness from his serious gaze.

Finally, Dozer rises, standing to his full, imposing height. "I'll get Vanessa to the airport as soon as the cops take her statement, and then I'll come back." He pointedly looks at me. "Don't go anywhere, Candy. I'm coming back for you."

Me.

I sit stunned. Maybe this is why animals freeze when they are scared, because right now something inside of me is screaming 'run while you can,' and another part is freezing me to the sofa.

Sometime while I sit there, the men leave with Vanessa.

"I guess it's just the two of us," Dannee says as she curls up in the sitting chair. Her brows are tight with worry.

For some reason I spill my most personal thoughts. "I'm thinking about running. But truthfully, I have a feeling that man would hunt me down."

She narrows her lashes. "I have a feeling you might be right."

What would it be like to be pursued by Dozer? Would he go to the ends of the Earth to chase me down? Or would he walk away, knowing that I've got serious shit in my past, things he should never tangle himself up with.

I admit, "These guys sure are intense."

Danee lays back on the chair and closes her eyes. "You have no idea."

Chapter Twenty-Eight

DOZER

All night long, I've seen the way Danee and Marshall look at each other. Marshall's my new boss, so I'm not sure what his rules are about mixing it up with clients, but it sure as hell looks like he's mixing it up hard with Danee.

That soft look she gives him...

Dead giveaway.

I open my truck door and help Vanessa inside. Marshall steps into the door and has a brief private conversation with the woman.

Obviously they share some kind of serious history, but right now I know the man only has eyes for Danee.

Smart man.

She's not only beautiful, whip-smart, she's also over the moon for the man.

He closes the door and I shake his hand.

"Good work, tonight," he says.

"You too." As I step back, I think better of what I'm about to say, but my mouth has other things in mind. "You'll take care of Candy?"

A slow grin slides onto Marshall's stony face. I haven't hid anything about my interactions with Candy, but I also haven't said anything about what has transpired. Or the things she makes me think about.

Those are my thoughts alone. Most of them are X-rated, the others just rattle the shit out of my core.

Not that anything has transpired, other than me being swept up by her innocent damned attractiveness. That and whatever story has driven her to the desperate situation she's living in.

Marshall reassures me with a quick tip of his chin. "Danee and I will look out for her."

"Appreciate that."

"She's an interesting woman."

I notice he's careful not to comment on her exotic beauty. Especially not on her banging body. Men know when to tread carefully.

"Makes me kind of crazy, to tell you the truth."

He busts out with a single, short laugh. "Brother, I feel ya. I can't tell you how crazy that woman has made me feel since she walked into my life."

"It's gotta get better," I grumble. "Because I can't fucking walk around like this."

He chuckles again. "Yeah, tell me when that happens. I've watched this play out in the men that work for me, thought I was immune, or I'd be able to keep my head straight. Now I'm beginning to think I'm the one failing. Or falling. As fucked up as this thing I feel for her makes me feel, I also know it's the happiest I've been in a long time."

I'm shaking my head as I round the truck. "You don't have to tell me. I'm right there with you."

He tosses his chin as I climb in and turn on the truck, feeling twitchy and ready to be on the fucking road to Mexico.

I've got business to finish with Candy.

Talking being the first.

Touching her pretty body, soon thereafter.

That is, if she'll have me. And that's something that remains to be seen. Maybe she's gonna be smart about it and tell me no. As much as that would sting, I'd be glad for her. She's had enough to deal with, and my under-fucking-stand-able need to claim her is the last thing she should be thinking about.

But none of that, whatever that is, is happening until this mission is a wrap. That isn't happening until I get my act in fucking gear.

If there's one thing I don't like it's open-ended bullshit. I like things tight, squared away, and locked down.

Only, a little voice in my head says, "Good luck, buddy. Women are anything but simple."

If only I knew how true that thought would turn out to be.

Chapter Twenty-Nine

Candy

I wasn't sure what I expected to happen after dinner, but it was not for things to escalate and go sideways so quickly.

Dozer had to leave on a dangerous reconnaissance mission immediately, leaving me with a spinning mind, and a hollowed out feeling in my chest.

After taking a bath, pacing, trying to watch television, I fell into a terrible sleep. Only to be awakened by pounding on my door and news that the sweet brunette, Danee Swann, had been taken from the resort against her will.

It's now twelve hours later and I'm still dazed and stunned when one of the Agile guys walks me up the steps of a farmhouse in Utah. After a private plane flew us to the mountainous community, I was escorted to a hold-out until things are resolved.

I'm more than a little unsure why I'm here, but with everything that's happened, I've just been swept along in the chaos.

Rubbing my eyes, I fight the yawn that would be rude. I haven't slept in thirty-six hours, minus a few minutes of a nap on the private jet.

How could I sleep, though? Danee must be terrified. Marshall was barely restrainable. The whole team is ready to tear the world apart.

The tall, brutally handsome man that's my escort knocks twice. The sound echoes through the big wooden door. With his shoulders square and jaw tight, he waits for someone to answer.

Shuffling sounds come from the other side. Soon, the door is swinging open to reveal a small woman with a pleasant, sun-weathered face. She's tiny, not even as tall as I am. With a flicker of a smile, she says, "Mako! Come on inside. It's good to see you, but I wish it wasn't under these circumstances. Nevertheless, thanks for bringing our guest over."

With a tuck of his chin, he holds the door and motions me through. "Yes, ma'am."

"This must be Candy. I'm Nolene Strong." She opens her arms and grabs me in a fierce hug, squeezing me to her flour-covered floral apron. "Honey, you come on in. I've got a room ready for you."

She turns back to my escort with narrowed eyes. Mako met the Agile jet at the airport and has taken care of me since. She asks, "How's Marshall this morning?"

"Rough. Chewing nails."

She shakes her head, clenches the dish-towel in her hands. "I can't believe someone just grabbed that girl, but I know the Agile team will get her back, though."

"We will," he replies confidently. I pray he's right. Danee's had trouble in her past, and I'm terrified for her.

Spinning on her socks, the woman motions for me to follow her. "Let's get you settled."

"You're sure you don't mind? I wouldn't want to be an imposition."

"Not at all. Marshall said that you'd be staying a bit while you sorted some personal things out. I knew he meant that you'd be here till the mission was done."

I'm kind of speechless for a second, then she smiles gently at me.

"I... have a lot of things up in the air right now."

"Well, you're welcome to stay as long as you need. This big, old farmhouse has lots of space. That's what happens when you raise five boys and they all marry and run off to have kids."

The screen door creaks open behind us. A man that I've never seen before steps in. He's wearing black scrubs, a stethoscope, and a pair of running shoes. "Hey Mom."

There's an instant transformation in the woman's face. "Liam, what a nice surprise. Speaking of one of my boys, this is my oldest." She hustles over and wraps her arms around the waist of the man.

He hugs her back. "I can't stay. Clinic's busy today, but I wanted to stop by to look at your stitches."

She tsks. "They're fine. Healing up well. Not stopping me, that's for sure. I'm busy as usual."

With a very unhappy look, the man scolds his mother. "You're not getting that cut wet, are you?"

She smacks him with the end of her dish towel. "No. I'm wearing my gloves. You sound like your father."

"That's because he raised me. But seriously, don't get that cut in dish water. I'd hate to have to sic Sophia on you."

His mom lifts a brow and pins him with a look. "You wouldn't."

Liam grins and replies, "You know I would."

"Get." She shoos him out the door, but he pushes her toward the kitchen. "Not until I have a look."

They wander off, and as their voices fade, she says, "Keep an eye on Marshall, will you? I know he's under an awful strain right now. I don't want anything happening to that boy."

The man replies, "I'm heading to his house next," then they start talking about her stitches.

Mako shifts his weight around. "I need to get going, but I have something for you."

He surprises me by holding out a cell phone. "Dozer and I talked. He asked me to give you this. His number's already programmed in there, but he's still in Mexico right now, so the satellite phone number might be better. It's also programmed in. The rest of the Agile team's numbers are in there too."

I'm speechless. I don't even know these people and they are making themselves available to me.

Mako studies me as I look at the phone with my heart in my throat. "He'll be back as soon as he can."

"I hope he's not worrying about me, everyone needs to be focused on getting her back."

Mako smiles slowly. "He's worried about you. But don't worry. I've known Dozer for a long time. If anyone will tear the world apart until that woman's home, he's the man."

"You served with him?"

"For seven years. Go ahead, I can see questions in your eyes."

"Of course, I have questions. I know nothing about him."

He glances toward the kitchen where there's a lively discussion going on, then meets my gaze again. He's far more serious now. I'm not sure how that is possible, but his eyes are flinty in the dim lighting of the vestibule.

"I'll tell you this, Dozer's the best man you'll ever meet. He's loyal to the thousandth degree, the kind of man you want to have your back. He's as brave as they come, and smart as fuck. I've watched him in battle for years and there's *no one* like him. This is something you need to know too, he is ferociously protective of the people he cares about, and that now includes you."

Ooooohkay. Breathless.

After I recover from that punch to the solar plexus, I murmur, "I kinda got that impression, but truthfully I don't want him worrying unnecessarily."

Mako looks down at me thoughtfully. "You're not convincing him or me that you're good. There's something going on and I know he's getting to the root of it."

"I didn't mean for him to get involved with my mess. I just thought I was helping him and he was helping me, and now... I don't know what's happening because it seems like he's getting attached or something. I can't exactly explain it, but he didn't want me to leave the resort... then here I am. He didn't have to do any of this for me."

"Too late to analyze, he is attached," he says matter-of-factly with a guarded grin. "I've heard the way that man talks about you. In all the years I've known him, he's never sounded like that when he talked about a woman. So... invested, for a lack of a better word."

"It's nothing. Maybe a crush, but nothing."

"For you maybe. But for him, I think it's gonna be far more than a crush."

Then the smile disappears from his face and a hard

façade slides over him. The transformation is instant and unsettling. "I want to tell you something, McKenzie. Dozer's not the only one who is protective of the people he cares about. That man is like a brother to me. Hell, he's closer than family, if you get what I'm saying. But my point is, if you hurt him in any way, shape or form, you'll have me to deal with."

A biting silence slams over us. After a stare down that feels more like a beatdown, he says, "He deserves to be happy after what he's gone through."

The air swirls when he takes a step back. "My number's in there. If you need anything, don't hesitate to call me. Dozer cares about you, that means I care, and the Agile team does too."

When the front door closes after him, I'm left staring.

It feels like something major has just transpired. A welcome into their fold, with a heavy warning on the side.

I would never hurt Dozer on purpose, but worry starts to bloom inside of my chest. I know *nothing* about relationships.

What if I do or say the wrong thing? What if I misread him? I don't know what's happened in his past, but whatever it is that made Mako give his warning must be bad.

I'm still standing frozen in the living room when the front door opens and another woman breezes in. She gives me a warm smile. "Oh, hello," she chirps, then continues her trajectory to the kitchen.

Apparently the kitchen is the center of the universe in this house.

A moment later, Liam passes through on his way out. He throws up a hand. Grumbling, he says, "Make sure she's wearing her gloves."

He also disappears out the door.

Giving my head a little shake, I mutter, "Feels like I'm in a different world." One where I have no point of reference. A place where a man is determined to help me. His friends warn me to take care of him, and where I'm swept up in the middle of a team of people in a town I've never been to.

When I walk into the kitchen, the women have their heads inside the door of what looks like a really big, well-stocked pantry.

Jealous. Admittedly.

Not just of the shelves of obsessively organized supplies that could feed a household for a year, but also at how close the two women seem. A fact that's obvious in the way their shoulders are pressed together and they are sharing a laugh.

Lump in throat—go away.

I drag my eyes away and look around the Strong family kitchen. It's a beautiful space, warm with sunshine, country accents, and cheery paint. There's an enormous wooden table in the adjoining dining area that can probably seat well over a dozen, and out back there's a wide, expansive lawn that stretches off to fenced ranchland.

A lot of love has been shared in this room. Lovingly prepared meals. Kids' laughter. Stories shared. Family bonds built that will never be broken.

Lump—you're not supposed to get bigger.

I choke down my silly emotions as the women return to the granite island with arms full of supplies. For a minute, I wonder if I should bow out and go to the room Nolene has prepared for me. But their chatter is grounding. Finally, I take a breath.

You can do this.

I've never spent time in a kitchen like this with friends to cook with and a big family to feed.

My mind drifts to Dozer. He grew up with a big family. I wonder if this is what his life was like growing up?

Suddenly, I'm warm all over and inside and out, like all the love is seeping right into my bones. It's the strangest feeling ever.

I want to make it last forever and running to the bedroom would just isolate me from the source. "Can I help with something?"

The older woman glances over her shoulder with raised brows. "Know how to bake?"

"I can make a mean loaf of bread."

Her smile beams like sunshine and she tosses me a pink checkered apron. "Well, that's the best news I've heard all day. We got a whole lot of men to feed while they work on that case."

And just like that I'm swept into the fold. But my heart feels guarded.

Don't get used to this, McKenzie.

Chapter Thirty

DOZER

I'm sleepy, grumpy as fuck when I hit Utah. It doesn't help that I have no idea when I'll get to see my sweet Candy. Work isn't done, so I head to Marshall's house.

With my pack in one hand, I swing open the front door, wishing like hell I was going to have Candy rush into my arms.

God, what is that amazing smell? Only fresh, home cooked meals can light up your tastebuds like that.

My stomach growls loudly. I scan the room expecting to find the usual suspects—the Agile team.

But I get my second shock.

Candy.

Her eyes collide with me and we freeze. I missed those warm beauties on me. *Fuck, let's go.*

The drive to pick her up, throw her over my shoulder and stride off to the closest bedroom is visceral.

My control is threadbare. Which blows. She is probably a virgin. That equals the absolute requirement to make sure her first time is slow, gentle, and the right kind of memorable.

But fuck. I'm losing the battle. We need some alone time fast.

I'm jolted back to the reality where I'm standing in Marshall's living room when Mako slaps me on the back. "Hey man, welcome back. How was everything?"

"Everything was good. Ready to help out in any way I can," I answer, completely talking out of my ass because I can't think.

I've got room for only one thing in my head. My eyes never leave Candy's. I need to take her beauty in. Need her light to get me through the next however many days.

"We're about to sit down, the whole team, so just throw your gear in your room and join us," Mako says as he walks toward where the other men are gathered around a table.

Nolene gives me a smile as she sets some food on the kitchen counter.

But all of that is secondary and unimportant.

Dropping my bag at my feet, keeping my eyes on my girl, I take a couple of steps forward and open my arms wide, letting her know where she belongs.

The spell snaps, frees her feet, and she runs to me and lands in my arms with a sigh. *God.*

"Babe," I murmur against her hair.

She tightens her grip on my arms which results in an equal tightening in my heart. Shit. This is exactly what I was afraid would happen.

Too bad I'm completely unable to control whatever this is that's growing between us.

"Missed this," I growl.

Some would say I'm stupid for missing the feel of her when I've only had it once. But that elevator kiss did it for me—seared the soft contours of her right into my mind.

She feels even better now. Soft sweet places against my harder angles.

I want to kiss her, take her, mark her. Brand her. But I can't. I won't. The mission needs to come first now, and if I do anything other than hug her, I know I'll be lost. Gone.

We've got a fucking audience too.

I set her back and look her over. "You're okay?"

"Fine. But we're not staying. I know you have work to do."

I nod because my throat is tight with words that won't help right now. *Stay. Don't go.*

Pensive, she bites her lip. "I rode with Nolene, I should go so she doesn't have to wait."

I want to drive her myself, but that's going to cut into working with the team. "It's okay. I'll come soon."

Quickly, before she can step out the door, I tag her and pull her against me again. "I'll be in touch."

Her gaze rises to mine and sticks. "I'll be waiting. I'm glad you're back safely."

When she's gone, I head to the dining table where the team is gathering. Damn if I can concentrate. That's something I'm going to have to deal with soon.

Later that night, when I finally get a second to take my shit to my room, I start to text.

Can't wait to see you again.

But I delete the message.

Fuck. I'm screwed. How is it that this girl I've just met has me so tightly wrapped around her finger?

All kinds of ugly nonsense start to rear up in my messed up brain. Should I just give her the money and let her go? Let her live her life and go back to the way things were?

Christ. Right. Now that I've had a taste of everything she is, can I really do that?

Pathetic that even just one second is too long to let her out of my sight.

What the fuck do I do?

I need to focus on the mission now. We need to bring Danee home safely.

All hands on deck, but my why on getting this done fast is big. The sooner we get her back, the sooner I get to see what this thing with Candy is all about.

Because fuck if I know.

Chapter Thirty-One

Candy

I stretch my aching back. Jeez, I thought I was used to work. Until I hit the ranch. Life here is different from home-steading. Different busy.

Leaning back over the sink, I massage suds into a thick head of auburn hair.

The common thread is there's always something that needs to be done. In Alaska, it might have been drying fish, hunting, or picking berries.

Here, a lot of the chores revolve around livestock. Not tonight. Tonight it's straight up beautification.

Salon night. A special occasion—a bachelorette party that most of the Strong men's wives are going to. Right now it's all hands on deck in the colorful little hair studio.

"Pass me that curling iron," Sophia calls.

Sierra, the Agile Team pilot, teases and makes a face. "You're a doctor, do you know how to use that thing?"

"You're a pilot, can you really apply color?" she counters.

"You're both my daughters-in-law, isn't that a given?" Nolene challenges.

So, I've been worked into the fold just like the other girls who have married the Strong brothers. For some reason that gives me immense pleasure. I've never belonged to anything. But here in this little spa, with the hair dryers blowing, makeup dust in the air, and the sound of chatter in between, I feel... something different inside of me.

A grounding. A warmth. A weird buzz of happiness. The sound of a timer going off drags me back. That's my cue to check the funny helmet-looking dryer.

The hum of happiness goes on around me, and I find myself smiling for no reason. Or maybe for every reason.

When there's a bachelorette party, the Strong girls go all out. Trimming, toner, bleach, waves, up-do's, you name it, it's happening. I didn't even know half of these things existed two weeks ago. I'm washing another head when heavy footsteps thud down the stairs.

Manly boots descend into sight. My heart falls in disappointment when it's Marshall Lake.

My throat was already dry as I anticipate seeing Dozer. But the tang of disappointment is biting when his boss steps into the room and hugs Mrs. Strong.

Darn.

It's been almost twenty-four hours since I saw him at the 'office' as they call Marshall's house.

As Nolene hustles up the steps with Marshall, my phone vibrates in my pocket.

Can you be hugged by a voice? Because that's exactly what this feels like when I hear Dozer say, "Hey, beautiful."

I'm addicted to that rumbly, gruff, deep sound. I crave it more and more.

Smiling like a little fool, I squeeze the phone on my shoulder and wrap the towel around the head I just washed.

"Just a second."

Nolene swishes back into the salon and looks at my grin. She waves me off. "I know that look. Go on, girl. Visit with your man."

My man.

What?

She gives me a knowing nod.

So maybe I do talk about him... once in a while.

"It's great to hear your voice."

"You busy? It sounded noisy."

"Believe it or not, I'm learning how to style hair."

"Nolene's keeping you busy."

"There's a bachelorette party tonight."

There's a beat of silence.

"You going out?"

"I didn't plan on it, but the girls are saying I have to go. But not if you're coming by."

A weird silence falls between us.

He rumbles, "I'm gonna sound like a dick, but I don't like the idea of you going out without me."

"Why?"

"Because you're fucking beautiful. All the guys will be making moves on you."

My face starts to heat. "Hardly. You should see these girls."

"I have," he counters immediately. "You get my vote. So when I say men are gonna be all over you, I know."

"I didn't picture you for the jealous type."

He's quick to say, "I never have been."

Well...

That makes my heart flutter. Bad idea. Don't read anything into it.

"I'd rather stay in. You know me. Simple. Boring. Homebody."

There's another long pause. "That's one of the things I love about you."

My breath feels oddly light.

Love.

Silly, I chide myself.

"So, you're working late?" I try to sound casual and change the subject.

But his voice rumbles against my ear. "I wish I could come, but we need to work double time to find a way to get Danee home."

"I understand. There's no pressure to come. Just stay safe."

His breath hitches and I don't understand the emotion that drove that sudden inhale. He lets out a slow breath. "Fuck. McKenzie."

"Is something wrong?"

"No."

But he doesn't elaborate.

Gumbly, he says, "Have a good time tonight. Text when you get back."

My body warms. It feels good for him to want to know that I'm safe.

"If it makes you feel better, I'll text you where we go."

"Do that." He sighs again. "Look, I gotta go, babe. Text. Don't forget or I'll send out a search party."

"Roger Ranger."

He chuckles softly and my skin tingles. "Over and out."

When I hang up, I can't go back inside for a minute. There are too many emotions swirling around inside of me. Every one of them will probably show on my face.

As I step through the door, I'm met with a big wide grin. "Someone is in love," says Summer.

"What?"

"You two are smitten. No woman has that look in her eyes that isn't."

"I'm not in love. Besides, who knows what he thinks."

Nolene kills the power on her blowdryer and announces, "I know what he thinks!"

Summer tugs my sleeve, "Girl, I can already see the beautiful babies you'll make."

"Lord, you're not kidding," Skye says with wide eyes and a laugh that causes the other girls to join in. "Those are gonna be some supermodels."

I'm startled at the idea. Babies?

"No, that's not what this is. We are friends. He is helping me get back on my feet."

But I can't stop thinking about that kiss. Apparently that makes my face turn red. Either that or my shirt is on fire.

Sierra starts, "Candy and Dozer sitting in a tree," and everyone else, to my embarrassment joins in, "K-I-S-S-I-N-G."

"Ladies, please. Don't you have someone else to antagonize?"

"Oh no, you're not getting off that easy. Next thing you know we'll be taking you out for your bachelorette night."

That hits me right in the solar-plexus.

These women would do it. The'd pretty me up and

make a fuss over me. They'd celebrate the wedding. They'd tease me about babies.

I'd love every minute of it. As much as those things scare me, knowing people were there to hold your hand along the way makes it seem so much more beautiful.

My eyes begin to mist, before anyone sees me, I head to the girl sitting at the washing station. With a wave of my hand, I mumble, "Whatever."

Everyone laughs and they try to engage with me to talk about Dozer and my feelings, but all I can think about is, I'm not in love with him.

Am I? That's ridiculous.

Too bad I fall asleep before I text him when I get back. Because Dozer doesn't take it lightly.

* * *

When I wake up, the morning light is filtering through the drapes.

I almost scream. But I realize that the shadow next to the bed belongs to Dozer.

Jesus.

After I throttle my racing heart back, I laugh.

But he's not laughing.

A scowl darkens his face as he looms over me. His hands are fists by his side. For an instant I feel afraid, then his eyes heat.

"Someone's getting a spanking."

Yes. *Please?*

God, what am I thinking?

Before he sees the fire burning up my cheeks, I cover my face with the blanket. "I'm so sorry."

When I peek a few seconds later, he's still staring down at me. This goes on until I'm hot from head to toe.

With a tip of his chin, he says, "I knew you made it home, otherwise I would have sent out the search party."

"How did you know?"

"Sierra remembered to call Cole. She told him you were exhausted when they dropped you off."

I push up into a sitting position and shove my tangled beach waves over my shoulder. They were really pretty last night and I wished Dozer had seen me, but now I'm worried I look like Medusa.

But he still looks like he wants to eat me.

And I feel like a total heel. "I messed up. I'm so sorry. I was dead on my feet after that 'three ring bachelorette circus,' as Sophia called it."

He leans down, plants a hand next to my hip, uses his other to brush my hair aside, and whispers into my ear, "I need to leave because I can't take looking at you in that bed."

Then he kisses my cheek. His scruffy jaw abrades my skin. I shiver as my eyes drift closed and my smile makes my cheeks rise. "I'm sorry, but I might have done it on purpose if I knew you'd come over."

He pulls back and steps across the room, where he shoves his hands in his pockets. His face is a mask of tension. "Careful, woman. You're playing with fire."

"Kiss me," I whisper and wonder where that voice came from.

His voice is rough and low. The tension in the room is palpable now. "*No.* No fucking way. I won't be able to stop and we are not making love the first time in the guest room of another family's home."

146

My breath leaves my chest and my pulse replaces it. Thud. Thud. Thuddddd.

Making love...

Dozer's next move is a big step toward the bed. There's something dark and dangerous in his gaze. He tips my chin up, drops his lips to mine and whispers against my mouth, "Next time I'm in a bedroom alone with you, I'm claiming you as mine."

Chapter Thirty-Two

DOZER

Taking a breather, I step onto the back porch of Marshall Lake's house. Behind his property, the mountains stretch off into the distance. The peaks hold a patchwork of snow that hasn't fallen victim to spring temperatures yet.

But down toward the valley floor at his house, the sun feels warm enough to make me groggy.

I take a seat in one of the chairs, fighting the sleep that's trying to catch up with me. Before I let myself catch a few minutes, I cue up my phone and call the only number I call these days.

"Hi." A breathy, welcoming sound comes through the microphone that makes my heart lurch.

"Hey sweetheart. You doing okay today?"

I hope she is because I'm not. I'm fucking dying to have her alone. Naked. And beneath me.

She lightly replies, "Good. I made something for you, swing by later if you can."

I'm grinning as I relax back into the chair even though the blood in my veins is hot as lava. "Yeah, what this time, babe?"

"Trying out a new cinnamon roll recipe with Mrs. Strong. It's kind of experimental, but so far the taste tests have been a resounding success."

A little smacking sound follows her words.

Hot. Damn. My throat goes Sahara dry. "Are you licking your fingers?"

"Maybe," she laughs softly. "I've got icing all over me."

Groaning, I close my eyes. Vision of sugar plums... *not.* Visions of very dirty fun fill my head. "We can't talk about that very distracting fact."

"Sorry, I'm just cleaning up."

Don't.

And bring an extra bowl of icing with you when I stop by tonight because I'm dragging you out to the car to devour you.

So much for waiting for a nice romantic bedroom. I'm not that strong.

I chuckle but keep my mouth closed before I say something incriminating.

"We're just starting on dinner, Nolene's making barbecue for everyone. I think she's planning on delivering it unless someone else is coming this way."

"I'll come," I offer instantly, just so I can make sure I get a chance to see McKenzie. We've been as busy as all fuck trying to track down Danee, but I'm trying to steal a moment or two with the woman every chance I can.

149

Like some junkie.

But fuck, *her hugs*. Best drug ever.

And that chaste kiss in her room. Mainline of the good stuff right into my veins.

Not to mention all the other things I've grown to love. The soft whisper of her voice as she greets me at the door. The way she tumbles into my arms...

I'm a goner.

Dunzo.

Officially fucked.

In the background on her end, women are laughing. The vision of McKenzie cooking with Nolene Strong and her daughters-in-law does something weird to my chest.

Not just that. The way she's coming to life, more and more each day. All that female friendship is exactly what she needs. I'm glad she went out, even if it drove me fucking crazy all night to think about her at a bar.

Little did she know that one of the guys, a friend of the Strong's, was lurking around the bar where the girls were partying in case there was any weird trouble. Creepy assholes are everywhere. Can't have the ladies in any danger.

It only made me feel slightly better.

"What are you thinking about?" she prompts when I lapse into silence.

"How I like seeing you making friends."

"Feels good," she admits. "Although, I wish I could do more. Mrs. Strong is being so gracious letting me stay. I feel bad..."

"Don't, sweetheart. She's got a big home, and you're doing all kinds of things to help with cooking for the Agile team."

"I've been helping around the ranch too, but I feel inept."

"Hardly. Every helping hand is valuable around a ranch."

She goes silent for a few seconds.

Then almost shyly admits, "I like the horses best."

Another ray of sunshine pierces my armor. My smile deepens. It's easy to picture her with sunset colors dancing in her hair as she rides.

I'll buy her the prettiest gelding. A big, gentle giant that would fall instantly in love with McKenzie. They'd be thick as thieves.

Although, knowing what I do of her, she'd rather have a horse with mad spunk.

I sound a little rough when I reply, "They're my favorite too. Always have been."

"Do you have any?"

"I have in the past, and I'm sure I will again. It wasn't fair for me to have someone keeping a horse for me while I was on active duty."

"Makes sense. But now, maybe."

"Maybe," I echo, Even though I have no fucking clue where I'll be. Work could have me anywhere, or possibly in an even better scenario, I'll be following McKenzie.

But we'll see.

I ask, "Didn't tell you about the wild horse rescue work my brothers do, did I?"

Through the phone, I can feel her focus sharpen. "That sounds incredible. Do you keep any of them?"

"Only if they are injured or sick. My family works with an organization to provide access to our land. It's been really incredible to be a part of."

"When are you coming over?"

I'm curious about her abrupt switch, but I'll ask later. "Not for a few hours still. We're digging through intel right now. I just stepped outside for a break."

"You sound tired."

It's hard not to sound tired when you're running on vapors. "Bone deep tired, babe."

"I'm sorry," she says plainly and those simple words mean the world to me.

"It's okay. Missions are like this sometimes. I'm good at running on the adrenaline of bringing a target home safely."

Softly, she speaks into the phone. "I love that about you."

For a beat, I'm silent. But my heart is having a party. "Thanks."

"So...," she brightens. "I'll save a big bowl of cinnamon buns just for you."

"What are you doing with the extra icing?"

"Why do you ask?"

I'm grinning like the dirty bastard that I am. "Oh, nothing."

Behind me, the door opens and Mako steps out onto the porch. When he steps around in view he's got a shit eating grin on his face.

He chuckles. "Icing?"

Fuck you, I mouth.

"Gotta go, babe. I'll see you in a few hours."

"Who's that?"

"Just an asshole also known as Mako."

"Oh, I like him. When he's not being over protective of you."

Huh?

But I table the convo for later, when my best friend isn't staring a hole in me.

His grin turns up a thousand degrees. "Tell Mac I loved the cookies she made for me."

Mac? What the *fuck*? Now he's got a nickname for my girl?

Hell. No.

Then I register the second part of his remark. She made cookies for *him?*

I don't have to say anything into the phone because McKenzie says, "Tell Mako I'm making some more tomorrow, just the way he likes them."

What??! I growl. Sounding like a ridiculous child, I mutter, "I didn't get cookies."

McKenzie shoots back, "You didn't ask for any."

Mako's laughing silently, holding his guts. Good fucking thing because I'm thinking about sticking my boot through his bellybutton.

"Gonna go now, and, babe, any time you make cookies, I want some. Feel me?"

"Loud and clear, pouty-McPouty. But I think you'll like the cinnamon buns better, and if it makes you feel better, I won't give him a single one."

I'm chuckling when we say our goodbyes.

Then I turn my acid stare on my SEAL brother. "What. The. FUCK," I slice out at him.

He busts into loud laughter. "Brother, I've never seen you so... stupid."

"Stupid?" I snap. "Because I'm digging her and you're digging your own grave?"

He continues to laugh, now he's got tears in his damned eyes. "You're too fucking easy, bro."

I kick his shin when he sits down next to me. He jabs me with a hard punch in the deltoid.

For a minute, I consider throwing him over the porch

railing and having a go with him on the grass. But settle on giving him a real, you-better-not-fucking-go-near-her glare.

He throws up his hands. "Doz, you know I wouldn't mess with your woman. I'm a happily married man."

Shit, I forgot that he's hitched. But that doesn't mean the handsome as hell SEAL won't flirt with McKenzie, a fact that grates me all to hell.

"Does your wife know you're eating *specially baked* cookies?"

He leans back in the chair and clasps his hands behind his head. A deeply satisfied smile settles on his face. I've seen it a few times, and have to admit, I like him like this.

"Shared them with Erika. She thought they were amazing. Wifey likes to bake for me too, but she's been so damned busy lately that the kitchen has been neglected unless you count me cooking."

First, *wifey?*

Weird. He really is a different man.

Him saying he shared the cookies with his wife takes some of the umph out of my childish tantrum. But not before he prods me.

"You're spun up about this woman."

"Is that a statement or a question, I'm not sure whether your voice went up or down as you finished."

He laughs as he kicks my foot. "It's a statement, asshole."

"I'm spun up. Okay, I've admitted it. Does that make you feel better?"

He instantly shoots back, "The question of the hour is, does it make you feel better?"

"Her?"

He smacks his forehead. "Yes, her, you idiot. But the

truth is, I don't know why I'm asking. I know it—*she*—makes you feel better. You seem..."

"What?" I demand.

"Like the darkness is letting go."

His shrewd blue eyes follow me as I lean forward and scrub my hands over my face. *Fuck.* Is that what's happening?

He clasps my shoulder with a meaty grip. "The right one will do that for you, brother. I know you've carried a lot of pain in you for a long fucking time. Don't be afraid to enjoy something so beautiful. You'd be a fool to stay in the shadows."

Christ. I draw in a breath so big it makes my ribs ache.

"She is beautiful. So fucking beautiful. And before you go and get yourself a mouthful of fist, don't agree."

He chuckles, and smacks my back hard. "Alright, I won't agree. But you're right. She's also very fucking into you."

Why does hearing that make me feel so... light?

"You really think?"

Mako whistles softly, "Doz, brother. She looks at you like you're about to walk on water."

"Hardly," I snort.

"Erika agrees."

"She hasn't even seen me with McKenzie."

"She doesn't need to. A few hours with your woman at the Strong's was all she needed. And just so you're aware, if your ears are burning to a crisp it's because the women have been prying Mac for information on you."

"Oh, fuck."

"Apparently she glows whenever your name comes up."

I can't stop the smile that erupts on my otherwise grump face.

He rises and looks down at me. "Brother, don't fuck this up. I've seen you alone for far too long. I like that star-struck grin you've got on your face. It's good on you. Just do me a favor, and go slow, okay?"

"That's my plan."

"Yeah, tell that lie to yourself again."

His smile is gone now and I pick up on the shift in his energy. We've worked in the most fucked up places in the world, in the midst of the nastiest battles, and reading each other kept us alive more than once.

"What aren't you saying?"

He takes a slow step to the porch railing, scans the distant mountains. "Truth?"

"Always."

"There's something I can't put my finger on. Something makes me uneasy about her. I'm probably just overthinking. Too many years watching your six got me acting like a momma bear."

Chapter Thirty-Three

Candy

Nolene Strong has a sixth sense for someone driving up her ranch road.

She sways her little round hips over to the big french doors that lead out the back of her house. A smile squints her eyes and I hold my breath, waiting for her to announce who it is.

It's not her husband. For that she wears a whole different smile. A radiant thing that makes her glow.

Her sons—depending on which one—also make her smile, however some make her narrow her eyes, depending on what he's done that day. But it's always with love when she announces their name.

She's the same about the daughters-in-law too. God and

there's so many of them. Five sons, five wives, and the others that she seems to have adopted from the Agile crews.

"It's yours," she announces with a sparkle in her eyes as she bustles back to the stove where her gigantic pot of pork barbecue is simmering.

"Mine?"

"That big, handsome man that makes you go all gooey-eyed."

My body lights up at the announcement, but I quickly snap, "He's not *mine*."

She chuckles a warm motherly laugh. "Not yet, sweetheart, but wait till he tastes those buns."

I choke on the glass of water I'm sipping and almost need CPR.

That amuses her terribly. "You okay, child? I was talking about the cinnamon buns. He's going to lose his mind."

"Sure. Fine." I choke and cough.

"Better get yourself right, your face is the color of a Christmas bulb."

Great, I'm dying and she's having a great time with this. I take off for the bathroom, hacking up a lung, to splash some water on my face. Like I didn't get enough water when she made that remark.

Tasting buns?

Heaven help me. I almost snorted an ice cube.

It's not long before the heavy footfalls that I've come to recognize as Dozer's, enter the house and go right to the kitchen. Lord, I know what his gait sounds like now. Obsessive much?

A pleasant exchange with Nolene ensues. He's so damn nice. I love listening to him say 'ma'am,' 'please,' and 'thank you,' to all the women. Never misses a beat. Faithfully kind and gentle to them.

So different from any man I've known. Namely my father since he's pretty much been the only man I've really known. Because the boys in school do not count. They barely entered puberty and had yet to stop making stupid jokes about how the numbers 7-7-3-4 spell hell upside down on a calculator, or how 8-0-0-8-5 spells boobs.

Except here it seems that's the norm for this house. The men are gentlemen. Although, I have a feeling Nolene would have beaten any disrespecting behavior out of her sons with her dishtowel. Her husband too.

They're delightful. Every one of them. So nice it makes my heart twist and squeeze. What would it be like to have a family like this?

A booming voice calls from just outside the door. "McKenzie?"

The tone sends a full body hot-flash scorching my insides. "I'll be right out." My voice is still rough from inhaling water.

When I open the door, Dozer's wearing a worried expression. "Nolene said you got choked."

I grin and wave a hand dismissively. "Did she tell you why?"

That frown deepens. "No."

Laughing at myself, I shrug. "Thank god. It was nothing."

He tilts his head and takes a step forward until he's in my space and I have to lean back to look up at his beautiful eyes. "You alright?"

"Better than alright, now that I get to see you."

I don't hesitate at all when he opens his arms. I've been waiting since his last visit. He draws me up tight, burying his face in my neck, lifting me so high, my toes leave the floor.

"Don't like hearing you got choked."

"It was just some water that went down the wrong pipe."

He squeezes me harder. "Still."

I wind my arms around his neck and breathe in his scent. Today he smells like clean cotton, warm male, and leather. A delicious, tummy-stirring smell.

He lets me down, and for a beat, I wonder if he's going to kiss me. Then I stop wondering and start praying.

I'm so desperate for him to kiss me that I almost attack him, but he's holding back for some reason.

I suspect it's got to do with the case they're working on. It's taking all of their energy. That's the only reason I can figure, unless all these hugs he's giving me are brotherly.

Crushing disappointment jolts me.

That would be the worst.

Then my worry vanishes when he slowly draws his fingers down through my hair with a throaty rumble.

Definitely not brotherly.

After that touch and growl he quickly steps back to hold me by my upper arms with a half-scowl on his face. "We gotta talk about you cooking for Mako?"

Oops. Um. So maybe he's not only kind and courteous, but also a tad on the jealous side too. I offer up a weak, "Huh? I didn't mean to upset you."

For a beat he lets me wonder, then he laughs and touches his finger to the tip of my nose. "I'm teasing you, babe. He's fucking over the moon with those cookies you made. Said his wife loved them too."

That makes a smile work its way up from my heart and

bloom on my face. "Oh, well then. I'll make them some more."

"Like I said on the phone, only if I get some." He loops an arm around my neck and drags me toward the kitchen. "Now, where are these famous test-recipe cinnamon rolls? I want to be a judge."

Nolene looks like she's about to bust a seam from her excitement when we walk in. She's practically floating above the floor. "I'll just run to the barn and check on that calf while you keep an eye on things in here."

She tosses her apron on the counter and practically sprints out. I had no idea the little compact woman could move so fast.

"That was convenient," Dozer says with a wink, and I fall a little more in love with the man.

I didn't even realize what was happening until the girls pointed it out. *Crap.* It's so silly. I can't be falling in love. I don't even know this man.

We've barely spent any time together. If you add up all the hours we've been alone since this whole madness started it's less than a single day.

Can you fall in love with someone in less than twenty-four hours over the span of a week?

I'm doing math when he eyes the counter behind me. I reach for the snap-container that's got a half dozen rolls in it. "Be warned, these could result in a cavity."

He chuckles and accepts the goods as his eyes darken. "Remember, dear, I like sweet things."

Blush. Ing.

Freaking blushing like mad.

"Um. Yeah?"

He tags me around the waist and pulls me into his chest again. I love crashing into that wall of muscle. He's so strong

161

and the heat that radiates off him makes my head swim. "Fucking adorable when you're blushing at my words."

"You do that a lot to me."

"I'd like to do it more." His voice goes grumbly. "But I've got to get back. Cole Strong came with me, he's out in the barn. Happy to say, though, we've made some ground on locating Danee. The team is getting close, which means I could be wheels up any minute."

That freezes my blood for two reasons. Please let Danee be okay. I also don't want to think about Dozer and the team facing down whatever monster has stolen her. "I'm scared for you, for everyone."

Dozer slides the bowl of treats back onto the counter and pulls me further into the warm hollow of his bent shoulders. "Every one of us is trained for this. Whether it was being in the SEAL Teams or some other Special Ops team, we've all been in the thick of danger our whole careers. But I won't lie to you, I'm scared for that girl. I hope she's okay."

A shudder violently contracts my muscles. "She seemed so nice."

Truth is, I want to go hunt that bad guy down too.

"Agreed. Shame what she's already been through, and now this. But Marshall will never stop. She's gonna be safe again, I promise you, babe."

I cling to him until he sets me away so he can look at me. Dozer's eyes darken to the deepest steel gray color. "Are you resting?"

"I'm fine. It's lovely here. But you on the other hand look like you need to sleep for a week."

"I'm used to this. I'll catch up when this is done."

A slow grin changes him from serious to devastatingly adorable. "Heard the girls are giving you a hassle."

"Oh, gawd. Yes. They always ask me about you."

"It bothers you?"

His expression conveys his concern and that emotion is so genuine that my heart makes a weird squeezing sensation inside my ribs. The thought of Dozer taking up for me makes me happy in ways I didn't know possible.

But that's not necessary right now, I'm enjoying the playful banter. "No it's not a bother. Truthfully, they are great. All of them. They love their men, and want me to find that one day too."

The pupils in his eyes dilate swiftly. "How 'bout you, do you hope you'll find that one day too?"

Biting my lip, I consider my answer. Now's not the time for crazy confessions of my puppy love. Finally, I settle on, "I *would* like that. A girl can dream, right?"

With that swirling between us, I almost miss the front door opening and closing. But I don't miss the booming voice of one of the Strong men—Dozer's coworker, a man named Cole. "Break it up, you two, no hanky-panky allowed in the kitchen. Nolene will skin your hides. That is when she's not kissing on our father."

The man strides past us and to the stove. "See, you're letting the barbecue stick." With his nose over the pot, he inhales deeply. "Hot damn, I've been waiting for this all day."

"Me too," mutters Dozer, and I have to wonder if he's talking about something altogether different, because he's eyeing his coworker like he's got a target on his back.

I'd like to think that Dozer has been waiting to see me just like I've been waiting to see him. With knots and shivers inside.

But big hard men like him? Nah. He's probably here for the barbecue or the promise of sweet things. But a girl can hope, right?

The next twenty minutes are chaotic. Nolene and Cole pack the food for the Agile team into big picnic baskets complete with all the side dishes we made.

I do what I can to help by checking the list she wrote on the whiteboard on the fridge. Dozer helps load everything in his company SUV, and then catches me for another quick hug as we walk out onto the porch. He's got his container of cinnamon buns clutched to him like they're some great treasure.

"I'll try not to have fantasies of you in a tiny apron while I eat these."

Oh my god. Definitely not brotherly. That was downright smoldering.

I bury my face in his chest. "You just like making me fire-engine red."

He chuckles warmly, stirring my hair as he does. "I'd also like to talk more about that icing you were licking off your fingers."

"Let's roll, home boy!" Cole shouts as he jogs down the steps. "Dinner's getting cold and we've got a team meeting while we eat."

"Copy," Dozer grunts back. Then he smiles down at me. "Stay sweet, beautiful. I'll be back as soon as I can, but try not to worry if I call and say we're going dark. That's gonna happen. Soon as we get a lock on Danee's location, we're going to get her."

I grab him for one more hug as something seizes my heart. "Just promise you'll come back."

"Always," he murmurs, then kisses my temple. "Careful around the ranch, keep your hair tied up when you're around the equipment. Don't go in with the livestock alone. Be sure someone knows where you are all the time."

I push him toward the stairs that lead down to the yard.

"Alright, alright. Just concentrate on staying safe and getting Danee home. Nolene's an excellent mother hen. I'm in good hands until you get back."

He strides to the SUV where Cole is waiting, then calls back to me. "Don't make any more cookies for other men."

I wave and give him a little shrug. He busts out laughing. But as soon as he climbs into the vehicle and they drive away, my smile vanishes.

I'm fine on the ranch. I love Nolene and her big, warm family. I'm just too new at this to know what's happening inside of me.

But now I know that part of the emotional melee is worry. I told myself I'd never worry about anyone else. It hurts too badly when they're gone. Especially when you're the reason.

Chapter Thirty-Four

DOZER

Millspring, North Dakota is a frozen, barren, wasteland. A forgotten town. A ghost riddled place with run down buildings and ice covered roads.

A place that no one would have ever looked for Danee, except the Agile Team.

Grim determination makes us silent as we climb off the plane.

Across the tarmac a man waits next to an overland vehicle, a truck with studded tires and big lights on the rack over the cab. Thick mustache, flinty eyed, the Sheriff stares across the space at us as we sprint the short distance.

The man wastes no time on formalities. Not even a muttered hello. Marshall launches himself into the passenger seat as I climb into the back cab. Before our doors are closed he's tearing across the pavement.

The man's grizzled voice booms. "Only one road leads to the mountains that faces west. There's an old factory on the edge of the town there. Someone's building a new business there supposedly. Not shit going on there if you ask me. A few meat heads hanging around with guns. Been trying to ferret out some information on them for months."

Every word he says multiplies the tension.

Looking over at Marshall he says, "I've already got the state police there. They didn't find a woman. They found a room where one had been staying though. There was a lot of blood, and a big angry man who's now in custody. Said she stabbed him."

Holy. Fuck.

Marshall's face morphs from angry to deadly furious.

"She ran," he growls, then his voice chokes, "Please god. Please let me be here in time."

The Sheriff says, "My men have been looking."

Marshall's jaw is locked tight as he stares at the road ahead, clenching his weapon in white knuckled hands.

"She'll hide," I offer. "She's going to be scared."

Marshall scrubs a hand over his eyes. "She's out there, I feel it. We don't have much time. Can this thing go any faster?"

Fuck. I can't imagine how he feels. The woman he loves is out there. Alone. Scared. Cold as fuck.

As the sun slips low on the horizon, my fear for the woman grows suffocating. She'll freeze to death if we don't find her fast. If that happens, Marshall will be gone too.

Chapter Thirty-Five

Candy

"Those men know what they're doing."

My eyes drift across the table. Nolene's expression is soft as the light coming from the night light that's sitting on the sideboard.

I don't know how long I've been sitting here now. But I'm sure I haven't breathed once. "We're going dark," Dozer called to say. My heart fell out of my body and slid onto the floor.

"They'll bring her home."

Thickening to the point of suffocation, the lump in my chest turns into a vice. "I can't imagine what Marshall is thinking right now."

"He's thinking that he's going to bring that woman

home or he will die trying. And that's exactly what he will do."

She waits for my surprised eyes to meet hers. I guess I shouldn't expect Nolene to sugar coat it, because she's a straight shooter.

"It's all so scary." I know she knows that my words mean so much more than the horrible thing that has happened to Danee and Marshall. I'm talking about the enormity of how it feels to care so much about someone that you would literally lay down your life for them.

"Honey, that's what true love is."

Tears coat my lashes again for the hundredth time in the last few days. The things I feel for Dozer are getting more complicated. How is that even possible?

I don't know what these feelings are. He makes me feel safe. Cared for. Wanted.

Christ. One look from the man and I feel beautiful all the way to my soul.

She stands up from the table with her cup of tea. "By morning you'll know. I'd tell you to sleep, but I know it's useless. Come get me if you need me. I'm going to lay these tired bones down."

I go to her, give her a hug. Because I need it right now and she freely gives them.

When I let her go she says, "Dozer's a good man. He knows what he's doing or Marshall and the others would never let him on that team. They're good judges of character, which to me says that you're safe to open your heart up to that man."

"I'm trying."

"It's work sweetheart, but it's so worth it. I know you've been through a lot and you haven't even told me about it.

But I want you to know that I've watched my sons and their wives go through the hardships that forge forever love."

"I just need him home safe. Then we'll see where this goes."

As she walks away, I turn off the nightlight, letting the quiet darkness surround me. But inside me there's a storm that's threatening to leave me in tatters.

Chapter Thirty-Six

DOZER

Radio chatter fills the cab of the beefed-up pick up, but the Sheriff drives with a singular focus. Getting us outside town to the road he and Marshall think Danee used to run.

"The terrain's too rugged for her to go far in the woods. Based on my experience she'll stick to the fire road. If she hears a vehicle coming she'll hide, but I'm certain we'll be able to see tracks in the dust of snow."

I clap Marshall's shoulder. "She strong. She escaped. We're going to find her."

But the light's fading fast.

Then something catches our headlights. "Fuck," Marshall spits.

The Sheriff mashes the accelerator. "Boys...," he growls as he turns on a bank of floodlights that shatter the night.

Holy. Mother. Of. God. My throats cinches. My gut dives.

The shape comes into clear view. A tiny female form is lying on the ground.

Jesus, fuck. She's wearing thin clothing. No jacket. No shoes.

Marshall leaps out of the truck and sprints the final few feet before he slides in on his knees.

"Get the first aid bag!" The Sheriff yells at me as he reaches for the radio mic.

When I close the distance, Marshall's got Danee in his arms. I can't see her face, he's got it buried in his neck. Her body is as pale as a ghost.

Brokenly, he whispers, "She's alive. Thank god."

Chapter Thirty-Seven

DOZER

My throat tightens. The urge to see Candy and have her safe in my arms makes me push the accelerator hard on the company SUV.

I voice command the phone to call Candy Sweet.

"Hello, you," she answers, sounding breathless.

"Hello, back, beautiful."

"Where are you?"

"Just driving in from the airport. I'm about ten minutes out from the ranch."

She sucks in a breath. "You're back?"

"It's done. We just got Danee home to Utah."

"Oh, god, Dozer. I haven't been able to breathe."

"I know, sweetheart. I should have called you last night, but it was too late."

"You're really coming here? Can you stay?" she rushes.

"I'm off work for a while. We're all taking some downtime."

The line goes silent. "That's good. That's really good. I know you are probably ready to get back to San Diego and wrap up things at your apartment since your lease is done."

"That's not what I'm eager about."

She breathes softly into the phone. I love that fucking sound. Want to spend the rest of my life listening to her breathe next to me in the dark night.

I say, "I'm eager to spend time with you."

"Me too," she whispers.

"See you in eight minutes."

"Copy," she replies with a laugh. She's been using all kinds of military lingo, joking around with me when things were bad with the case. It helped me so fucking much. Those moments of light in the darkness.

"Over and out," I say and disconnect with my damned cheeks hurting from the big ass smile I have on my face.

Chapter Thirty-Eight

Candy

I'm already on the porch, fidgeting with my hands, pacing around, when the black SUV turns down the lane. Dust kicks up in the morning sunshine like a mini tornado.

My insides flutter. Heavens. Every time I see the man something strange happens inside of me.

Stop it, McKenzie. This is going nowhere and you know it.

Dozer's become more than a friend. But that doesn't mean there's any future to this.

He's probably going to see me along until I start to climb out of my dilemma. But that's as far as this thing goes. He'll go on working and traveling. He's going to be back to doing what he does best. Kicking ass, taking names, and being a

SEAL through and through even though he's in the private sector now.

Me... well, I don't know what that future looks like yet.

The black Suburban rushes up the driveway between the tall trees, slams to a stop on the grass, and he bolts out of the driver's door. He takes five long strides toward me, then stops.

We stare at each other.

He looks *so* good. Tall and lean. Strong, but not too bulky. A black polo shirt is tucked crisply into black tactical pants. Clean, lace-up boots cover his feet. A black baseball cap with the Agile Security logo is pulled low over his brow. I can't see his eyes, but *my-oh-my*, I feel those gray knives slicing up my will power.

Nothing about getting more tangled up with Dozer makes sense. But something inside of me screams that it makes perfect sense.

A flare of anger tightens my lungs, fires me up to think about depending on a man. One that could leave. Or die. Or... break me.

No. I'm not going there.

As much as I love the way he looks at me, a mix of hunger and possession and protectiveness, I have to figure out how to stand on my own two feet. I've always had a strong backbone and right now that means selling my father's belongings and figuring out where I can live and finding some kind of job I can do.

"Come 'ere, beautiful Candy Sweet."

I keep my feet rooted on the deck even though his nickname starts to warm something inside of my chest.

He grins. "What do you think you're doing?"

I jut my chin. "Looking at you."

He crosses his arms and shifts his weight to one side. "Yeah? Did you miss me while I was away?"

I fold my own arms, mocking his stance. "No, I was busy helping around the ranch."

Really, I was, but I was also running circles in my own brain trying to figure out how to use the ten thousand dollars, and what that would do to help me turn my broken life around.

He chuckles as he looks me over. I'm wearing jeans, a cute flannel shirt that's sleeveless, and a pair of cowboy boots. All courtesy of the Strong boys' wives. They rallied around me when Dozer went head deep in his mission of helping Marshall and the team find Danee.

With appreciation in his voice, Dozer says, "Turning you into a real ranch wife."

I make a scoffing sound. "Hardly. I have no clue what to do other than what chores they give me."

He unfolds his arms and puts his hands on his hips. "What's got you up there, when every time I've been here since we got to Utah, you've rushed into my arms."

I shrug as my nerves start to tingle. "I don't know."

But the truth is, he's now off from work. While he was working, we had a reason to stay away from whatever was simmering between us. Things I don't understand. He'd come for a short visit, then go back to working twenty-two-hour days. I don't know how the man survived on so little sleep, wherever he was crashing during the crisis.

But right now, all I know is my body is rioting. For him.

Of course I understand the birds and the damned bees. But these complicated desires, the emotions, the uncertainty about my future, those are things I don't understand how to process.

The screen door bumps open behind me and Caleb

Strong, the local fire chief and one of the Strong sons, steps out onto the porch.

"Dozer, good to see ya. Heard that things all turned out good. I'm glad as hell to hear that." He holds up a mug of his mother's strong coffee. "Breakfast is about to hit the table, let's celebrate."

Then Caleb glances at me and I'm not sure what he sees other than me on the porch, and Dozer on the lawn with his hands on his hips.

"Ohhh," Caleb says slowly. "We'll save you two plates."

Then he turns and the screen door slams closed behind him as he disappears into the house.

Dozer crooks a finger at me. Much to my surprise, as if I'm in a trance, or a puppet on a string, I trundle down the steps and stop in front of him. Inches away. He reaches for me, wraps an arm behind my waist and tugs me against his chest.

"I missed you," he murmurs, against my hair. "You look so pretty this morning, I'm glad as fuck to be back here and be able to finally spend some time with you."

Melt.

Butter on hot toast.

Then he leans down, flips his baseball cap around backwards, turns my face toward his and does what I've been dying for.

He kisses me.

With freaking gusto.

That melting I felt a moment before was NOTHING.

The man's lips are gentle but—whoa, he knows what he's doing. That first kiss wasn't a fluke.

Nope. Dozer kisses like a freaking rockstar.

His hand laces around the back of my neck, calloused

and warm, and before I realize what's happening, he's dipping into my mouth with his tongue.

He tastes like mint and hungry alpha male. At least that's what my ovaries say that flavor is.

Whatever. I love it.

I open with a little moan and realize I'm inhaling him as delicious heat tears through my body. It's like I've got coals spilling down inside me from my scalp toward my toes, landing in places where my girl parts take fire. My nipples. The bottom of my tummy. Between my clenched thighs.

It's the most unnatural, natural thing I've ever felt in my life.

Oh, I've had a few stolen kisses with a teenage boy, but never have I been kissed by a man until I met this man.

If Dozer's anything, he's all man. Almost six and a half feet of hard, commanding alpha.

His kiss is nothing teenagery. It's completely sexual, and totally, blisteringly emotional all at once.

I'm flayed open instantly.

The dam inside me that's been straining to hold everything back snaps. A flood of emotion spills over, coating my insides with too many sensations to name.

"Hang on, sexy girl." He loops my arm up and around his neck, lifts me up by grabbing my hips, and sets me on the hood of the company SUV.

Then, he's right back at it, as if he's never broken the kiss, we're locked together again.

We're eye-to-eye now, nose-to-nose, no more neck breaking contortion needed. Our height differences are on the verge of ridiculous. But apparently he knows how to solve that problem.

Up here, with me on the hood, Dozer can kiss me straight on. It's different. Deeper. Hotter. Possibly because he's wedged his waist between my thighs. With a swift tug, he pulls me flush against his hard body as he kisses and kisses and kisses me.

I distantly think about the fact that everything has changed. Am I ready for that? I don't know.

The man invades my mouth, my heart, my soul in a way that sucks me under into a dangerous and foreign current.

The kiss unravels me. Soft and slow at first, soon building higher and higher. Burning. Growing demanding to the point of us both being breathless. Our teeth bang, our lips get pinched, our tongues mercilessly tangle.

I'm swept up in a storm in his hands but he's the anchor.

"So. Fucking. Delicious." It's a growly comment from him on words punctuated by ragged breaths.

Dozer's hands range up my back, molding, exploring, memorizing the little details of my ribs, my shoulder blades, tangling in my hair, making me purr, then swooping back down to my hips.

His chest vibrates with a primitive rumble. Clenching my hip bones hard, he makes a low, rough noise. "Dreamed about this a thousand times."

I'm so breathless and dizzy, I can't answer. All I can do is touch my fingers to my trembling lips as he watches me. Piercing me in his storm-colored gaze, analyzing every breath I take.

Then he touches me tenderly, so gently. Pushing a wisp of hair off my cheek, trailing a knuckle down over my burning skin, until his fingers are wrapped around my jaw.

I'm putty in his hands now. He could convince me of anything at this moment.

Never taking his eyes away, he says, "We have a lot to talk about."

I blink at him. *T-talk?* Not happening. My brain is

drowning in a bath of sex hormones. Nothing but oohs and aahs will be produced by my vocal cords right now.

He smiles gently. "Not now, sweetheart. Now we should go in there and eat some breakfast, celebrate with everyone, and start our morning off right with some good sustenance because it's a big day."

"It is?" I whisper-croak in my delirious state, even though I know it's because he's off from work and we're officially going to spend time together again. The thought alone makes me breathless all over again.

He presses a lingering kiss to my forehead. "It's the first day of our new relationship."

My heart tries to turn around and run. "Dozer..."

"Say my name, McKenzie. My real one."

I try the name out in my mind first. *Justin.*

"Justin," I say roughly.

"Remember my name, sweet girl." He grins devilishly. "You can call me Dozer any time you want, but I'd like for you to be comfortable with my real name too. Especially when you're beneath me in my bed."

Ungh.

This feels important. We've been getting closer and closer and now I feel like I'm sliding down a slope of marbles. I gulp a little swallow, then find my voice.

"Justin, you can't just swoop in here and declare something about a new relationship. That takes two people."

He chuckles softly in a warm, deep tone as his hands move to my thighs where he rubs circles on my denim. "Like that kiss?"

I huff out a breath and push a finger into his hard chest, he immediately wraps his hand around mine.

Mocking a frown, I say, "About that kiss, you ambushed me."

181

"SEALs are known for using unexpected tactics."

So serious. The big strong warrior. That fierce look he wears so well.

His expression makes me giggle. What the heck? I can't remember *ever* giggling. "Well, you got me with that one."

He leans in and kisses me again, swiftly. Once again he makes my head swim with the intensity. He holds my face in his palms, tilting me to the right so he can own me until my toes curl in my borrowed cowboy boots.

"Gotcha with that one too," he murmurs against my mouth before he starts all over again, like he can't get enough of me.

I let him kiss me.

Okay, *I'm lying*, I get into it. Not that I know what I'm doing, but my body wants IN on the game.

When he pulls me off the hood and sets me on the ground, he's grinning smugly and his eyes are sparking. "Wait till you see what other tricks I've got up my sleeve."

"God, give me strength," I mutter.

He laughs as he loops an arm around my neck and pulls me against his side, directing me toward the house. "That's why I said you needed a good nutritional foundation for your day."

Chapter Thirty-Nine

DOZER

"Where are we going?" McKenzie asks from the passenger seat. She's had a worried expression ever since we got in the Agile SUV.

"The bank," I reply as I signal to turn into a parking lot for a national bank chain.

She goes quiet then, and it's obvious her nerves are raising hell. I lean over and kiss her, wrapping my hand around hers, weaving our fingers together. It feels so fucking perfect.

"Since we left the ranch, you look like you're about to shatter into a bunch of sharp pieces."

She lets out a little breath. "Sorry."

"Relax, babe. Now I'm coming around to get you, so stick tight."

She frowns. "Huh?"

"I'm opening your door, and helping you down from the vehicle."

"Why would you do that?"

I give her a look. "Because it's the thing men do for the women they care about."

That leaves her blinking.

Once I've got her out, I wrap my arm around her shoulder and walk toward the bank entrance.

We walk up to the teller and I advise her we want to open an account. McKenzie goes stiff beside me as we wait for the other banker to help us.

"You okay?"

"Dozer, I... I don't know what to do. I've never done any banking."

My heart contracts. I love all the facets of this woman, but my heart goes out to how big this world must feel for her. I still don't know the ins and outs of what's had her life tangled up like it is, but we're getting to those conversations soon. "I've got you. Don't worry. Just stick close and I'll make sure everything gets taken care of."

After half an hour, we walk out with the documents for a new bank account in the name of McKenzie Rush containing ten thousand dollars.

Once we're back in the vehicle, I catch McKenzie staring at the documents. "This... is big," she whispers.

"It's all yours."

She blinks away a few tears.

Emotion swells up in my chest. Now that we've got her account set, I have other plans in play. "I think I know where we need to go."

Chapter Forty

DOZER

Two hours later, we stop on a small, deserted road. The sky is a bright wild blue against the cinnamon, green, and charcoal landscape. I stretch, yawn, and turn the vehicle off. "I need some fresh air."

She waits for me to help her out and we walk away from the vehicle toward the open expanse in front of us.

For a long time she turns around, taking in the vast, uninterrupted landscape. I draw a deep breath, feeling some of the unease of the last weeks draining away.

This isn't sweet-home-Montana, but it's just what I need. *Fuck.* I gotta get back to Trident Ranch soon. It's been too long. So long, I started to forget what a view like this could do for your soul.

"Nice out here, huh?"

She nods, twists the end of her hair around her finger, then turns her face up to the sky, letting the soft golden rays slide down over her skin. "It's *really* quiet. The Strong ranch was quiet... but this is next level. I love all the open sky."

"Just the way I like it."

"Where do you live?" she asks without looking at me because she's still soaking in the sunshine.

"I was living in San Diego while I was in the teams. I don't really live anywhere now that I'm ending my lease in California, no need for me to stay there. I grew up in Mustang, Montana. How about you? Alaska your whole life?"

I could have had Marshall's guys at Agile run her prints and get a full rundown on her, but I didn't. This moment was too important—her trusting me enough to open up.

On a deep inhale, shoulders clenching, she rubs her hands over her face. "Born in Nebraska, but I've lived most of the years I can remember in Alaska."

Now some of her story makes more sense. She's been in back-fucking-woods of Alaska. Thus, no cell phone. Thus, the pale skin. Also, the steel backbone.

Alaska's no fucking joke.

"What drove you out?"

She turns and looks at me. Hitching her hands in her back pockets, making her shirt draw tight across her full breasts.

But any and all focus on them screeches to a halt when she says, "My dad got killed in a hunting accident just over a month ago. He was all I had."

My senses shut down like a switch has been flipped. It's suddenly hard to breathe as I try to recover from the sledge hammer I just took to the chest.

Through my fog, I register the searing pain that crosses her face, fleeting as lightning, before she hides it from me. Somehow that snaps me back from the dark as fuck place I was tumbling toward.

But I'm unsteady on my feet as my heart pounds and my stomach tries to choke the fuck out of me.

Has this woman been sent to my life as some kind of lesson from the universe because of the shit I've never truly dealt with?

When she turns her eyes to me, I squeeze some air into my lungs and manage a weak, "I'm so sorry."

I'm so, so sorry.

So fucking sorry.

A million nights I've fallen asleep with those words choking me.

Looking off toward the horizon, she pinches her lip with her teeth. "Yeah, me too," she finally replies, before turning and walking off.

I don't know how long I stand there with my eyes stinging, but she doesn't look back. When I can finally take a breath, I trace her footsteps, keeping her in sight as she walks down the gravel road. There's no one around, but the need to keep her safe makes me follow.

Finally, she stops, wraps her arms around herself and toes at the ground with the cowboy boot she has on.

I'm still not sure I can talk when I reach her, but she's ready.

"When my dad died, I found out that the stash of money he kept at the house was basically gone. I don't know anything about his bank accounts, he was very private. Even from me. I guess he hid that information, locked it up somewhere, but I couldn't find it. Not that I would have been able to access his money."

Her gaze swings back to me, this time it's tinted with embarrassment. "I didn't have a big supply of food, so I panicked and called Bob Claymore. The only guy my father was still in touch with from the SEALs. He told me he'd fly me down and give me a job. I felt like I was out of options, so I came."

The urge to have her in my arms grows too strong, but I'm not sure if it's to soothe the pounding ache in my chest or to comfort her. Or both.

She doesn't move away when I step up and wrap my arms around her. The energy around her is prickly as a cactus, but so is mine.

Now so much makes sense about her. Holy fuck... her father getting killed in a hunting accident is devastating.

I know. I've watched people that I care about try to recover from that my entire life. It was gut wrenching. All I wanted to do was take that hurt away.

Then with my father's accidental death in a blizzard, I saw that pain even closer as my brothers, sister, and mother tried to cope.

A cloud of familiar grief settles over me. Death sucks. Especially if her father was her lifeline, like it seems the man was.

"You've been through a lot," I offer. "Hunting accidents are such a sad fucking way for a life to end."

She sighs heavily and burrows a little deeper into my chest. I want to curl myself around her and save her from the world. Only, I'm not sure I'm strong enough right now.

But McKenzie makes me crazy protective. Irrationally so. I'd go to bat again and again for this woman. But I know that as much as support and being surrounded by people who listen helps, the healing has to come from the inside. There's no doubt that takes time.

I've yet to figure out exactly how long. It's an open-ended question.

Shoving my own pain back into the recesses where it festers, I try to help her. Like I always do. Helping the people around me. Maybe because I've never been able to help myself through the darkness.

"I'm here to listen if you want to talk, babe."

"Thanks, that means a lot," she murmurs as her shoulders rise and fall again on a sigh.

As I hold her, my mind starts to reach for comfort. For me that's Montana. I used to think I felt better when I was away from the memories there, but when I was away, I wanted one thing—to be home on the ranch.

The craving to get home claws at me. Even if I've never found my peace, I know where I'm a helluva lot closer to it. Trident Ranch.

"How'd you like to go to Montana to meet my family? I think you'd fit right in with them."

After a beat, she steps away from me. There's something new in her expression but it's gone so quickly I can't get a read.

Then she says, "It sounds nice, but now that I've got the money, I'm buying a ticket to go back to Alaska."

Knife, meet gut.

Twice.

Chapter Forty-One

DOZER

I try not to jolt like I've been hit with a sledge hammer when her words slam into my soul. I guess I fail because she slips out of my arms, but not before I grab her hand.

"If you're ready to go, I'll help you get back home."

Fuck if those words don't sting all the way down my spine.

Pale green eyes look up at me. The shimmer of tears makes them ethereal.

Let go, Dozer. Let her fucking go.

If that's what McKenzie wants, give her that. She doesn't need your shit tied up in a knot with hers.

Chapter Forty-Two

Candy

Dozer's fingers circle my wrist. A big, warm cuff that refuses to let me pull away, when I want to.

He knows I'm trying to hide from him. Probably smells my fear like a wolf. Only this time, I catch a scent of something he's holding tucked in a dark, hurting place.

Dozer is not an easy man to read, but the flash of pain he didn't hide is from something that cut him deep.

Even as torn up, and upside down as I am, my first instinct is to reach inside this big, strong man and soothe that pain. To shoulder some of his burden. Turn a light into the dark places that burn from wrongs and haunting memories.

But if he's like my father in any way, he probably refuses to open that door. It took a lifetime for me to finally unravel his darkness, to finally understand that the terror I saw in my father was almost equal parts whatever haunted him, and the fear of letting it go.

Holding so tight because that darkness might come out and never be contained.

John Rush had so much pain. Ghosts rode his back from his time in the service. A volcano of rage boiled in his heart. For all those years afterward, he was swirling with a tornado of paranoia.

People knew he was disturbed, even if I didn't. Little girls are observant, but they can't understand what they live within. Like the tree can't see itself in the forest.

Sometimes there were strange looks from people at the hardware store. When that happened, a simple supply run could turn into a night of agonizing behavior: checking locks, loading weapons, peering out a tiny crack, punctuated by hours of pacing.

Then there was the cautious way parents would skirt out of the way with their kids when he showed up at my school.

When I was young, I thought it was because we weren't native to Alaska. Then Hattie Cullen told me my dad was scary.

That day at lunch, I dropped my Spam sandwich and it tumbled on the floor when she told me she had nightmares about his beady eyes and snarly teeth.

The memory still causes me to flinch.

That's the very first time I saw him in the light others did.

He was scary to me too, I just figured dads were like that. Loud. Uneasy. Always a breath away from an explosion.

Guess I was wrong. Not that I have much experience

beyond that. Only a friend from high school rocked my understanding of what family was. Her stories of family were nothing like mine.

Holiday meals with aunts and uncles. Fishing trips with her dad. Talks by the campfire. Him taking her to the city to purchase things to decorate her room.

This was not the man that I lived with. The survivalist with a dangerous glint in his eyes.

I watched my father struggle with it my whole life. He never let me close enough to truly understand in a way that I could help. I never saw behind the façade he wove so tightly that it became the brittle, volatile definition of his existence.

Looking over the beautiful landscape, I reach for the peace it should bring me. Instead, a shudder runs through me. Cold starts to seep into my bones again. A reminder of the icy feeling that settled into my heart the night before my dad died.

Our house was a house of pain. Just like many times before, he'd argued with me that night when I tried to get him to eat. Eating helped him calm down. But I lost my usual patience after a long day of chopping and hauling wood and snapped at him when he refused dinner.

That's when things went nuclear.

It took days for the bruises on my arms and back to start to heal, but the real pain cut deeper. He'd never threatened my life with a gun before.

Until that night.

That's when I knew we'd hit a hard stop. That was the last time.

I would never be beaten by my father again. I didn't care if he was sick or in agony. I was done.

Bile stings at the back of my throat and I turn to find Dozer's gaze on me. It makes me flinch.

What can he see?

Too much. That scares me.

Feeling raw and exposed, I cross my arms tighter. When he calls out, "We should roll," I nod and follow him back to the SUV on legs that feel disconnected.

When we're settled inside, I'm still fighting the ache in my chest when I find Dozer looking at me.

His eyes soften as he reaches for my hand. But he's silent, and I wonder if he's done with me. Relieved to have my baggage off his shoulders.

That should make me happy, right? I don't want him saddled with my life when he's got his own pain.

Chapter Forty-Three

DOZER

After walking around for a while, her hand tangled in mine with both of us in a silent funk, I drive to a hotel. A nice place. Somewhere I had originally thought we could sit by a pool, have a quiet dinner, almost like a date, then...

Hell, I didn't know what might come after that.

After that kiss, I had high hopes—

Fuck, yeah. That's what I get for thinking. Any imaginings I had about something between us are obviously on ice in her opinion.

My renowned people-assessing skills feel like a flat-out failure.

"So." I tap my fingers on the steering wheel, then kill the SUV engine. "Since I doubt I can get you a plane ticket and get you airborne tonight, and I'm not rushing back to California, it seems like neither of us has anywhere to be tonight. I thought we could chill, catch some dinner. This seemed like a good place to stay, or I could take you back to the Strong's ranch."

"Staying here sounds reasonable."

Her tone is normal enough, but she won't look at me and that makes me wonder if she felt my proverbial face-plant when she broke the news her father had died in a hunting accident.

That was so far from left field that it caught me right between the eyes.

Now, I don't know what the hell I'm sensing in her. This new cool detachment adds to the mixed bag of signals I'm getting off the girl.

Or maybe it solidifies that what I thought was some-thing happening between *us*, was something just happening inside my head.

I'm not a patient man when it comes to lack of clarity. I like to get to the bottom of shit. Another reason, amongst many, for the nickname, Dozer.

McKenzie starts to open her door, and I grab her wrist.

Startled, she says, "Oh, I forgot, *youuu* like to open the door."

"I do, but it's not that. I need to talk and I think you need to listen. Then I want you to talk back. Because I'm not feeling very clear on what's happening right now."

Her eyes round. "Oh. Okay."

"That kiss..." I start and have to swallow as I'm flooded with a wash of memories. Good memories this time, not the black shreds of memories that coat my brain and have since I was sixteen.

This time, they're all about McKenzie's soft body in my hands, her sweet little moans, the taste of her. *Perfection.*

Grumbling, I dive in. "That kiss wasn't just a drive-by liplock."

Her gaze falls to my mouth quickly and darts away as her cheeks grow a dark shade pink. "I didn't think it was."

"But you just said you're ready to trot off to Alaska."

She looks up at my eyes, assessing me with a hint of stormy wariness, but doesn't say a word.

I continue, "You don't know me well, but when I want something, I don't just let it waltz away from me without putting up a fight."

In a flash, her pupils dilate, but she's locked in silence or giving me a chance to say everything I have to say.

"I kissed you because I *want* you. Not just a fast fuck. Although I do love a fast, hard fuck. I also like a long, slow morning of lovemaking. But that's not what this is about. After all the talking we've done... and haven't done yet, I'm curious about you. I want to peel away those layers and learn what makes McKenzie Rush tick."

She opens her mouth to say something but I hold up a finger. "You also make me protective as fuck. Being a protector is something I'm born with. I'm watchful as hell over my sister and the people I care about, but this is a level I've never felt before and can't explain.

"Which means, I'm not just going to let you go easily. I'm not trying to scare you, but I want to lay the truth out there. I know we didn't start on a great foot, and you might think I intentionally deceived you like that fucker Bob did, but that's not how I roll. I lay the facts out, as hard as they are to swallow, and I expect you to do the same with me. I want you. I want to get to know you. I want to protect you and keep you safe in the dark hours of the night. I don't care if it's in Alaska, Montana, or some island in the Pacific. I just know I'm not ready to let you walk away. Now, I have one question for you."

The expression on her face is now one of complete disbelief. She blinks rapidly as I pause, then I ask, "Did you feel anything when I kissed you?"

A rush of air leaves her lungs. "Feel anything? *God.* Justin, I felt *everything.* I just don't know what it all was. I felt like I was being pulled to the heavens and drowned at the same time."

After rubbing her palm on her jeans, she shakes her head. "It was scary. It was amazing. It was... something that I have no idea how to deal with."

Fuck. Relief is the best feeling in the world.

I once heard it is the strongest emotion. Now I understand why someone would say that—nothing is sweeter than relief.

I feel a grin start to tug at the corner of my mouth. "Pretty much the same for me."

We watch each other for a few seconds as a heaviness settles around us. "Don't run from me, McKenzie. Don't hide your feelings or your fears."

I reach out and cup her velvety soft cheek. "Ms. Rush, I want to know you. In every way a man can."

Her gaze transforms from shocked to soft and vulnerable. She fully blushes now. The color is warm and sweet and reaches to her beautiful eyes. Her mouth opens, but she's breathless.

When she can't speak, I lean in and brush my lips over hers, inhaling her sweet, mind-blowing scent as I do.

"Sweetheart, we don't have to go fast. If you really decide you want just a friendship from me, then that's what happens. I'm not going to make you do something that you don't want to do. Just don't expect me to go away. To back down. To leave you unprotected or in dire-fucking-straights. Because that's not the kind of man I am."

Her hand skims up my arm and her fingers come to rest on my neck, pulling me close.

"I never expected someone to say things like that to me."

"Babe, I'm the kind of man that won't let you fight your battle alone. The kind that will go to the ends of the earth to keep the people he cares about safe. The kind of man that loves hard whether you're my brother, my friend, or my everything."

She draws in a shuddering breath and I kiss her again, gently tasting her, then I pull back.

"I'm taken by you, Candy Sweet. One kiss, hell ten-thousand kisses, will never be enough," I roughly whisper.

I don't know when she unbuckled her seatbelt, but suddenly she's crawling across the console and into my arms. A wicked grin curls my lips.

We barely fit in the driver's seat, but Christ, she feels good. Our mouths meet and our breath mingles, and we're all tightly wedged against each other.

My heart nearly splits wide open.

She's panting when we break apart. "I didn't want to just leave. I just didn't know how to stay. But, Justin, I have to go back. There's unfinished business there, my whole life is there..."

I press my forehead against hers. "I'm going with you."

She stills. "You would do that?"

Of course I would. What kind of man does she think I am? "Woman, didn't you just hear everything I said?"

"I did. I'm just a little shell-shocked."

"Well, get used to me being around, sweetheart. If I'm not working, I'm going to be glued to you."

She laughs softly, skimming her hand over my chest. "Your intensity surprises me."

"This is nothing, babe," I murmur, then I unlock my door, climb out with her in my arms, and stride into the hotel lobby with her laughing the whole way.

Chapter Forty-Four

Candy

The clerk stares open-mouthed at us as Dozer lowers me to my feet.

"We need a room," he booms and I'm thankful the lobby is empty.

The woman jumps into action, barely able to keep her eyes off his gorgeousness. I can't blame her. With his five-o'clock shadow and his hair mussed in a devil-may care style, paired with his tight T-shirt that does nothing to hide his build, the man is fire.

I have the urge to stand in front of him, but restrain myself. This jealousy thing is new for me. But he is going upstairs with me after all.

Less than a minute later, we're heading to the elevator.

Hand in hand, his strong fingers gripped tightly around mine.

The connection feels so right it's surreal.

As soon as the elevator door closes, Dozer turns to look down at me with a heart-stopping intensity. Storm clouds swirl in the gray of his irises. He rests his calloused palm against my cheek. "What happens tonight is up to you, babe."

I feel a flush of heat from my head to my toes and all those places in between. I gulp down my nerves. "We could eat."

His eyes heat to a barely contained simmer. "We could."

"We could talk," I offer.

He smiles slowly as the elevator dings as it passes a floor. "We will do that."

"We could..." I start to burn at the idea of the things I could do with this man. Or he could do *to* me.

"Whatever you want," he murmurs hotly.

My words shake as I ask, "What if I don't know what I want?"

When the elevator door opens, he tugs me into the hallway and lowers his mouth to my ear. "I can tell you about all the options."

He inhales deeply, drops his lips to my neck where he softly nips, before he swipes his tongue against my burning skin.

A rush of emotion and want surges in my veins.

It's so primitive, so raw that it makes me shiver, contradicting the fact that I'm raging hot inside my own skin. I push his chest with the palm of my hand. "We should go inside now."

Pupils dilating, Dozer wraps his hand around the back of my neck as he looks down at me. His breathing is faster now. Heat is pulsing off of him in thick waves. "Fuck, yes, we should."

A few seconds later, the door thuds closed behind us, sealing us into the cool, dark quiet of the suite, and I barely register the beautiful hotel room before Dozer's hands go to my hips. Then he lifts me and carries me to a dresser, where he deposits me onto the top.

We're eye to eye again and I love it so much when I see him this way.

Growly, he says, "As much as I want to rip your clothes off, and throw you on the bed, we need to take this slow."

We do?

What am I thinking? I'm not sure I could take Dozer fast. I nearly whimper at the thought of him advancing on me with all the intensity that's swirling around him.

I don't know if I find the idea more scary or thrilling. For some reason that makes me laugh. "Slow could be a good idea."

I'm playing with fire for the first time here and I'm about to light a match the size of a rocket ship.

He threads his fingers into my hair and looks at me with a fierce but tender energy in his expression. "The first thing I need to know is if you're a virgin."

What?

Fair enough question, but it still takes me off guard, mainly because I'm not sure how to answer. "N-no," I stutter although I'm not sure I define myself as other than a virgin. Because what happened between me and Devin Newman was not the least but intimate. Not that sex has to be intimate, but can you really count two idiotic teens fumbling through kind-of-sex?

He lets out a held breath and something dark crosses his already tight features. "Christ, I'm not sure if I like that you're experienced or if I fucking detest that I'm not your first. But you said you'd never been naked in front of a man, so..."

Oh. That. "Ah, I understand now. I've had sort-of-intercourse. So, by definition, I'm probably not a virgin."

Embarrassment burns me to cinders. "It wasn't what you think. Truthfully, I'm mortified to talk about this."

He holds my face and makes me look at him. Suddenly, he's bristling mad and the animal inside him is tearing at the cage he keeps it in as he seethes, "So help me god, if you tell me it was rape, I'm going to hunt someone down and filet them."

I grab his wrist, "Shhh, no, calm down. It was nothing like that. It was just a stupid teenage thing. We didn't even take our clothes off. It was one time and I'm horrified to even think about it."

Dozer drops his head and blows out a hard breath. "Thank fuck."

When he looks at me again, I quietly say, "This is the first time that I'll be with a man."

Dozer's stormy gaze intensifies as his thumb strokes over my cheek slowly. "We're definitely going slow."

"You're in charge here," I whisper.

He growls and curls his fingers into my hips. The power of his touch is so delicious that it makes me want that feeling all over my body.

With a thick voice, he says, "*Slow*. I can't go hard or fast with you until you feel comfortable with me."

I move his hand to my stomach and under my T-shirt. "Then just don't stop."

Chapter Forty-Five

DOZER

Just don't stop.

Three words that unravel me. A bulldozer couldn't stop me right now. I have one mission. To feel everything she will give.

I lift McKenzie off the dresser with one hand under her ass, as I glide my other hand up the soft skin of her stomach. She wraps her legs tight around me.

A constant, low growl builds in my chest. A resonant sound that feels like it's coming from the core of the earth. Reaching through me, straight up to the stratosphere. A rocket ship heading for the heavens.

McKenzie's so damned sexy and doesn't even have an idea what a perfect package she is.

Armies have fallen over women like her.

Men sell their souls to know what it's like to have eyes like hers on you.

To taste the heady flavor of her kiss, to know what it's like to feel her lush body surrounding you.

"Justin," she murmurs against my lips in a throaty purr. Her legs wrap tight, cinching me closer, right up against the heat that's escaping her jeans.

I can't get close enough. I want it all. Everywhere. Everything. Velvet skin, warm and soft. The throaty purrs. The breathless words. Give me every fucking thing.

"McKenzie, holy sex kitten. You're driving me mad, squeezing your thighs around me like that," I whisper against her throat.

The muscles of her stomach flutter as my fingers explore her delicate curves. So womanly. So small compared to my size.

I was fully intent on laying her on the bed, but I can't make my feet move a single damned inch. I'm locked up in a lust-filled haze. About five seconds away from bending her over the desk chair and slamming a home run.

But I can't even take a single step. A throaty laugh forms inside me. For a man of action, it's pretty fucking funny that all I can do is hold her tight.

She smells like sunshine, warm desire, I bury my face against her neck as I fight the weird storm of emotions inside of me.

What *is* happening to me?

This was never supposed to unfold this way. I wasn't shopping for a relationship. Hell, I was staying clear of women. After seeing the chaos that my friend Mako and his woman dealt with getting to their happy ever after, I knew I wasn't ready.

Probably'd never be ready. Especially when I know dark

memories eat at the part of me that should be able to love. But fate is a bitch. Or a gentle hand. Or a slap and a shove.

Sometimes all of the above.

"You feel so good, I love how strong you are." McKenzie's fingers slide into my hair as she trembles in my hands. Those sweet fucking legs are wrapped firmly around me, holding me tight.

Legs made strong from hiking in the Alaska wilderness. That turns me on even more.

With every inhale, our chests rub. The tips of her nipples pushing against me. "You feel so fucking perfect," I whisper throatily against her lips. "I need to get these clothes off of you."

She beats me to it and yanks her T-shirt over her head. It floats to the floor, forgotten as I hoist her higher up and bite at the mound of her left breast.

A short keening sound comes out of her throat, instantly tightening my groin. "Off," I growl. No need to tell her what I'm asking for, the black bra falls between us when she releases the clasp.

"God. *Damn,*" I breathe as systems in my body start to rev. "I've been thinking about this moment since I first saw you."

She laughs shyly as I circle one nipple with a lazy swirl of my tongue. Then I do the other before I tuck my nose between them for a deep inhale. "Oh, McKenzie. *Fuck,* what are you made of? Because it's the most delicious thing I've ever been close to."

"Justin," she rasps against my mouth when I kiss her again. She's breathless and laughing when I pull back.

That gentle, easy laugh she has makes my body heat and purr like a well-oiled engine.

I spin and stretch her out on the bed, pressing her hands

higher. "That's it, stay right there," I murmur roughly as I lean back on my knees. "Let me see you spread out before me."

Her hands flutter above her head like she wants to cover herself, but she resists. Chills rise on her skin and her nipples peak even tighter, making my throat constrict. I'm shaking inside as I slide my hands down her stomach.

Then I say the craziest thing.

"I want you to be mine."

Her eyes leap.

I span her waist with my hands, dipping my thumbs below the edge of her jeans. "I know that's fucking insane, but I've been consumed with this need and I can't shake it. I'm not sure what's happening here, but I know that I don't want to pretend."

She watches me carefully for a beat, then quietly says, "Me either, but it scares me..."

I lean over her, planting my hand next to her shoulder and look down at her beautiful, angelic face, at the clear, lucid awareness in her pale eyes.

My voice is thick, I'm breathless. Hell, I sound like a man that's been possessed by some force much greater than himself. "We'll fall together. I won't let anything happen to you."

"I know you will keep me safe," she replies with solemn eyes that trace my face.

She shivers beneath me as I trace my hand down over her body, grazing her collarbone, the curve of her breast, down to the nip of her waist.

"Your body is safe." I press my hand over her breast-bone. "This too. I'm a man of my word. I won't hurt your heart."

She blinks back a tear that's on her lashes and the tightness in my chest grows when she whispers, "Justin..."

"I'm not an easy man, I have demons. Ugly, dark baggage. I have a big, complicated family. I'm possessive as fuck. I'll want things from you."

Uncertainty enters her eyes, and I lean down and kiss her. It's a hot, possessive tangle of our tongues that makes my blood burn.

"Honesty." I brush my mouth across her cheek and whisper in her ear, "Total fucking honesty at all times."

She nods.

I go on with my heart pounding in my throat. "Faithfulness."

Her hands leave the place I put them above her head and come up to cradle my neck as she arches against me.

I roughly whisper my next word against her ear. "Surrender."

She turns her mouth to find mine. We kiss so deeply that my heart spasms. *Christ.*

I growl, clench her hips roughly, and roll her on top of me. She straddles me naturally and her hands land on my chest, pressing my T-shirt against my electrified skin.

"We need to talk about some things."

She stares down at me looking like a vision. Her irresistible mouth is painted wet from the kiss we just shared. The light shimmers off the pale tumble of hair. Nipples begging for my mouth, she studies me with a small smile. "Do you always talk so much during sex?"

I laugh. Deeply. I want to flip her back beneath me and show her there's a whole world of things I can do to her without saying a single word. However, I don't because we need to get some things straight. So, I say, "No. But this isn't just sex."

That mischievous smile falls in an instant. She dips her head, letting her eyes fall to where her hands are on my chest. "I agree."

"McKenzie, I need to know with one hundred percent certainty that you're ready for this."

Her brows shoot up as she meets my gaze again. Then I see understanding dawn in her eyes.

"Am I giving you a mixed signal here?" With the question, her hands go under my shirt, and she scrapes her short nails over my scorching flesh.

I shudder.

Uh. Talk about getting right to the damned point. "Fuck, McKenzie."

She grabs my belt. "Or how about this?"

I hiss as she unbuckles me. When my cock springs free, her eyes flare, then she blinks a whole bunch of times. There's admiration in her voice. "Whoa. I thought I imagined how big you were when I saw you at the resort. Now I'm thinking I was underestimating the size of this beast."

I'd be lying if I said I don't love the way she's looking at me.

"I'm big. That's one of the reasons we need to go slow... the other is because damned if I'm going to let our first time be me taking you like a rutting animal."

Those tantalizing lips turn up again as she tentatively wraps her hands around me. "You say the funniest, weirdest things. Just so you know, I happen to think animal rutting is quite natural, but let me see if I can help you relax. I think you'll also realize I'm onboard here. *Completely.*"

Her playfully excited eyes hold mine as she makes a long stroke against my very willing and ready cock.

I lose another piece of myself as I watch her watch my face. Jesus. What is it about McKenzie Rush that breaks down my walls and drives spikes into every part of me all at once?

She wiggles and slides her body down mine, straddling my knees and lowers her torso until her hair is grazing my lower stomach and my cock. "Your body is unreal, Justin."

Then she leans down, licks her plump, deliciously rosy lips, and takes the head deep in her mouth.

Just like fucking that.

Bam.

I clench the bedspread and curse through locked teeth. I didn't see that coming. "Holy fuck. Baby. *Mc...Kenzie*."

She laughs, sending a vibration through my electrified cock. My brain is shutting down. Zone by zone. Soon there's gonna be a total blackout.

Before I'm too gone to move, I fist her silky waterfall of hair, but just let her drive this show. Her touch is a little awkward, but it's the sweetest, sexiest touch I've ever felt.

Her mouth is hot, wet, delicate heaven. Tracing her tongue over me, kissing the head, breathing against me as she whispers, "It's so perfect."

Her lips slide over me again, taking me deeper this time. I growl or groan, I'm not sure which, but it starts at my toes and ends locked in my throat. When she comes up for air, she wipes her lips with her fingertips. "Embarrassed to say, I have no clue what I'm doing here."

I grin. "Hell, you're wrecking me, that's what you're doing."

She lowers her mouth again, this time swirling her tongue over the slit in my head. "Salty," she murmurs.

And it hits me. Fuck. I have to taste her. STAT. When I flip her beneath me, she gasps.

"My turn. I'm going to take your jeans off now. Then I'm going to eat you until you scream. After that, I'm going to fuck you deep and slow. But I want you to know that no matter how into it I am, I will stop if you want. You're safe with me. One hundred percent. I make you uncomfortable, you tell me."

I take her chin in my hand. "Understand?"

She nods and whispers, "Thank you. I already feel like I'm flying."

Giving her a devilish grin, I reply, "Just wait, sweetheart."

I yank her jeans down her hips, spread her knees, not even bothering to get her ankles free because I can't wait a second longer. Then I bury my nose against her sweet slit, pressing against her black panties.

I groan in relief as I inhale her while I press my thumbs into her spread thighs, holding her wide for me. Fuck. Fucking. *Fuck.* I'm dying for this woman.

She's shaking already, then when I press that thin layer of fabric aside and swipe into her with my tongue, she goes crazy. Jolting, whimpering, breathing my name over and over.

God. She's so responsive.

I devour her, slide my fingers all over her sensitive places, slowly until I know what she likes, and murmur against her pussy until she's on the verge of falling.

Then I penetrate her with two fingers. Sinking my flesh into her. "Let yourself come, relax into it."

"Justin. I can't!"

"You will." I curl my fingers tighter against her thickened g-spot, slick my thumb over her clit, dancing the line between pain and pleasure, and the release slams into her.

Her thighs clench my shoulders as she contorts beneath my hand. It's the hottest thing I've ever watched.

A knot inside my chest releases and I take a massive

breath. Somewhere there's a rainbow in the sky. A choir is singing. Holy. Shit.

I climb her body, kiss her through the aftershocks. "That was so damned beautiful. I can't wait to do it again."

She smiles leisurely and skims her hand over her face. "What was that?" With a laugh she adds, "I'm floating."

"That was what you get when you are mine."

Gliding my hands down her body, I free her ankles from her jeans and panties, throwing them aside, I shuck all my clothes in record time. Through hazy eyes she watches me as I get covered.

"I love the way you look. All those powerful muscles." She reaches for me, wraps her arms and her legs around me as I settle in the cradle of her body.

"All for your pleasure, baby." My words catch as I press against her for the first time.

I want to catch the moment in a bottle. Remember the way she breathes against me, the rise and fall of her nipples against my pecs. The sweet smell of her lingering on my lips, the heat of her body wrapped all 'round me from the wrap of arms across my back, to her calves around my hips, to the tease of her entrance throbbing against my cock.

When I slip inside of her, merging more than just our bodies for the first time, I kiss her intently. Taking my time to show her how amazing she's making me feel, showing how much I want this. "That's it, sweet girl, take me. Your body isn't used to my size. Just breathe and let me all the way in."

Soon, I'm seated to the hilt, her nails dig into me, and I start to move. Every stroke is pure and amazing. Tight, slick heaven.

We lose ourselves in between ragged breaths, sweet growls, and heated touches.

Christ. I'm so thankful.

Fuckin-A.

I'm thankful I took that job with Agile.

Grateful she said yes to the fucking nutso deal.

Thankful for whatever drove her to this place, because now I'm going to build her life back up. Piece by piece, until she's walking on fucking sunshine every single day.

That's what she deserves. That's what I'll give her.

Somehow I manage to stay slow until she unravels around me. Her voice tears, shreds to thin remnants, falls low and hot. "Justin. Oh, god. Yes. Yes. I need—"

Then I let myself move harder, but only until she arches, clamps her eyes and screams so loud it shakes the room.

I freeze in place, watching. Absorbing. Memorizing the first time that I get to watch her come apart with me deep inside her.

I don't ever want to forget.

Throat tight, body vibrating, I fist her hair and kiss the maniacal pulse at her throat. I'm not even sure how it happens, but a blinding orgasm wallops me, without me so much as moving an inch.

I bark out a sound that I've never heard before. My chest locks up. My vision goes black, but my heart is telling me something loud and clear.

McKenzie Rush is it for me.

Chapter Forty-Six

Candy

Fed, sated, and happier than I think I've ever felt, I fall into a perfect slumber wrapped in Justin's arms.

I didn't know that I could feel like this.

Warm, safe, happy, and adored.

Who knew? I guess those romance novels were onto something.

But I awaken when Dozer—Justin—slides from the bed.

His sleep-rough voice is across the room when he says, "What's up?"

I blink and try to orient myself. "Justin?"

"On the phone," he replies from somewhere in the heavy darkness. Then he's spitting out a rough string of curses.

My body goes stiff. My heart pounds as he's obviously listening to someone on the other end of the call.

Finally, Justin bites out, "They're wrong. Shit. Do you think? Got to be *fucking wrong*."

I've never heard the violence in his voice before. It makes me bolt upright in the bed. Holding the sheet to my chest, my heart throbs.

"No. Yes. I'll send the address."

I jolt off the bed when he yells, "Fuck."

Something crashes loudly, and when I scramble for the lamp, the room is flooded with light. The coffee table is on its side, the items that were on the top are now broken or strewn on the floor.

I freeze.

Justin's staring at me with narrowed lids, his brow locked down. His jaw is clenched. The phone is in a white knuckle grip as he listens to whoever called.

"Yes. Send the jet. We'll go to them," he says in a voice that would freeze hell over as he disconnects.

Chapter Forty-Seven

DOZER

Wrong. My mind was screaming as my best friend told me the news. But Mako is never wrong. He's the most right SEAL I've ever known.

His intel is solid. Agile takes their shit as seriously as we did when we were in the teams. I want the bomb he just dropped to be wrong, but I know he's telling me the truth.

When the call ends, I'm staring at McKenzie with my throat completely closed like a vault door. The coffee table has a snapped leg. The vase that was on top is broken. Pink and red flowers are scattered on the hotel rug. Water has made a dark stain.

I can't breathe. I can't fucking move. I definitely can't process.

McKenzie's body's shaking, which is obvious completely across the room as she tugs the sheet tighter to cover herself. "Justin, what's wrong?"

"There's a warrant for your arrest in Alaska. For murder."

Chapter Forty-Eight

Candy

Oh. God.

Justin's words land like a nuclear detonation.

My body reacts by shutting down. I faint before I can reach for the bed.

I'm not sure how long I'm out, but I wake to find Dozer holding me. Anger, hurt, and fear blend into a frightening mask on his face.

"I'll go with you," he roughly says, and I'm not sure exactly what he's saying.

Murder.

Oh god. I didn't imagine it. I sound like I aged eighty years in a span of moments. "Where are we going?"

"To Alaska to meet this head on. Otherwise, they'll arrest you here and extradite you."

Nausea whips through me and I clench my stomach. I'm suddenly freezing. My teeth chatter.

Dozer helps me dress. Then we're at a small airport getting on a private plane. I'm numb. I'm terrified. I have no idea what's about to happen.

Murder.

Murder.

Murder.

The word repeats in my head, an eviscerating chant.

As we climb the stairs to the plane, Marshall and Mako are waiting.

"Brother, you okay?"

Justin doesn't reply, but shakes his hand and steps into a half-hug. Mako's brow is creased. His eyes are full of worry for the man I've just made love with.

The group of men ushers me into the jet and I take a seat. Justin stays close, but even though he's beside me, I feel a million miles away. A wall slammed down between us when that call came in, and I'm not sure if it's me or him, or both of us.

All of them are eyeing me warily. Like a murderer.

Things go from bad to worse when Marshall puts some documents on the table in front of us. It's the warrant where I'm being accused of murder.

"Ohmygod. *My father?*" I gasp. I hadn't even asked who I was charged with murdering because getting told you're wanted for murder scrambles the hell out of your head.

My breathing gets labored, even to my own ears I sound like I'm sprinting. A wave of cold terror fills my body completely, every cell, every fiber.

"I'm here with you." Dozer's voice is rough, his hand flexes on my thigh as he stares with narrowed eyes at the papers on the table in front of us. The cords of his neck are tight. His breathing is shallow.

I can't read them, my stomach will pitch if I do.

"You don't have to talk now, but if you want our help, you need to."

"I know," I reply shakily. "You think I could have—"

I fight the anger in my throat, but can't finish my words.

Dozer grips my shoulders and turns me to face him. His brow hardens into a slash. "You need to tell me everything."

I don't know why I expected him to have my side, but I did. And I'm crushed at the bite of his words. "You really think I could kill my father?"

"I don't know."

Those words shred what was left of me.

I shut down on the inside. Organ by organ. Until I'm nothing but a block of dirty gray ice.

After a crushing silence, I whisper, "I loved him even if he was mean." My eyes drop, then lift to meet a penetrating inspection. "Justin, he was sick from being broken when he was in the SEALs. I took care of him."

His brow draws together. "What are you saying?"

I press my hand over my pounding heart. "No one knows this. I didn't even know what was wrong with my father until I happenchance read a book that had a character with severe PTSD. Then I understood everything."

He shifts and faces me, questions burning in his eyes. "Did he assault you?"

"He was paranoid. He was angry. Things set him off. Noises. Sudden flashes of light. Me saying the wrong thing. Sometimes he'd just wake up in a rage."

Dozer drops his head as his hand clenches on the table.

I want to reach for him, but I don't have to because I can feel him. A thousand miles away, but there at once. It's hard to explain, but if I hadn't felt what it was like to have his energy open to me before, I'd never know what it was like to feel it closed.

He's my one lifeline and the thread between us is as delicate as a spider's silk.

Dozer stays like that for an agonizingly long time. "That's why you stayed with him even when you were old enough to leave?"

Tears pulse out of my eyes and fall steadily on my hands. "He didn't have anyone else. Even if I wanted to leave, there was no one to look out for him. When things were bad, he wouldn't eat or clean, or do anything to care for himself. There was no way I could move and leave him there in the mountains alone. Unless something drastic happened, I was going to be living in that cabin for the rest of my life."

He nods.

"Okay. Once we land, we need to meet with the sheriff," Dozer says solemnly.

The word sheriff strikes terror in my heart. I've never dealt with anything related to law enforcement. My mind is filled with scenes from the fiction books I've surrounded myself with. Every one of them is nightmare material.

I'm so crushed by the prospect of being locked in a cell, I barely have the strength to ask, "Am I going to jail?"

Marshall leans forward and lifts one of the papers. "We will do our best to avoid that. We already reached out for Agile's lawyer and he'll be here as soon as he can. Besides, I have contacts. I'm seeing if I can get any additional information."

"You are not alone in this, I promise." Dozer tries to reassure me.

I sit frozen as the plane engines begin to roar. When I

thought my life was destroyed before, I didn't know how shattered it could really get.

Christ.

Murder.

I'm going to *jail*.

Chapter Forty-Nine

Candy

My body jerks when the metal door slams closed. The air is frigid. The jail-issued scrubs are a pathetic shield against it. Or maybe I truly am frozen from the inside out. Heartbreak is a real bitch.

I shiver for a while until finally the interrogation room door swings open.

A man in a suit strides in. Behind him is the man I haven't been able to stop thinking about.

The sight of him steals my breath and slices through my heart like a machete. He flinches, locks his jaw tighter, then looks down as he moves into the room.

Justin's hair is slicked back with styling products and he's dressed in a business suit today. It's tight on his biceps and the sleeves are a little short, making me think it's borrowed. Inane thoughts at an insane time.

When Justin finally looks at me again, his eyes are filled with fire. Burn-cities-down fire.

The jailer closes the door and locks it with a loud clunk.

"Ms. Rush, I'm Abe Wilson. Agile Security & Rescue's lawyer. This is my assistant, Mr. Roark."

I look between them, confused. He goes on, "I'm sorry that the other members of the Agile team haven't gotten to see you. County policy. Only attorneys and their staff."

Keeping my eyes off Justin, I say, "Okay." So, the suit probably is borrowed if they are sneaking him in.

The attorney is immaculate. With a military precision haircut and a tailored suit. He's also wearing an apologetic expression. "Sorry it took me so long to get here. I came as quickly as I could."

"Thank you," I reply in a brittle voice. The last forty-eight hours have taken everything from me.

Justin says, "It's good to finally get eyes on you."

I know he can't say anything personal, but that little statement rocks me.

The man takes a seat, opens his briefcase and pulls out a sheath of paper. "You're charged for the murder of your father."

I hold onto the table in front of me as a full body shake starts. I'm already speaking the instant he finishes. "He was killed in a hunting accident."

"Your father's death was reported to the sheriff in Smoke County, then when they discovered you had fled, charges were filed against you."

"T-this is a mistake. He was killed in a *hunting* accident."

The attorney asks, "Did you see the accident?"

I shake my head as tears burn down my cheeks. "I didn't hunt with my father that day. We had a fight the night before and he left during dawn, still moody. I let him go alone. He often hiked and hunted on the days his demons were worst. Truthfully, I wondered if someday he'd just not come back. Not because of an accident, but because he couldn't take whatever hell was inside his head any longer."

I try to inhale, but mostly fail. "I was home. Around noon a man came to the house to tell me about the accident. He lives nearby and was hunting in the same area. Mistook my father for a deer."

Justin shifts in his seat and asks, "And you believed him?"

There's a hitch in his voice, revealing a crack in his stony expression. I don't want to see his emotions. I can't. I cannot bear another thing right now. I'm too weak.

In a rough voice, I go on. "He brought me my father's pack, his gun, and his watch. It was all covered in blood. Hunting accidents happen all the time. It is just a fact of life where we live."

Now I've got two sets of eyes on me, as they analyze my expressions.

Justin asks, "Do you know this man well?"

I'm shaking my head as I say, "Not well. But I know who he is. Mark Forester. His cabin is on one of the ridges near us. But I've never been there. My father knew him, but not closely."

It's the attorney's turn. "What state of mind was he in when he came to you?"

I think for a few seconds. "Disheveled. Pale. His voice was rough. Like someone that's just tragically killed a man."

He continues, "You accepted the belongings, then what?"

I close my eyes as horrible memories flood me. "Then he left. I couldn't really speak. I was stricken. He left me standing on the porch. I stood there until he vanished into the woods. It was snowing that day and biting cold, even though we were into spring. Sometime later, I got so cold I couldn't feel my hands. After putting the bloody gear in the shed—" I choke on my words as emotion fills my throat. "—after that, I crawled into bed and I slept because I was destroyed. My whole world had collapsed. A few days later, I called his old Navy contact and flew to California."

"You didn't call the authorities? Or someone else?"

My eyes flip up and hold his. "Why? Mr. Wilson, in Alaska we take care of our own problems. What was there to report? He was shot in a hunting accident at the hands of a man that at least had the decency to come and tell me. In Alaska, the land, the accidents, or the animals will get you. It's a hard place. We all know and accept that. When someone goes out hunting, there's a chance they won't come back. That's a hard fact of life. I'm sorry if you don't understand that, but I do."

"What about family?" Wilson asks.

"We have no family."

Dozer leans across the table, spreads his hands on the surface. I know he can't touch me, but I want to curl up in his chest and disappear.

Right now, I don't know if he'll ever hold me again. Does he think I'm a murderer too?

I can't look at him and I can't read the attorney's eyes. Is that mistrust? Icy unease?

Interrupting my thoughts, the attorney asks, "Did you ever see the body?"

"No."

Terse, he demands, "Why?"

227

"My father had hiked that morning. The place where he was killed was hours away by foot, and by the time I got there, an animal would probably have already had at him."

The harsh realities of living in the wilderness. "Not everywhere in Smoke Valley was accessible by road. Good hunting grounds often require hiking, ATV, taking a boat, or even a plane."

"Did this guy say he buried your father?"

"He did, but I'm sure it was a shallow grave. The ground is unforgiving and he wasn't prepared, he'd probably be using a small trenching tool. He said he marked the spot and told me where it was, in case I ever want to go."

The attorney shares a look with Dozer, then says, "Someone needs to get the body."

My stomach revolts. Bile surges to my vocal cords. I gulp air. Dozer clenches his fists and says, "Steady." I hate that I can't touch him, that he can't hold me in his arms and make me forget this nightmare for even a second.

We are so close and yet miles apart right now.

The questions keep coming from the attorney. "Do you have any alibis?"

"No," I reply roughly as I scrub my eyes. "No, no one."

"Do you own a lot of weapons?"

"We had several in the house. Very normal for life in the wilderness."

Dozer asks, "Do you know exactly what kind and model they were?"

"The kind that shoot," I reply angrily. "I'm not that kind of person that cares about guns beyond the fact that they put food on the table and protect you from Grizzly bears. I didn't memorize what models of guns my father bought. I just know how to use them."

After a long silence, the men shift and share a glance. I know I'm so screwed.

The attorney lays his pen aside and holds my gaze, his mouth pinched with thought. "Thank you so much for answering our questions. I'm going to make some calls."

He rises and his deep set eyes are unreadable. "We'll try to post your bail as soon as a judge is available."

When the door closes after them, leaving me to be escorted to my cell again, tears are scorching my eyes and my insides are struggling between despair that I'm here and hope that someone out there seems to be fighting for me at least.

Now I just have to wait. And the waiting is killing me inside.

Chapter Fifty

DOZER

Cabin is a relative term. Remote is also a relative term. But this...

What the *fuck* am I seeing?

"This place is rough," Mako mutters as he rolls to a stop and shuts off the engine of the truck Agile rented.

"It's basic. I guess the guy built it for himself," Marshall says from the back seat.

I scan the property, taking in the piecemeal house, the ragtag wooden shed, the stacks of firewood, and the racks where they probably dry fish or other game. An older model truck with a flat tire is on the edge of the property.

The scene is bleak as hell, and the fact that the ground is muddy from the spring melt only adds to the dismal effect.

Growing up in one of the poorer states, I've seen my share of ramshackle homesteads, but this makes me truly fucking sad.

Mako interrupts my need to punch something as I think about McKenzie's father dragging his baby daughter out here to get away from the world because he had PTSD. "I think that's pretty routine out here for people to build whatever."

I grumble. Fuck. I can't even imagine living like this, way the fuck out here. Shit, our family ranch is remote. This is next level. "Is that an outhouse?"

"Probably," Marshall says as he swings his door open, "But I'm guessing they had some indoor water."

Mako asks, "Are you sure? Because McKenzie said they are off-grid."

Marshall says, "Off-grid could still include some kind of cistern that could be pumped into the house."

The guys get into a debate that I want no part in. All I can think about is the shitty living situation in that apartment in San Diego and how that probably felt regal compared to this. Only McKenzie was there out of desperation.

Living a legacy of desperation that drove her father here.

A federal agent in a blacked out pickup truck stops next to us. He climbs out, adjusts his cowboy hat and scans the property with shrewd eyes. We join him at the front of the trucks.

Marshall makes a quick intro, "Guys, this is Agent Sebastian Beckett."

I shake his hand. "Thanks for getting us access."

"Sorry it took me this long."

I'm glad he thinks twenty-four hours is long, because I

sure as fuck do, since that is how long it's been since I last laid eyes on my sweet Candy. But we couldn't just go trampling a crime scene. Beckett had to get through some red tape before we could go into the house.

All while McKenzie's still sitting in the Smoke County jail. While I chew fucking nails. The metal kind. Not the finger kind. That's just disgusting, thought that ever since I was in high school with a guy that would gnaw on his hand non-stop. *Nasty.* I shudder and my gut goes back to twisting itself around like a pretzel because I'm obsessing over the fact that McKenzie is in jail. Scared boneless. Alone.

I told her I'd be with her.

The look in her eyes when they took her... Christ, I'll never forget the fear etching her pretty face. I offered to go instead of her.

Marshall had to drag my ass out of the sheriff's office.

They didn't even let me see her the morning after she was taken when I showed up demanding that I put eyes on her.

Thank fuck for the Attorney. He got me in when he was there for a short visit. She was looking like a fucking ghost, but she was holding on. Fuck. I wanted to take her in my arms and break her the fuck out of there. She has no business being locked up. She belongs with me. By my side. And it fucking kills me that there is nothing I can do to get her out of there.

"Let's go have a look," the fed says, breaking me out of my reverie, and we fall into step with him as he climbs up the slope toward the cobbled-together wooden structure. Mismatched lumber and different kinds of roofing make a patchwork façade.

It's surprisingly sturdy, a fact that's not obvious until we get closer. The door is locked, but Beckett kneels down. A few seconds later, he's picked the knob. "Alright, boys, don't touch anything without gloves."

Marshall tosses some nitrile gloves to me and Mako and we walk into the murky interior.

Books. Everywhere. That's the first thing that hits me. McKenzie loves to read. Her only escape from this tiny world.

The second thing—the inside of the cabin is better than the exterior.

It's small, but comfortable. A corner kitchen, a sitting area with clean, but worn furniture. A reading nook by a window.

That's where McKenzie spends her time. There's a quilt and the little containers that were once filled with tiny plants. Now they simply hold carcasses of living things neglected.

This is where she tried to make life as best she could.

Now even this simple life has been taken from her.

Mako picks up a book. "Someone had an obsession with murder mystery. That could be used as evidence."

I growl, "Just because someone reads murder mystery doesn't mean they are a murderer."

I hold up a romance book with a brightly colored, mystical cover with a woman wielding a glowing spear. "When someone reads fantasy romance doesn't mean they're a wizard."

"A sorceress," he corrects.

"How do you know that?" I demand.

He chuckles and walks away. "Oh no, I'm not sharing how I know that."

"I found a lot of ammo," Marshall calls from another room.

He's in a sparse bedroom. It's a masculine space with a

navy blue comforter on a single bed and a plain dresser. On top of the night stand is a dish with a few shotgun shells.

A wooden foot locker is open on the floor and protruding halfway from beneath the bed. Inside is shit tons of ammo. Lots of different kinds.

We didn't find any guns, but that makes sense, given that the scene has already been investigated.

"I guess someone took the guns as evidence," I mutter as I pass by Marshall and stop next to the wall where several photos are hanging. "SEALs."

Mako appears at my elbow and makes a rough sound in his throat. "I have some of his records if you guys want to take a look."

Marshall asks, "Anything stand out?"

"Clean."

"Something doesn't add up. Which just reminded me of something. McKenzie has a Navy-issued duffel with J. Rush on the side, but there's something off about the writing. I could be wrong, but it just looked different."

Beckett walks into the room. "Gentlemen, I think I might have something."

Silently, we file out and follow him to the kitchen where there's a package of something frozen laying on the small round kitchen table.

He nods to the table. "This was in the freezer."

"Don't tell me that's people's parts," Mako remarks as he gags.

Beckett says, "Pansy. Retching like you're some softie. But no, it's probably bear meat. Read the note on the freezer paper."

I turn my head so I can make out the sideways text. "Poliverco." I scan the rest. "A name and a phone number."

Beckett's looking at us with a glint in his eyes. "Herman

Poliverco's the right hand of a guy known as The Dark Ghost. A bad fucking stain on Alaska. Based on all the blank looks on your faces, I take it you've never heard of the fucker. He's a dealer. If that woman or her father were messed up with him, then there's no wonder he got whacked."

"Organized crime? Drugs?" I demand.

"Dealer of everything. Secrets being the number one."

Mako and I look at each other and I ask, "I thought he was a good SEAL?"

"Shit. People do turn bad," Mako says with a scowl.

Chapter Fifty-One

DOZER

When the jailer opens the door and ushers McKenzie into the lobby, we lock eyes. For a beat the world and all the horrible crap that's happening disappears. But when she leaps at me, throwing herself into my arms, I'm jolted back to reality because she's shaking uncontrollably.

As I lift her off the ground, I bury my face in her hair. "Christ, it's good to see you."

Her broken whisper nearly undoes my last control. "Thank you for getting me out."

After hugging her tighter, I set her down so I can get a good look at her. Dark circles mar her skin. Her hair is tangled. There's marks of stress all over her. "Come on. I've got food and clean clothes in the truck."

Gripping my hand like a lifeline, she tucks in against my side. "That sounds like heaven."

"Far from it, but a helluva lot better than what you've had access to in the last eighty hours.

"I'm just so grateful to be getting out. I don't imagine people charged with murder get bail very often."

"Marshall's contacts scored us a solid. Besides, I have a feeling the judge doesn't believe you did it. I mean, not to say you look like a kitten... but you kind of look like a kitten. Not the picture of a deranged killer."

"All kinds of people kill people," she mutters as I click the key fob for the truck. Once I've got her settled, I pass her a white paper bag.

She peeks inside. Her eyes soften as she shivers. "A burger? Oh my god. This smells so good."

Memories of the day we met wash over me. It feels like a lifetime even though it's only been a few weeks. Once again, McKenzie eats ravenously, tearing through the burger as I drive.

"Christ, didn't they feed you?"

"I wasn't hungry. My stomach was in knots. But seeing you, getting to walk out that door, made that ache go away. Now I'm starving."

Like she didn't just rock my world by saying that seeing me was part of what eased her worry, she dives on the burger again. My heart starts to beat normally for the first time in days.

As she chews, I say, "I have a lot to catch you up on."

"Mmm?"

"Marshall's contact got a fed to take us to your cabin."

Her eyes round. She finishes chewing slowly with a look of alarm growing on her face. "You've been to my house?"

After stealing a look at her, I try my damndest to keep my eyes on the road. But what I really want to be doing is touching her. Watching her every little move in my desperation to figure this woman out. "We did a search."

She lays the sandwich down on the wax-paper wrapper on her lap. "I didn't know you were going there."

"We wanted to get our eyes on as many potential leads as possible."

I feel her looking at my profile with hope and desperation. "Did you find anything?"

I want to say more, but I've been put on lockdown. "The Fed thinks so. He's working the lead now."

"What did you find?"

When I don't answer, her voice gets rough. "Please tell me it was nothing against me?"

"No, I don't think so, but we don't know what other evidence the cops have. They must have taken your father's pack, gun, and the watch because the shed had been searched."

Folding up the burger wrapper, she leans back in the seat. "Now I feel sick."

"I'm sorry. I didn't want to upset you, but I felt like it was only fair if you knew we'd been making moves. Just lay back. I'm taking us to a house Marshall rented. You can rest there while we work through some things. Just know it's going to be chaotic there. There's a team of people working round the clock."

"For me?" she asks in a hushed voice.

"For you, sweetheart."

McKenzie's pensive for the rest of the ride. Half of her burger goes untouched. She changes clothes, though, wiggling around in her seat until she's got on a pair of track pants and a sweatshirt. I'm torn up inside, but it makes me feel better that she's clean and comfortable.

"We're here," I announce when I push the door open and guide McKenzie inside.

"Yo," Beckett calls but doesn't raise his head from his laptop. Mako's on two phones at once *and* his computer. He cuts his eyes toward us and then goes back to what he's doing.

The attorney is there, with his shirtsleeves rolled up and his hair looking like it's been fingerfucked. The Fed has been here the whole time too, as his truck was sitting in the same spot it has since yesterday, out in front of the house.

I flex my hand on McKenzie's low back and she leans into my touch. "Sorry. I told you it was chaotic. Maybe you can go upstairs and take a bath? I've got some of your things in the back bedroom for you."

Arms crossed over herself, she stands frozen for a minute, then shakes her head briskly. "Yeah. Okay."

"What's wrong, babe?"

"I was just remembering something."

"What did you recall? It could be important."

She closes down. "Nothing really. It was just kind of a déjà-vu moment." Glancing away, she says, "I will take you up on getting a bath. It's a luxury I haven't been afforded very often."

Without looking back, she trots up the stairs. Marshall strides into the room from the kitchen where he's got his laptop office on the kitchen table. He's in mission mode. "Think she's up for leading us to that grave?"

"Truthfully, no, but the clock is ticking and the sooner we get there the better chance we have at getting to the bottom of this shit."

He nods once. "I'll head to the local mercantile and get

some supplies together. Sounds like it could be a long ruck. We should leave early tomorrow, it's too late for a safe out and back today, given that we don't know what we'll find."

The last thing I want is for McKenzie to have to lead us to her father's grave after what she's just been through, but Marshall's right. Someone needs eyes on that body ASAP.

I turn to Beckett who's scanning over something on his phone. "Any luck finding the neighbor?"

His grim expression gives me an answer before he says, "His house was locked up tight."

I grunt. Fuck. Our one witness is M.I.A. and the only other lead is rife with shit I don't want to think about. Espionage.

Angrier by the moment, I voice a question that's been bothering me. "Nobody's been out to look for this guy's body?"

Beckett says, "Going out there and tromping around would be as effective as looking for a specific penny in a fountain."

"So, that means we have to rely on her or the neighbor to take us to it?"

Beckett pockets his phone and his displeasure shows when his gaze meets mine again. "That or another lead."

Holding Beckett's stare, I ask another question that's been brewing. "You personally think we'll be hauling a body out?"

"Not likely. The animals will take care of any carcass if it wasn't buried well. We might find a few bones, some clothing, but nothing big or heavy if that's what you mean."

Not finding a body means little if any evidence which could help with the case. Which could go either way, for or against McKenzie. But unless something pans out with this Poliverco, then all eyes will stay on her.

I shake my head as those bitter facts settle into the pit of my stomach. "Which means there won't be much chance for ballistics."

He tips his chin up. "You're right. Welcome to my world."

Chapter Fifty-Two

DOZER

The upstairs is quieter, thanks to thick carpet and a floor plan that separates it from the main living areas below. When I peck on the door of the room I selected for us, McKenzie calls, "I'm in the tub. Is it you, Doz?"

"Yeah." I turn the latch and slowly push the door back feeling guilty for wanting to see her silky wet body in that tub. "Mind if I come in?"

Her voice echoes in the bathroom. "No, I don't mind. I'd like that."

The bedroom is dim, with the curtains pulled low, the bathroom the same, only a scant few inches of sunlight slide under the blind that McKenzie has lowered.

Steam is rising. The light filters through it, casting the room in a warm, almost mystical glow. In the midst is my fairy woodland creature with her hair piled on her head, and her brows lifted in a curious expression.

For a beat, I'm stuck, frozen with my heart surging. I want these moments to last forever, but I know time is like hounds closing in on prey. Tomorrow we'll hike to her father's grave. If we don't find evidence that frees her of the charges, she'll eventually face a jury…

God damn, I swear silently.

I will not let that thought invade this moment. No, my worry will not ruin the little time we have.

I walk slowly to the edge of the tub, unable to resist the pull. "You need anything, angel?"

"Some company?"

"Careful, sweetheart. You look too tempting in that warm water."

She smiles sweetly with a hint of embarrassment in her eyes. I love that she's not a brash, experienced tease. Women like that bore me, they're all the same.

With a little bit of breathiness, she replies, "Thanks. You're looking really good there yourself." Her gaze slowly saunters down my body. Lingering on my biceps, my pecs, my abs. The fly of my jeans—or what's growing behind the zipper—and down my thighs.

When she's finished, she ducks her head as her cheeks burn a little bit brighter.

I rest a hip at the edge of the tub and dip my fingers into the suds, avoiding touching her skin, because that isn't a slippery slope, it's a guarantee to me having to have more.

This is her space. Even if only temporary. She needs this. To feel safe, warm, and relaxed.

But what I really want is to slip my hand under the water and into all her secret places until we've soaked the whole damned bathroom floor and ruined the ceiling downstairs.

"I'm going to get some dinner together. Sounds like we're going out to your property first thing tomorrow. Too late to go today."

Uncertain, she asks "What do we do in the meantime?"

"We rest. Eat. See if we can find any other leads in the intel the guys are gathering."

"Is it okay if I stay here a while? I don't really want to think about that stuff right now."

"I think that's perfect." Perfect. A word that was on the fringe of my vocabulary until one blond pixie sat across from me and looked at me over a Flamingo pink smoothie.

Kill shot.

Right between the ribs.

McKenzie watches me as she stirs the water with her fingertips and tiny ripples catch the light as they form rings around her hand. I hope like fuck that I'm not an open book right now. Because the things she'd see might scare her.

I'm mesmerized for a few seconds watching the clouds of bubbles part, revealing skin before they form again and conceal her treasures.

"I've never had a tub like this." She focuses on the swirls, drawing little figure eights with her fingertip.

"Nothing better after a long hard day."

I'll give her this. When all this is done. She'll have a big tub in a lavish bathroom.

Now I know exactly what I'm putting in the master bath at the house I'm building in Montana. McKenzie's never had a soaking tub of her own and I have the crazy need to give her one. A great big two-person tub. One that looks antique but has all the lush features of a modern spa. Hell, maybe I'll even put in a big roll-up door so we can enjoy each other while we stare at the misty blue mountains. Watching as thunderstorms roll in while we make some lightning of our own.

Looking at me through her lashes, the woman that's wrecking my plans of a long bachelorhood tentatively asks, "Do they need you downstairs?"

I consider my answer for a beat. I should leave her in peace after her ordeal at the jail. But I reply, "No. They're doing their thing."

"Good, because I don't want to be alone."

Unable to resist any longer, I lean down, grasp her chin, and take her mouth. She inhales sharply, but leans into my touch.

I'm so hungry for this woman, I'm barely one step above an animal. For a second I lose my control, but then I make myself go slow.

Stoking the coals.

The kiss stretches out, our lips and tongues exploring each other. Savoring. God, I didn't know if or when we'd get a chance to do this again and it felt like part of me was dying in the waiting to find out.

Now I can't stay away from her, even if I'm the last thing she needs.

McKenzie reaches for me, her wet fingers twisting in my shirt tugging me forward more until I'm on my knees next to the tub and her slick wet body is in my hands. "Come," she whispers.

You'll never have to ask twice.

I toe off my boots as we kiss, which is hard as hell when you're on your knees. She tugs my shirt over my head. I unbuckle my belt, stand up, shove my jeans down, taking my briefs with them. In five seconds flat, I'm as naked as she is.

Her eyes devour me. *Yep.* It feels so damned good to see her innocent hunger as she eats every nuance of me, making my skin scorching hot. "You're so crazy beautiful," she says in a rough voice.

"No, Candy Sweet, you're the crazy beautiful one. I can't believe how you steal my fucking breath and wreck my brain every time I see you."

After biting her lip, she looks right at my now fully erect cock. "Same, cowboy. I'm shocked how you make me feel. I don't understand. But all I know is I want more of you. *All* of you."

Her words are medicine to my dark soul. McKenzie doesn't even blink at my scars. She seems to memorize them, catalog them, and just file them away as part of me. Part she doesn't see as a mark of the horrendous things that put them there.

Flipping her gaze to mine, she swirls the water so that the clouds of bubbles clear, revealing her shimmering, sexy as hell body to me again. She smiles and hotly says, "Touch yourself, I want to watch."

I chuckle at her boldness. It amps my lust up by a thousand degrees. "You do, huh?"

She nods as she quickly licks across her lips. When my hand goes to my shaft, her eyes widen.

"Like this, babe?"

With a little moan, she focuses on me touching myself, the place where my fingers are locked around the heavy base of my cock. Heaven above, I love the way she looks at me. All fucking innocent spiced up with that need to explore.

"Just. Like. That." Her reply is all breathy as those pale greens hold on my throbbing cock.

Damn, what that does to me. Blood surges hard toward

my shaft, growing me to epic proportions as I stroke up and down.

Up. Down.

Tugging just hard enough on the head to fill it even more with searing blood. The skin is taut and the color is violently red now.

When she leans to the edge of the tub and commands me to let her taste, I groan.

Fuck. Me. Like I can resist that.

I'm supposed to be comforting her right now, not shoving my cock down her throat.

But her eyes are pleading, so I obey like a puppet and sidle up to the edge of the big porcelain tub.

When she traces her little pink tongue over me, I hiss, "Sweet fuck, *baby*. Your mouth feels like pure sin on me."

She leans up, splashing some water over the rim. It slaps against the tile floor when it hits. Yes, indeed. Gonna make a big wet mess.

I close my eyes and fall into a hypnotic trance from the silken feel of her tongue, the sounds of the water, and the satiny strands of her hair tangled between my fingers.

Those delicate little things are my very big undoing. "McKenzie," I growl. "You're getting me too damned close."

Whisper-soft, she laughs. "I know. I love watching you climb higher and higher."

My muscles go rigid. My chest vibrates. My hands shake, but I force myself to stay still. This is about her. Not me.

She unravels me more when she tells me, "You don't have to hold back."

"Yes. I. Do," I grit out. But things are getting serious now. My balls are starting to draw up, my pulse feels like bombs exploding inside my chest. The countdown to detonation is off and running.

"Justin, let me... I want to."

When I peel my eyes out of the back of my head, she's looking up with those translucent green eyes shimmering softly in the evening light.

"Come on," she teases with a little grin tipping her lips.

"Fuck." Fisting the base of my cock, I move the tip across her kiss-swollen lips. "Squeeze your tits up."

Instantly, she complies with a breathy little sound.

"I'm gonna jack off all over you."

Her eyes dance as she watches me. Her body trembles in the water causing little tiny tsunami waves.

"Give me your tongue, baby."

After rising quickly on her knees, she laves her tongue around my engorged head as I pump the shaft. A deep, animal growl forms in my throat. "Ah. Chr—, fuck, Mc..."

When I jerk stiffly and explode, she holds her breasts high, knowing exactly what I want without a word. Oh. Fuck. Yes. I get off hard on her fascinated expression as she watches my body contracting.

Shock after shock tightens my body, clenches my glutes, jolting me, forcing pulses of cream to shoot out onto her porcelain white skin.

I can't drag my eyes away.

Quakes rock my body. I'm hollowed out, enamored, teetering to keep my shit together. From the enchanted expression she has on her face to the way my seed is all over her, the aftershocks nearly crush me to the floor.

When I catch a ragged breath, I rumble, "Babe, look at you, I love you wearing my cum all over you."

My hand is still shaking as I drag my fingers through the creamy trails on her chest, spreading it all over her luscious mounds. She opens her mouth eagerly when I press two fingers to her lips. Moaning, she slides her tongue over my fingertips and sucks me inside her hot little mouth, and I lose the battle.

I wanted to pretend me ejaculating all over her wasn't me marking her, but I'm not a big enough man.

It was.

She's mine.

Clear and simple.

Fucked up and so right at once.

No matter what happens with McKenzie, she's mine. I'm hers and we'll go to hell and back together.

Chapter Fifty-Three

Candy

Hot. Over the top masculine. The sexiest thing on earth.

None of those descriptions capture the awe of the moment we just shared.

Dozer's eyes are pure fire as he watches me suck his fingers. When I'm finished cleaning him of his salty release, he motions for me to slide forward.

We make a gigantic mess—the second one—when he folds his mammoth-size body into the tub behind me.

His deep voice rumbles against my back, sending a delicious shiver over my skin. "Your turn, sexy girl."

I'm so close already. Watching made my body turn to pure heat.

He tugs me against his chest and without hesitation dives his hand between my legs. Oh. *Oh.* Okay.

The man knows how to find my clit. Which pulses hard as soon as his calloused fingertips collide with the delicate bud.

"Lean back on me."

I love his commanding voice.

His other palm cups my breast, branding my electrified nipple.

"Mmmm," I moan roughly and fall back, letting my head rest on the thick muscle of his shoulder.

"Let me hold you," he hotly whispers against my temple. "Let me catch you when you fall."

A shard of hope pierces my heart. The sting makes me roughly swallow.

"You already have," I reply tremulously.

He tenses, breathes once against my shoulder, then tightens the grip he has on me.

The next stroke of his fingers makes my whole body go electric. A wave of heat and pleasure, and something much deeper when he whispers roughly against my ear, "Always."

I know it's fast and it's crazy, but Justin "Dozer" Roark caught my fall the minute I grabbed his thigh at the café. He saved me, in every way, physically, emotionally. But he didn't just arrest the fall, he caused an all new one.

Never having felt what love could be, I didn't know it existed. Sure, I 'loved' my father in a duty-and-loyalty sense of the word. I loved the simple life we had, even though I craved more, but I loved it still because I didn't know any different.

Now... this.

This is something deep. Powerful. Not understandable. A slipping, an aligning, a rising and a falling.

How is it possible to float and fall at the same time?

That's exactly how I feel, like I'm on a cloud and diving into the depths of a dark sea all at once.

Is this love?

Maybe *this* is all the things I've read about. The thing that people give their lives for. The thing that makes you and destroys you, all in a blink of an eye.

When I read those books, I always thought it was creative license. Or maybe I wished it was, because I never saw it in my future.

But Dozer roared into my life.

Now I want something that can't be.

Especially now, with my father dead and gone, my world wiped off its map, and my face on a warrant for murder, I shouldn't be feeling this.

But I am. God. How I am.

So when Justin demands an orgasm from my body this time, it's more. So much more. It's me surrendering to a power that's so strong, I'm just a reed in the water being swept away in a raging current.

When I come apart under his fingers, with my head thrust back into his warm, protective shoulder, tears shred my throat, blind my eyes, and baptize me by fire.

Welcome to love.

Your soul has awakened now.

There's no going back.

Chapter Fifty-Four

Candy

It's eerie being back. The home I've lived almost all my life in feels foreign and cold to me. There's a hush. Not just the silence. Something has been laid to rest. An anguished soul released. I'm not sure if that's me or my father. Maybe both.

Dozer looks up when I step onto the porch. He does a quick scan. Boots. Canvas pants. Coat. Pack. He looks pleased.

I tried to hurry while I was changing, but it felt like I was walking in wet sand with a weight of dread in my stomach.

Yet at the same time, I was burning alive from the inside. I'm on fire to find out something. Anything.

The last thing I want to do is look at my father's grave—

or heaven forbid, his body—but I know this is the only way I can help shake this criminal charge against me.

When I close the door, Dozer is still inspecting me from beneath the brim of his black baseball cap. I'm a far cry from the woman he met in San Diego in my worn hiking boots, heavy canvas pants, field jacket, and pack.

For a beat our gazes hold and I thank whatever power brought him into my life. I'd be totally alone, sitting in a jail cell right now if he and his team weren't here to help me.

"Do you have weapons?" I ask, looking between the group of men.

All of the men reply in unison with some variation of yes. "I expected as much, but since we're walking into bear country, I wanted to make sure."

They make room for me to descend the steps. "This way." I motion toward a trail that is barely visible. I'm heads down watching where I step as we navigate the muddy terrain when Dozer tugs my sleeve. "I'll take point. I need you to stay behind me."

I puzzle and look at him askance.

"I need you safe," he murmurs as his intense eyes hold me frozen.

He's protecting *me*. I've hiked these woods thousands of times. Alone. Sometimes with my father, but he never made an effort to take point. Yet, Dozer wants to look out for me. "Alright," I concede as my chest warns this feels too good. "But you're not used to these woods."

He squeezes my upper arm as he looks down at me. Something inside of me goes soft at the intensity of his expression. "Sweetheart, I've been in forests and jungles all over the world. Often with someone shooting at me. These guys can attest to that."

It still makes me nervous. "You have a point. But just be careful. We have bears."

That makes him chuckle warmly. "I'll be careful. Now, just keep me posted if there's something specific I'm looking for."

"It's going to take a while to get there, but we're going to an old hunting tree stand. It's not my father's but the man told me he buried him under that tree so it would be easy to find."

"Copy that." He leans down and kisses me in front of the other men. It's not a simple smack of lips. This is a kiss of ownership. Deep and hot.

It rocks me. As fire licks up my neck and encases my cheeks, I clear my throat and pretend they don't exist.

"Give me your pack."

I blink up at Dozer. "Say again?"

"I'll carry your pack."

"You don't have to. I'm used to hiking with weight."

"Not when I'm with you. I carry the heavy shit."

I can tell this is going nowhere fast so I shrug out of my bag. "If you insist."

He slings my pack up, adjusts the straps, and settles it on top of the one he's wearing. When he's done, he's a camel with two heavy packs on his back.

"Seriously, you don't have to..."

His snarly expression makes me snap my mouth closed. "Okay. Do what you want."

I'm happy to see the men took the hike seriously. In Alaska you have to be prepared for anything. Drastic changes in the weather. Food and water for an extra day at least. You never know when you'll have an emergency or a sudden change in your plan.

All of the men have new gear except Beckett. From the

looks of his well-used pack and hiking boots, not only is the man kitted out for Alaska, but he's spent a lot of time in the woods. My curiosity about the man grows. He's a Federal agent—obviously assigned to this area, but his accent makes me question his origin.

Dozer does some kind of hand motion that I guess is a military signal and we fall in line and start down the trail.

An hour later we stop at an overlook for a water break and short rest. Dozer looks no worse for wear from our combined gear. The man looks as fresh as the moment we started the hike. As if carrying the weight of the world on his shoulders is something he does every day.

He hides his stress well. Physical and emotional. Until I catch a glimpse of his fear, worries, and demons. The man doesn't carry the world without baggage. A foolish part of me wonders if maybe I can help him carry his load too, just in a different way.

Giving myself a shake, I walk to the edge of the cliff, careful to stay a safe distance back from the lip. The expansive Smoke Valley stretches out below us. Tranquil even though I'm not the least bit calm inside. Cool, moist air fills my lungs as I take a deep inhale. Wishing that the knots behind my ribs would ease.

"Fucking unreal," Mako says as he holds up a bottle of water in a mock toast. "Never been to Alaska."

Dozer catches my hand and tugs me away as Marshall, Beckett, and Mako start talking and pointing at far off landmarks.

His expression is full of caring concern. "How are you holding up?"

"Fine. The hike isn't hard."

His eyes scan over my face, searching. "I wasn't talking about the hike. Now talk to me."

"I..." My shoulders sag as I let out a big breath. "I'm sad."

He tugs me into his arms and I cave, falling against him, burying my face against his flannel shirt. Softly, he says, "We're going to figure this out."

"I hope so. Being in jail was horrible."

"Fuck, baby," he mutters as he tucks my head under his chin and strokes my hair. "I'm sorry you had to stay."

I laugh humorlessly. "I can see why people try to escape. Can you imagine going from the kind of life I had where we worked hard to live off the land, to a concrete cell with a cot and a steel toilet?"

"No. I can't," he rumbles, then falls silent.

Shaking my head, I pull out from his arms. "Beckett said he was going to ask me some questions."

Dozer tucks his knuckles under my chin, forcing me to look at him. "He is."

Slowly, he lowers his mouth to mine. A little thrill wobbles to life inside of me. I love the way he looks at my lips when he's about to lean down to me. Like I'm some kind of precious thing to be savored.

The kiss is tender and makes my heart ache. It adds fuel to those knots that are gaining strength inside my chest. How can life be so cruel that I meet someone so amazing and then get locked away for a crime I didn't commit?

He brushes a thumb down my cheek, and tucks my hair over my shoulder. "I suspect Beckett's waiting to see what we find at the grave site."

"I thought so." I shiver and tuck my hands deeper into my pockets. "We should keep moving."

Chapter Fifty-Five

DOZER

We're nearing the end of our second hour of hiking when I hold up a hand. Frozen, mid-step, I ask the guys, "Hear that?"

Mako, Beckett, and Marshall spin, listening to the sound rumbling through the woods.

"McKenzie, how close are we to the tree stand?"

"Maybe a tenth of a mile."

A flicker of a light catches my eyes and I recognize the shape of what's caused the refraction. I never doubt my sixth sense. Right now it's screaming.

I grunt as my senses go laser sharp. "*Fuck.* Take cover."

With a shove, I hide McKenzie behind a stand of trees as the other men fan out around us, finding their own places to take cover.

"It's an ATV," McKenzie whispers.

Pressing a finger to my lips, I nod. The others acknowledge me as they ready their weapons. I don't know what's got my hackles up, but we're ready.

"No one's ever out here," she whispers as she tries to peek through the trees.

"Shhh, babe."

When the outline of the four wheeler comes clearly into sight, I press her closer to the tree, shielding her with my body.

"You're scaring me."

I growl and cover her mouth gently with my hand. "Shhh." She nestles deeper into the hollow of the tree, her trembling lips against my palm.

The noisy, oversized quad rumbles toward us. Followed by a second. They slow as the engines drop to an idle and men's voices carry through the woods.

Beneath me, McKenzie goes rigid. Before I realize what she's doing, she's scrambled free of my hold and is leaping out from beneath me and right into the path of the oncoming quads.

My fucking heart leaps out of my chest.

Before I can catch her, she's falling to her knees on the ground, clutching her heart, yelling, "Ohmygod. *Dad!*"

Chapter Fifty-Six

DOZER

All fuck breaks loose. Marshall, Beckett, Mako, and me rush the clearing, guns raised.

We're met by two barrels pointing back at us.

"Dad!" McKenzie wails, and I step between her and the armed men.

"Get up. Stand behind me," I hiss.

I feel her moving beside me, but I sidestep, putting her body behind me again without taking my eyes off the bastards. We're in a fucking standoff and I have no idea what the hell is going on. McKenzie's sobbing. The man on the front ATV looks murderous, and the man on the back ATV is even angrier.

The second guy's face is familiar from the photos in the cabin.

I steady my breath and drop into war mode—where everything slows down and your senses heighten to their maximal level.

The most subtle sounds are so loud. McKenzie breathing rapidly. My pulse in my ears. The idle of the ATVs. Wind in the trees.

Then a booming voice.

"Federal agent! Drop your weapons," roars Beckett.

But his words are drowned by gunshots ringing through the woods from an unknown direction. I act on pure reflex. Lunging, I take McKenzie down to the ground as we roll.

The ATVs roar to life, their tires spitting mud and dirt as they disappear down the trail.

Chapter Fifty-Seven

Candy

I blink and try to focus on the stream of light leaking down through the tree canopy. Dust motes, or tiny insects, or something is floating in that tiny shaft of sunshine.

It's all my mind can do to see them. Beyond that, I'm nothing.

"She's in shock," a distant voice says.

Then a very worried face appears in front of my field of view. Dozer kneels down in front of me and holds a bottle of water to my lips. "Drink, babe."

I obey, because my throat is dry, my chest hurts, and I feel like I'm in an echo chamber.

Carefully he helps me drink, then catches a drop on my lip with his thumb before taking it in his own mouth.

"Scared ten years out of me back there. You're sure you're not hurt?"

My hand nervously picks at the mud on the knee of my canvas pants. My brain on the other hand is so over-whelmed it's stopped working. That ray of sunshine catches my eye again, and I have to force myself to look back at Dozer. "Just some little bruises."

Leaning down he rests his forehead against mine, "I'm *not* sorry I tackled you, but I'm sorry I hurt you."

A few of my cognitive functions start to come back online. "You're not the one who should be apologizing. I was so stupid. Emotion overcame me. I could have gotten you and the other guys killed, but you threw yourselves in harm's way to protect me."

I have to stop for a breath because I can't continue. Suddenly, I'm a wreck. The dam has broken. A flood of fear washes over me, making me dizzy. "I can't believe you rushed out there and jumped in front of me."

Dozer's throat works as he swallows twice. "It was dangerous, McKenzie, I'm not gonna lie to you. I couldn't fucking understand what was happening, and then you were just standing out there in the open with those men roaring toward you. Then the guns. *Literal* cardiac arrest. I still don't understand exactly what just happened."

He looks away, clenches his jaw, then meets my gaze again. "I only know one thing, I'm not letting anything happen to you."

"Please don't get hurt because of me."

"Let me take care of you."

The intensity of his words rock me.

All of the feels try to tear open my poor destroyed heart. Even though my head's a mess, apparently one organ is still working. It likes the way Dozer looks at me. It loves the way he puts me before his own safety even when my heart hates that he's in danger.

The feelings he stirs in me are so strange I'm not even sure what category they fall into, but it's far more than like.

It's want and need.

Desperation.

Completion.

Looking at his beautiful, strong face and the intensity in his stormy eyes, I whisper, "I'm so lucky to have you."

He gently rests a hand on my shoulder and watches me so intently that I feel it stirring my soul. That look leaves me breathless.

Dozer doesn't deserve to be caught up in whatever disaster this is, whatever chaos my simple life has become. But I can't imagine what would be happening right now without him.

Without another word, he stands up and moves a few feet away, but never goes far.

"She's sure it's her father?" Marshall asks as his eyes scan the trees surrounding our location, checking over and over again for signs of another threat.

After the ATVs took off, Dozer grabbed me up in his arms and ran. The men all followed until we were in a safe holdout behind a cluster of boulders.

Still watching me, Dozer tugs an extra jacket from his pack and returns to wrap it around me. "She's convinced."

"Do we continue on to the grave?" Mako asks.

Beckett squats down on his haunches in front of me. "McKenzie, doing better?"

I nod. "My ears were ringing, but not as much now."

"You're one hundred percent certain that it was your father on the second ATV?"

My hand trembles as I push my hair back and realize

there's mud clinging in the strands. "Yeah. I know. I've lived with him all my life. As soon as I heard his voice through the woods, I knew it was him."

Beckett looks off into the woods for a few seconds like he's planning his next words. "How far is the grave?"

"Just down that hill, maybe a quarter mile now that we've left the original trail."

He scowls. "I don't like being out here with an unknown threat in the woods. We need to call for extraction."

"Agreed," Dozer says as he tightens down the straps on his pack. "And make it yesterday."

I don't know how long it takes, but we make it to a small clearing where a helicopter touches down. Its arrival is surprisingly quick, but apparently Beckett has powerful contacts.

"Stay low." Dozer tugs me toward the open door of the monstrous machine, keeping his hand on top of my head as we run.

He lifts me without even straining and shoves me inside, the other men quickly follow. Once he has me buckled and in a helmet, the radio static changes to voices. After a quick exchange between Beckett and the pilot, we're lifting off.

My stomach drops as we bank hard to the left and scream across the Alaskan landscape. Far up here it feels safe. Away from whatever terrible thing is happening down on the ground. Even though I'm rocked to the marrow, I take my first full breath since I looked down the barrel of two guns. One of them in my father's hand.

"We've got the coordinates now, so returning to find the grave will be cake," Mako says as he looks out the window, down to the passing ground.

"Roger that," Marshall says into his mic. "We can come back with more backup."

Beckett drinks from his water bottle, then asks, "What do you think they were doing?"

Dozer's murderous intensity flips to the federal agent. "Probably knew someone was heading to that grave. They knew McKenzie would be going along because no one else knows this area. So, it was a chance to do... *something*."

Like kill us. My veins are sloshing with ice water now. Every thought is more terrifying than the last.

Mako points out, "Except the guy who showed up and said her dad was dead. He knows this place too."

"And my father. Who is alive and pointing guns at me," I remind them with emotion squeezing in on my throat.

Dozer laces his fingers between mine. "I don't know what the fuck is going on, but I hate it."

After a long silence, Marshall asks, "Why would he draw a gun on his own daughter?"

"Fuck if I know, that's what's been burning me up," Mako mutters into his mic as he shifts in his seat. "I mean, Dozer was on her, standing in front of her by the time they came to a stop. So, maybe the gun was for Dozer's melon?"

"Oooh. That's horrible," I screech.

Dozer squeezes my thigh. "Guy talk. But he's right, the guns could have been because of me, not you."

"I can't understand why he'd want to aim at me. I know my father. *Heavens*. At least I thought I knew my father. But now I'm starting to question everything."

With deep frowns the team of men fall into analytical thought. The chopper blades whirl overhead, making the whole aircraft whomp-whomp, which I find works like a tranquilizer. Or maybe I'm just spent. Regardless, I sag back into my seat. Never thought I'd ride in a helicopter, but that fact seems so unimportant given the situation.

As I replay everything that happened in my head, I realize I don't know who actually fired the guns. "Who was shooting?"

"Someone that was creating a diversion for the guys on the ATVs," Dozer replies.

"But why would my father let me think he was dead, then..."

I can't speak anymore as my chest squeezes all the air out of me. *Then point a gun in my direction, and speed away.*

Dozer lays his arm across my shoulders. "Sweetheart, do you think his PTSD caused him to have a psychotic break?"

That's when it hits me... the déjà-vu that I couldn't quite put my finger on. A name. "Did someone at the house mention the name Poliverco?"

"Yeah." Beckett sits up attentively. "Do you know that name?"

"I don't personally... but after my father had a very difficult period—he actually disappeared in the woods for a few days over the winter—I heard him say that name. He was having a nightmare."

My stomach falls and it has nothing to do with the helicopter flight. It's the look that the men exchange.

Chapter Fifty-Eight

DOZER

The sheriff and two deputies are at the house waiting for us when we get back. Three of their winter-ready trucks are jamming up the street in front of the rental house. If we were in the city anywhere else in the U.S., they'd be in cruisers, but in Alaska they're in trucks with racks, overland lighting, with extra gasoline, and shovels strapped onboard.

As we climb out of our rental, they meet us on the lawn. After handshakes, we all step inside. I'm worried about McKenzie. The need to shield her from any assholes in uniform has me ready to tear heads off.

Everybody wants answers.

I take up a stance near McKenzie as they question her. She's not to be fucked with. My patience is starting to wear thin. I suspect Mako's is too from the twitchy way he's standing against the kitchen counter, that or he's worried I'm gonna go apeshit and is ready to rein me in.

One of the deputies pushes a piece of printer paper with a bad color image on it across the kitchen table. "You're one hundred percent sure you saw this man?"

"If you saw your father out in the street, would you recognize him?" she counters, obviously tired of this question. "That's my father. I'm sure it was him."

"You sure it wasn't some play of light?"

She stiffens and replies tightly, "Sir, I looked a man in the eyes that has sat across the dinner table from me since I was a little kid. I know."

I step up and rest my hands on her shoulders. "We all saw the same man."

The deputy holds the photo up so Beckett, Mako, and I can see the grainy image. "This is the man you saw?"

I nod. "He had a hat on and a thick coat pulled up around his neck, but it was those eyes, those cheekbones, that nose."

Beckett takes the photo in his hand, turns it toward the light. "The likeness is indisputable."

Marshall walks into the room. His hair is disheveled, but he's got this laser focus intensity that I'm beginning to recognize in my boss. He's fucking on. All the time.

I'm thankful as hell to have someone like him working on this case. I want this done. The charges to be dropped and for McKenzie to go back to Montana with me where we can figure out what's next.

Marshall tips his chin at the deputy. "I saw him too, same." Then he sets his computer on the table and turns the screen so we can all see it.

On the display is a grainy scanned image of a gray piece of paper with black text. There's an overlay of arrows and circles in red drawn on it, highlighting certain areas.

Marshall says, "McKenzie, do you have any idea why your father's birth certificate might have been faked?"

The confusion on her face is all the answer that I need.

Chapter Fifty-Nine

DOZER

There's a night light on in the kitchen, but otherwise the house is dark. Everyone's racked out. Catching some much needed downtime.

McKenzie is tucked into the big bed we've been sharing. Warm and soft. I should be there, but I couldn't stare at the ceiling any longer.

Something big is eating at me. Or maybe it's not me, I admit when Beckett strolls into the kitchen, shirtless, in a pair of gray joggers.

The energy of the house could be what I'm sensing.

"What's stirring?" I ask as I close the fridge, cutting off the harsh light.

"Can't fucking sleep. Something's under my skin."

"Me too."

"I know what's under your skin. A five-foot mystery wrapped in a tight little package," he says with a smug grin.

For a second my hackles rise. I'm not sure I like Beckett recognizing that McKenzie is hot. But it is what it is. She's gonna be turning heads. At least he's got the balls to say it out loud with a teasing grin on his face.

I sigh and sweep away my jealous bullshit, for now at least. "Can't deny that."

Beckett leans a hip against the counter and studies me. His cool gray eyes remind me of a shark. He's cunning and fast like one too. I like the man. Could see myself being on a team with him.

He tips his chin. "You're a lucky man."

"I'm trying to remember that, even though everything is a motherfucking cluster right now."

After a beat, he says, "You'll get through this and be even stronger for it. I've seen it before, that girl's gonna be by your side forever after you survive this together."

"You never thought she killed him, did you?"

"No. I didn't. She's got honest eyes. Besides, a hunting accident is a very real cause of death here."

"How long have you been in Alaska?"

He opens the fridge, grabs a bottle of water, and returns to the leaning stance again. "Four years. I was Army Spec Ops for eight years before that."

"What brought you here?"

"Needed space. From a woman."

I chuckle. "There's plenty here. Isn't the male-to-female ratio FUBAR?

"Yeah, every swinging dick with a penchant for a piece of wooded land and a mission to avoid eye contact moves up here."

"Kind of like Montana," I joke. "Same. It's the great escape. I get it. I don't like being crowded in. Nearly choked to death living in Southern California, but I was there for a purpose, my career in the teams."

"You got out early."

I point to a scar on my chest. One of many. "Ate a shitton of metal, decided to listen to the docs. There's a piece of shrapnel close to my spinal cord that they can't take out."

"Fuck, dude. I got my scars, but they're inside here." He knocks on his cranium.

"Got ya, brother." I change the subject and let sleeping ghosts lie. "So, you like this place?"

"It's a hard place. But I like the simple, no-bullshit bones about the place. Except this fucking Dark Ghost. That's the thing that runs our department in circles chasing our asses."

"How long you been working on the case?"

"Whole damned time I've been with the Feds. My first assignment was here, on that fucker's case. Burns me up that he's trying to buy military secrets. Hell, not just trying, he's succeeding. But red-fucking-tape is destroying any and all chances of taking him down."

"That's why I didn't go for a government gig. I'm out of the game and I'm settling into this private security and high-stakes rescue thing."

He nods knowingly.

After a beat, I say, "Believe it or not, I met McKenzie on my first assignment with Agile."

He chuckles. "No shit. You parachuted right into the thick of things."

We share a laugh, then he falls silent. When Beckett

scrubs his hand through his hair, he growls. "Oh, fuck. Now I know what woke me up."

He vanishes, and I consider following him, but he comes back in a few moments with a glowing laptop perched on his hand.

Chapter Sixty

Candy

I yawn and stretch. My elbow bumps into a warm, hard chest.

"Good morning, beautiful." A rough whisper stirs my hair, then I'm folded into the magical cocoon of Dozer's arms.

"I woke up earlier and you were gone."

"Sorry, babe. I hope I didn't wake you up when I got up."

"A little, maybe. But I figured you couldn't sleep. I'm just glad you're back now."

He rumbles a positive sound against my temple. "I was hoping you'd wake up."

I wiggle around until we're eye to eye. My breath catches when I see the worry. "What's wrong?"

He shakes his head tightly. "Let's not talk about it right now. I want to make this moment last as long as I can."

Worry has been planted in my belly now, and tiny, cold tendrils creep outward to my limbs.

But he's silent as he touches my face. Looking slowly from my eyes to my lips and back, as if he's never seen me before.

The river of thoughts behind his intense gaze is foreign to me this morning. But his energy is swirling and powerful. I'm helpless against whatever is churning in his mind. Laying in his arms with his hand caressing my jaw, with his eyes tracing every fine line of me, I plunge further into fear.

His breath stirs my hair as his almost-rigid chest rises and falls. Something is seriously wrong.

"Talk to me. *Please.*"

He blinks, refocuses. "I'm building a house. In Montana. On our family ranch. I haven't lived there in a while because I was serving, but now it feels right. Feels like where I belong. I have four brothers and a sister. My mom is there too. They are challenging, infuriating, but utterly loyal. They do everything hard. Love hard. Fight hard. Work hard. The spot where I'm building my house over-looks these great big mountains. The snow falls on their peaks most months and lingers there into the summer. The land is wild and unforgiving, just like here, but so different. It's in my bones, as much as the ocean. Which means that I've got a restless soul. I need to be there, but I also need to be at the sea."

He takes a breath and I touch his face, gently tracing the strong angle of his jaw with my fingertips. Absorbing the soft, prickly feel of his beard growth.

For a few seconds his lashes dip closed and I expect him to relax into my touch, but he doesn't. He draws a sharp breath. His eyelids snap open and he bores into me with that sapphire gaze. "I have shrapnel. The scars are bad, but what's inside of me could be worse. I have ghosts. Baggage. For a long time I've been lost to life. Focusing on the next mission. On anything else but myself. My life. But things changed. Now I just feel determined to live every moment."

Inside I'm cold, I'm shivering, I'm scared. Of whatever's happening right now. Of what this could mean for us.

They asked me if my father snapped. Now I know why I saw Dozer flinch. He's scared. Oh my god. Every fiber of my soul hurts for him.

When I open my mouth to speak, he touches my lips, gently pressing his thumb to the bottom surface. "There's more."

"Okay," I breathe.

He shifts me closer, looping his thigh over mine, securing me to him. I worry he'll feel my shivering.

"I've killed a lot of people. I'm always going to remember them. Every single one of them. Sometimes there's nightmares. Sometimes there are days I feel like fuck. I believe in what I did when I was in the teams, but it doesn't mean I liked killing people. *Fuck*. Some guys, they loved that. They wanted trophies. Not me. I wanted justice. I wanted peace and safety. That's why I'm working for Agile. I still want that. But that also means I'm going to be gone sometimes. I'll be working with a team to rescue people, or assigned to guard someone who knows where for who knows how long."

He swallows roughly. "I'm saying everything, but not what I need to say right now."

"It's okay. I love listening to you, honey."

His eyes soften. "I want to make love to you right now."

"I'd like that."

"Afterward we're going to go downstairs and meet with the team."

"That's fine."

He growls and pushes me flat until I'm on my back. Hovering over me, his voice drops low. "I want this done. I want you alone with me in my house for weeks on end. I'm a selfish bastard, McKenzie, but I'll tell you right now, things are gonna get rough before this is over, but *I'm with you*, and when it's done, we're going to build a life together. *Fuck* the demons. The ghosts. *Fuck* the timebombs inside of me. I want to live, and I won't be really living unless you're with me."

Holy. Mother.

This man.

My heart climbs up my throat.

All that was leading up to him telling me he doesn't want to live without me. He was bearing his soul. Laying it out there, what he is. All his dark demons, his fears, his dreams.

I lash my arms around his neck and pull him down onto me as I fight for breath. He rumbles against me. Buries his face in my neck. When his mouth goes to my collarbone, and the warmth of his palm hits my quivering tummy, I arch into him.

Silently, he tugs off the T-shirt I stole from his bag. Then goes right back to kissing his way across my chest, down my ribs, to the place where my hip bones rise.

Tears burn through my lashes as I relax into his touch, letting his mouth, his fingers ease away all the worry that was knotting me up.

He lingers, but not too long, before he pushes down his gym shorts and rolls me to my side. "My McKenzie," he murmurs as he stretches out behind me, curling his body around me.

I'm new to sex, but I've got to say, I love this. Dozer's thick bicep makes the perfect place to rest my head as his other hand slides over my skin. And his cock... god, when he guides himself into me, I'm instantly swept up in a storm of pleasure so beautiful that it colors my tears in sprinkling rose and gold.

Slowly, he builds us up.

When we fall, it's together, it's to his voice, rough in my ear. "I swear, I'll always protect you."

Chapter Sixty-One

DOZER

We're both silent in the shower. Now that all my shit's out there, I hope I didn't scare McKenzie.

But she's got to know what she's getting with me.

All that messy truth must be hitting her hard because she's locked down. Silent as I am, as I wash her hair. She closes her eyes as the long strands glide over my fingers.

Her body is relaxed but her mind is whirring. I know this because like sees like. That's one of the things that draws me to her.

When we're clean, I wrap her in a towel and kiss her with my heart thudding and aching. Every damned thing I said was true. Especially the fact that this is gonna get hard before it gets better.

I dress while she does and we descend the stairs hand in hand. Together we take this on.

"Rally up!" I call as we hit the kitchen.

A few moments later, everyone is settled around the table. In the center is a platter with baked goods. Mako passes out coffee in to-go cups. He's obviously been to town while I've been tangled up in the sheets with McKenzie.

I owe him.

But his shrewd expression reads me in on the fact that Beckett and him already talked. "Thought everyone could use a fix this morning."

"Thanks, this smells divine." McKenzie lifts the cup to her nose, then abruptly sets the cup back down on the table. "*However,* I don't think I can drink it with all of you guys scowling. I'm starting to get really worried. Not that I haven't been worried, but you guys never looked like you were about to go in front of a firing squad."

After looking at them one by one, she glances at me. "Time to tell me what's up."

I hate this moment. I fucking want to go back up those stairs and go back to bed. Back where we were in our cocoon of stolen happiness.

I wish it was me sitting in that chair. I'd take it in the teeth. Bring it on. Mow me down. Destroy me, but leave her the fuck out of this.

Only, I can't protect her from this hurt. That pisses me off like I've never been fucking angry before.

Marshall shifts in his seat, Mako drinks the scalding hot coffee and hisses, and Beckett just looks at me.

Let's get this the fuck over so I can clean up the pieces.

I give Beckett a nod. I've got her. No matter how hard she tumbles.

He straightens his shoulders and pulls an image up on

his phone. With the lines around his mouth tight, he pushes the phone until it's sitting in front of McKenzie, next to her cup of coffee.

"That's an image I've cropped."

She looks at the phone and back up at him. "That's a portion of a photo of my father."

He's used some kind of software to mask the image with black borders until there's only a small rectangle of the original image showing. The eyes, the nose, the brow and cheeks.

It's what he showed me before, but now he's taken the time to edit the image instead of holding his hands over the screen of his laptop.

"It is." He lifts the phone and opens another image. This time it's of two similarly cropped images, side by side. The eyes, the nose, the brow and cheeks.

"They're both him," McKenzie says.

"Are they?" Beckett asks as he lifts the phone again. This time he opens a split image. On one side is a man in a black balaclava holding an assault rifle next to a modern pickup truck. The other is an image I instantly recognize from the wall in McKenzie's house. He's relaxing with his SEAL teammates, leaning against a camo Hum-V.

I lace my fingers between McKenzie's, holding our clasped hands tightly against my thigh.

Beckett draws in a deep breath. "The image on the left, that's a photo of a known criminal, a man that's known in the criminal world as the Dark Ghost. He's wanted on fourteen counts of espionage for selling secrets to foreign governments. In addition to seven counts of illegal arms trafficking."

"You're wrong! You are. *Wrong*. My father never... he

can't even take care of himself." McKenzie's voice rises until the last words are shouted at Beckett.

She jerks her hand, tries to break free from my hold.

"Let go. Just stop," she seethes at me. "I don't know what's happening here, but I'm calling this bullshit. That cannot be my father. Period. So what if they have similar eyes? It's not him. My father can't keep his act together to even keep the house stocked with the provisions we need, and you think he's capable of selling secrets and moving illegal weapons? Wrong. Fucking wrong."

She yanks her hand as her face reddens with her fury. "Let. Go. Dozer."

I stand and pull her into my arms, locking her flailing arm down. Her feet pinwheel and she makes a damned valiant effort to kick the shit out of me, but I take us down to the ground, cradling her in my lap.

Against her ear, I murmur, "Easy now. Slow down."

"You slow down, Dozer! Let me go. Let *me* GO."

She's shaking violently. Her angry tears are falling on my arms. But I'm not letting her go. No way in hell.

The other men rise and leave us alone. Christ. It's coming. I feel the storm bearing down on us. I don't know what I'm going to say or do next, but I'm sure as hell not letting her storm out of here alone. We will get to the bottom of this. Then McKenzie and I are getting down to the business of building a life together. Fuck her father. Whoever he is.

Chapter Sixty-Two

Candy

The sheriff's office looms in front of us. I hate this place. The place makes my blood run cold. If I didn't have the guys with me, I'd never be able to willingly walk in that door.

Dozer grips my hand against his side as a slender, young cop escorts us to a conference room at the back of a rundown building. The offices aren't much better than the cells were.

After a tense ten minutes, the sheriff and the same two deputies that came to the house walk in. Each takes a seat at the table with us. All total, there are nine of us. Mako, Marshall, Beckett, Dozer, myself, the Agile attorney, and the three county officers.

"Thanks for meeting with us," Beckett says as he taps

the keys on his laptop. He was as comfortable in the woods as he is here.

Beckett launches into the meeting he's called. Arms crossed, I stare at the screen on the conference room wall where the same images I was shown a few hours ago are now shown in an almost life-sized display.

"Gentlemen, I've got an analyst workin' on this right now, but it looks like Mr. Rush and the man we suspect is the Dark Ghost are one in the same."

Beckett's got some kind of light pointer and is highlighting the similarities in the images as the sheriff and his deputies nod and whisper amongst themselves.

"In addition to analyzing the image, the forensics team are running the prints from McKenzie Rush's house now to compare them with the fingerprints we suspect belong to the Ghost."

The sheriff leans back in his chair, causing the spring to creak. He rubs a knuckle under his chin as he stares at the images. "That there's quite a development. You don't know for sure if the prints you have on file are the Ghost's?"

Beckett's expression darkens. "He's very evasive." The laser pointer wings to the image of the heavily covered man who is holding an assault rifle.

"As you can see, he's got gloves on. Also note the face cover. We've never gotten a full image of his lower face."

The sheriff's own scowl deepens until his jowls are hanging low. "But the girl," he motions to McKenzie, "says her father can barely take care of himself. Could have been some kind of act she fell for."

One of the deputies angles forward with a glint in his eyes. There's an unmistakable coldness in those pale blue irises of his. He's one of the ones that booked me. "Could be why they wanted to shoot her. She knows too much. I think we should retract her bail and put her back in the hold. Transfer her to the women's facility down in Anchorage until we can get this sorted."

A flood of fury makes my body go hot. My skin tightens. I can't keep this bottled up any longer. It takes a solid thirty seconds before I'm able to form a coherent word, but when I do, they fly.

"I am not involved. I didn't kill my father, I didn't take part in selling anything. Secrets, guns, even bubble-gum. Does my house look like the domicile of a person that's making money off of anything? We lived off my father's disability. That's it. He's sick. He has PTSD, and you're out of your mind if you think he could be some kind of evil-mastermind. Call the damned V.A. and get his records if you don't believe me." I spit the last words at them.

The attorney looks like he's going to need CPR any moment. His eyes flare at me. I get his message loud and clear. Don't say *anything!*

Well, that's horse shit. I'm not sitting here any longer without stating what's more than obvious. Somehow they have the wrong man. I don't care how much the images look alike.

But deep inside of me there's a terror. It's building like a hurricane, swirling, turning, growing strength off every stab they make at my father. What if?

God, the thought is sickening.

What if he *is* the man in that photo?

The criminal. The thief. The man who's betraying his country and endangering lives.

SEALs get hurt and die when men like him share intel.

That thought makes my heart stop completely. I may not know how the underworld or even the military operates, but I know enough to realize that when secrets get sold, people's safety is stolen.

I blink back the anger that's searing my eyes. Christ. Could my father be living a double life?

I flinch and look around to find the room staring at me.

Dozer's icy cold next to me. I've never seen him like this and I'm not sure if he's so angry he's gone glacial, or if he's also coming to some crazy realization.

But as I struggle, he glances at me, then gives both men, the sheriff and the deputy, a look that could decimate whole countries.

"You heard her. Now what other evidence do you have that could help get this bullshit with McKenzie cleared up? Obviously, her father's alive. She didn't commit murder. Whether he's some fucking traitor or not, she's not responsible. I want the murder charges dropped *now*."

One of the deputies sneers his lip at me. "She could be in on something. Could be hiding all his dirty secrets like a good little daughter."

Dozer slams his fist on the table. The impact is as loud as a gunshot.

"*She* is in the room. *She* has a name. Why don't you show her some respect. She's not a girl. She's a fucking woman. And all the condescending eye-balling better end right now, because I'm sick of it. McKenzie Rush has been caught up in some kind of hell she didn't deserve and now you're dragging her through the fucking mud. I'm not gonna stand by and let you do it. So, be warned."

The room crackles with fury.

For a few seconds I wonder if there's going to be broken bones and bloody noses. I don't want to see any violence, but god, I feel like smashing something.

Marshall's the first to break the crackling silence with

an oddly calm statement. "The other thing we need to consider is the altered birth certificate."

"It's falsified, you said?" the sheriff asks, with his face still burning with anger.

Marshall motions to Beckett who brings the images up on the screen. "My document specialist noted several inconsistencies. You'll see the oddities highlighted here." Marshall takes over the pointer and aims it at the screen. "Name. Location. Time."

"So, her father's not who the world thinks he is," Mako says thoughtfully. "The man might not know who he is. Or sometime later in life he tried to cover up his tracks."

The conference room door swings open and all eyes snap that way. A woman in uniform steps inside and quickly takes in the scene. "Sheriff, a word with you. Agent Beckett should join us as well, it's about Mr. Rush."

As the two men stride from the room, the air leaves with them and my heart turns into a pretzel.

Chapter Sixty-Three

DOZER

"Let's go." I pull McKenzie up from her chair, using her hand to drag her with me. "We're getting some air. Come find us when you figure out what the hell is going on."

Marshall and Beckett nod.

We cross the lobby, I shove through the doors, and don't stop until we're far from the building.

McKenzie's pale and trembling. Motherfuckers. I pull her into my arms. "Baby, I'm so, so sorry that happened."

I've never wanted to bash heads together so badly. Those assholes treated her like dirt. My voice is a ruined growl when I whisper, "We're gonna take care of this."

"What if..." She burrows further into my chest. "What if he *was* deceiving me?"

Her shoulders collapse forward as her fists clench my

jacket. The sobs come. Wracking, agonized, ghostly sounds. People stop on the street and turn our way. I hold her tighter, but I know that nothing I can do will hold her together as she shatters.

A guttural roar comes out of my throat. Fuck. Fucking motherfucker. I will destroy that man for doing this to her.

Marshall appears on the doorstep of the sheriff's office. Fists clenched, he watches us for a long minute. Then he steps off the landing and trots down the steps. Beckett sweeps out of the building next with Mako on their heels. All of them look like they are ready for war.

Marshall circles his finger in the air, "Load up."

I bury my face in McKenzie's hair. "Babe, we've got to move out."

Her breathing is still ragged, her body locked against mine. I sweep her up in my arms and jog the short distance to the SUV. Mako holds the door open for me. "Beckett and Marshall need to get to the Rush property to help gather evidence."

"What did they say?"

Mako's gaze drops to McKenzie who's cradled against my chest. His eyes are agonized. "Not now."

Fear leaps up and seizes my throat. My blood turns to sludge. How much worse can this get?

Chapter Sixty-Four

Candy

I know it's horrible. Whatever happened in that office is going to be a nail in my coffin. Mako wouldn't tell us.

Which is why the second Dozer walks into the bedroom door, I'm on him.

"Tell me." I clench my fists, to stop my hands from vibrating. "Don't look at me like that. Don't hold back. I deserve to know what's going on."

He draws in a long breath. Those steel gray eyes of his are filled with agony. "The cabin burned down this morning. Arson."

"Oh. God." I stumble back until my legs hit the bed.

"That's not all."

"What?" I croak.

His eyes nearly undo me. Then he knocks me flat with his words. "There was a body inside."

I swallow but can't breathe.

"There's no I.D. yet."

"My father..." I breathe as the world starts to crumble beneath my feet.

"We don't know," he says as he takes a slow step toward me.

"I feel sick."

I've already mourned my father, but now I don't even know who he was. My guts are in knots, my heart cold and aching. But my deepest pain comes from thinking he could have been deceiving me all those years.

"I understand, sweetheart." His arm loops around my neck and pulls me until my forehead is resting against his stomach. As his fingers thread into my hair and cup my head, he roughly says, "I wish I could protect you from this."

When I gather the strength, I wrap my arms around his waist. "Take me away. I never want to come back here."

"I will, sweetheart. As soon as we can. Right now the sheriff is demanding you stay close."

"Please, as soon as we can, I can't be here."

"I'll make some calls and get us to Montana the minute he says you're clear to leave."

He holds me for a long time. His breathing is steady, but his body is tight, coiled with dark energy.

"Can you rest? I want to see if I can help the guys. I won't leave. I'm just going downstairs."

My marrow is chilled, my bones aching. "I'm going to take a bath."

"Let me help you."

Like I'm made of glass, Dozer gently guides me to the

bathtub, starts the water, then leans down to brush a kiss over my cheek. "I'm sorry. So damned sorry."

I nod, but can't speak. It feels like he doesn't want to let go. I don't want him to, but I know being alone is best for me right now. He doesn't need to witness me unraveling.

"It's okay. I'm not going to disappear."

He stands in the doorway for a long time.

"I'm fine. I just need some alone time."

He brushes his hand over my head once more, leans down to kiss my lips softly, then turns to leave.

But he doesn't go far. He's torn about something, and that makes me uneasy.

"There's something else I want to tell you. It's premature, because Beckett is getting a second opinion, but I think you should know. All this ugliness needs to be laid on the table at once."

"Just tell me," I utter around the massive lump that's threatening my airway.

"Looks like your birth certificate was also forged."

The tears that come into my eyes aren't hot. They are ice cold.

Chapter Sixty-Five

Candy

It's hours later when I numbly walk down the stairs. The house is chaotic. But all eyes pivot toward me. Only, I don't see Dozer.

"Can I get you something?" Mako asks because he's the closest person to me.

"Food."

He rests a hand on my back and guides me to the kitchen. "I make a decent grilled cheese, want one?"

"Whatever," I reply, and my voice is flat.

"Dozer's gone out to pick up some things."

That stings, he said he wasn't leaving. But the bite is gone a second later. Not much left in me to sting.

Mako rests a hand on my shoulder. "He didn't want to go, but the sheriff asked for him specifically."

He goes to the fridge, sets about making a stack of grilled cheese sandwiches while I numbly stare out the window. The sky is gray. The ground is gray. The world is slate and sadness.

When he's done, he slides the plate in front of me. The yellow cheese catches my eyes.

So, not everything is gray.

"Want water or milk?"

I scrunch my nose. "Milk with grilled cheese?"

"Sure," he comments with a laugh. "Dairy and more dairy."

My hand goes out and lifts one of the sandwiches without me telling it to. Mechanically, it moves to my mouth. I take a bite. Chew. Take another.

He puts a glass of water on the table and takes a seat.

"Are you eating?" I ask as he watches me. "That's a lot of sandwiches."

"I wanted you to have plenty."

"One's enough," I counter and take another bite.

He selects one and proceeds to eat it in two man-sized bites.

"Hungry?"

"Always. My wife complains about it all the time." Then he launches into a story about how they met. I know it's to distract me, but by the time he tells me about hunting her all around the globe for fourteen months for Agile Security & Rescue, I'm caught up in it.

She's sassy. I like her already.

Then he tells me about the hell they went through because of the dangerous criminals that were chasing her. They almost didn't make it out alive. Maybe his wife and I will have a lot to talk about.

There's such kindness in his eyes, deeper than I noticed

before. "You know the Agile Team will get to the bottom of this, and we'll keep you safe while we do it, right?"

I hold his gaze. He's so sincere. "I think so."

"I understand why you're wary. Everything you've ever known and trusted has been—"

He reaches across the table and grips my hand. His hold is strong.

"Justin is all you need now. He's gonna give you everything."

Marshall Lake explodes into the kitchen. He's got his phone held out. It's on speaker.

"Where are you?"

There's a roaring engine sound in the background.

Dozer clips, "Fuck, I think this is route Seven-Twelve. I'm passing a mailbox now. Number four-sixteen. I've got three trucks on my tail. Sheriff is mobilizing SWAT."

Chapter Sixty-Six

DOZER

It happens fast. A truck roars up beside me, I slam it with the rented SUV. Another gets on my bumper, shoving me sideways.

Grass and tree limbs fly as we leave the road.

The suspension on the Ford bottoms out, but I keep the gas pressed to the floor. The truck that was pushing me loses some speed. Another road comes into sight, I swerve onto the pavement and gain some ground.

Then another truck catches up.

This one's painted in green camo and is decked out in tactical equipment. Burning spotlights flash in my mirrors.

"Come on!" I growl. "You want some of me? Come. Fucking. Get. It."

He might have gear. I've got experience.

There's a curve ahead in the road. Just in the perfect place.

When the truck edges up beside me, I jam on the brakes, swerve against it, sending it into the thick stand of trees.

My SUV skids, and everything turns into a blur.

I think two things as I start flipping upside down.

I love you, McKenzie.

This seatbelt better fucking work.

Chapter Sixty-Seven

Candy

People scatter when I rush the desk. "Justin Roark, where is he?!"

"He's that way, ma'am. But you can't go back—"

Beckett's hand tightens on my shoulder in futility. I rip free and sprint through a set of swinging doors, nearly mow down a nurse in a pair of hot pink scrubs. She's sputtering as I grab her. "Where's Justin Roark?"

"You're not supposed—"

My knees hit the cold tile floor as I grip her hands and beg, "Please. You've got to tell me. I can't breathe. I have to see him."

In a flash, her eyes go soft. "Oh, honey." She squats down and gives me a strong hug.

"I'm sorry," Beckett says from behind me. "I'll take her outside if you need me to."

That's what he thinks, but he's going to have his hands full. I am not leaving until I see Justin. I'll claw the place apart before he can drag me outside.

The nurse shakes her head. "No, sir. That won't be necessary." She gently helps me up until I'm standing on wobbly legs. "Poor dear. He's been asking for someone. Are you Candy?"

Tears explode out of my swollen eyes, but I'm smiling deliriously. "Yes. That's me."

Thank god, he must be okay if he's asking, right?

With her arm around my waist, she says, "He'll be fine, sweetheart. But you can't stay long. He needs to rest. He took quite a beating."

"Promise," I croak through my aching vocal cords.

A beating. Her words echo in my heart. God. He could have died.

When we reach room twelve in the tiny Smoke Valley Hospital, she stops me. "Now, he looks bad, but it's mostly bruises. No bullet holes or anything like that."

"Thank god."

"The SWAT team took care of the bad guys. That's what the sheriff told me. But don't you tell anyone because no one knows he and I go out."

She hugs me again.

"Your secret is safe."

Her eyes flip to Beckett. "Anyone finds out, I'll know it was you."

He grins, "Yes, ma'am."

As she studies him, her head tilts. "And who are you?"

"ATF Agent Beckett. For the next month at least. I'm about to be done with the government soon."

She smiles slowly. "Handsome devil. The ladies around here are gonna go crazy. I can barely keep them out of Mr. Roark's room."

When my eyes go wide, she says, "Don't worry, sweetheart, he hasn't stopped talking about you. Now, let's get you in there to your man. Wash your hands first, and I'll take you right in."

Chapter Sixty-Eight

DOZER

Mashall's phone is going straight to voicemail. Fuck. Beckett's too. And Mako's. And Candy's.

Who the hell is everyone talking to?

I am officially freaked out. I haven't been able to talk to McKenzie.

I sit up, but shudder. Christ, my fucking shit hurts. All of it. Right down to the hair follicles on my scalp.

But hell if I'm sitting here in a hospital bed when I don't know where McKenzie is.

Right as my hand wraps around my IV to rip the thing out, voices outside make me curse.

Nurse 'No-don't-do-that' is gonna have a hissy shit fit when she sees me up. Been nagging me for the last hour to rest.

I could care less. I could also care less if I have to prance naked through the hospital lobby because she's holding my clothing hostage. I'm leaving. I'm going to my woman.

Only, the door bursts open before I get the deed done and McKenzie skids into the room like she's been shot out of a cannon.

Mother of god.

She steals my breath.

"Hello, beautiful," I growl.

She sobs and leaps over the rail on the side of the bed and tumbles into my arms.

Not a single nerve cell that was screaming before registers pain now. I'm in heaven.

Instant bliss.

McKenzie's voice is shaking almost as much as her body. "Thank you, god. I'm never letting you out of my arms. I was terrified."

I bury my face in her hair and inhale her sweet scent. When I take her face in my hands, her lashes are brimming with tears and her pale green eyes are agonized.

"I'm fine."

She winces. "You look terrible. I shouldn't have jumped on you, but I was overcome."

"I'm fine," I say softly. My body might be abused, but my heart is filled with the most indescribable emotion. All my life my heart has felt heavy. Today it feels like it's flying.

Her eyes close for a second, and she shivers in my hold.

"I love you," I whisper. My voice is raw and filled with my heart.

Her eyes snap open as her bottom lip begins to tremble. So damned beautiful. So mine.

I smile, making my busted lip tug tight. "I love you," I repeat and kiss her lips gently even though my mouth is pretty fucking mangled. "All I could think about was that I hadn't told you."

Tears spill over her lashes and I catch them with my thumbs as they cut paths down her soft skin. "Don't cry, baby. You've already shed enough tears."

She whispers, "I love you too. More than anything. I was terrified that I'd lost you."

"I'm just banged up."

Her eyes go hard. "Who did this to you?" The protective growl in her voice makes my heart thud double-time.

"Technically, I wrecked."

That makes her frown harder. "Don't sugar coat it, mister."

"It's the truth, no one did this to me. The truck flipped over a bunch of times. That's why I'm beat all to hell."

Beckett steps closer, he's been watching, but giving us space. "SWAT got them all."

"How many?"

"Four."

His eyes hold mine and I know there's more that he's not telling me. He's protecting McKenzie and I appreciate the hell out of that.

"Thanks, brother," I murmur as I pull McKenzie to my chest.

Beckett tips his chin. "I'll just be outside."

"Don't go far. I'm sending her with you."

"I'm not leaving you," McKenzie snaps and clings to my neck.

"You are not sitting here while I argue about them discharging me."

She tightens her arms around me, snuggling closer, and damn if I don't love her more for it. She grates, "Don't argue, Justin. You need to listen to them."

I grin and kiss her. "Whose side are you on?"

"The smart side," is her retort.

"What I need you to do is go make some cinnamon rolls for me. Those really good ones, because the food here is gonna suck."

"Is it, now?" the head nurse asks from the doorway. Her arms are crossed, her hip is cocked, and I know I'm in for more hell.

"Guaranteed," I shoot back.

With a grumble, the nurse says, "He's right, honey, go on and make something good for him. If he behaves, we might let him out of here this evening, just because he's such a pain in the behind. You can argue with him, instead of me. I got enough troubles around here without a big ole grump ringing the bell all the time. You can take over as soon as the doc reviews his chart."

McKenzie laughs and it's the best sound I've ever heard. "I think I can handle that."

Chapter Sixty-Nine

DOZER

The kitchen smells like sweet Nirvana. Christ. I can't wait to have those amazing scents in my kitchen and have my woman baking in her panties. After I've had my way with her until we're both starving.

But thank fuck she's got on jeans and a T-shirt right now, because the kitchen is full of men.

Marshall pulls a chair out for me. "Sit down before you fall down."

I give him a glare. "Nah. I'm fine."

He grins, and shoves the chair back in. "Stubborn ass, I like you, by the way. Those driving skills will come in handy on the Agile Team."

I give him a chin lift.

"Beckett, let's get on with this," I urge as I lean a

shoulder against the wall. I probably should sit, but I'm not planning on standing around long. I'm dragging McKenzie off to bed and I might not let her out for a week.

Beckett pushes off from the kitchen counter, chewing something and moves to the table for his laptop.

"Is that one of my cinnamon rolls you're eating?"

His eyes flick to McKenzie and he flashes a sheepish grin. "Nah. She warned me. That was one of the Preacher Cookies she made for me. Special request. Gotta say, damn, the woman is good."

A thick, warning growl leaves my throat. Only to be met with a sweet smile from McKenzie. "It's okay, honey, I made some for you too."

There's a round of laughter, and all of us savor the moment. The normalcy of sharing food and the company of people that have your back.

But the mood sombers as Beckett flips open his computer. "Are you guys ready?"

McKenzie moves to my side, loops her arm around my waist, and tucks her head against my chest. "I guess."

She's nervous. Her body is trembling.

Beckett knows it too. "Mac, I hope you don't mind me calling you that. I heard Mako using the nickname. You know how us military guys are about nicknames. Anyway. I just want to say that I know this has been hard. I don't have all the answers you're going to want, but I do have some that I think will make you feel better."

Beckett reveals that the man who looks like her father has been arrested and it appears the threats against her safety are gone. Thank fuck.

At least he's behind bars.

"We're going to get to the bottom of this," he says solemnly. "I won't stop until I know everything."

McKenzie stares at the mugshots on the screen of his computer. She's numb. It's written all over her.

We all understand. She's already mourned her father. Now she's dealing with the fallout of a lifetime of lies.

She can't correlate the criminal with the man she cared for, that she loved. But it still breaks my soul to know what she's been through and everything she's got left to deal with.

In a rough voice, she says, "I'm still just so shocked he could have led a double life."

Beckett's quick to reply, "You can't blame yourself. Men who live like that are very good at hiding things. I've seen it time and time again. They can have very elaborate schemes to keep families separate from their criminal lives."

Marshall flicks a quarter between his fingers, stares at the ceiling, letting his mind work. "Why would he keep her around if he was living some other life? Why not just go do his shit and let McKenzie go on with her life?"

"A cover?" Mako asks.

McKenzie shudders against me. "Would someone really go to all that trouble?"

Beckett raises his eyes from his computer. "We won't know until we learn his motives. That probably won't happen until we know who John Rush really is. Right now, this is a puzzle with a million pieces." Questions that could take years to answer.

Holding McKenzie tightly against me, I share my thoughts. "So, this guy, his birth certificate is a fake, he's been living under the name John Rush for at least nineteen of McKenzie's twenty-four years. She's lived here since she was at least five, as best she can remember. Her school records go back that long, based on what Beckett found. So, the pieces we need are old. Nineteen to twenty-four years old, maybe older."

"You think he could have assumed an identity and moved here with her all those years ago?" Mako asks Beckett.

He leans back and crosses his arms, taking the time to let his thoughts form. "It's logical. I've seen other people create a new identity and move to Alaska and basically try to disappear. That could explain why her birth certificate is also forged."

Tapping my fingers on the table, I ask what none of us know, "Where was he from before that?"

Becket tips his chin, "That's the million dollar question."

McKenzie presses the heels of her hands against her eyes. "If the house hadn't burned, there might be more evidence."

Beckett makes a note on a pad in quick, slashing strokes. When he's done, he taps his pen for a few seconds, then looks at me. "Do you know any of his contacts outside of this area? Maybe someone from his past?"

I'm wracking my brain, when Dozer says, "Sweetheart, Bob Claymore. He was in the SEALs with your dad, at least that's what you said when we met." He turns back to the group, "He owns the Pink Palace in San Diego. Real piece of shit."

Marshall shoves back from the table and stands. "Anyone wanna go to San Diego?"

Mako grins wickedly. "I'll bring some SEALs along to play." He cuts me a quick look. "Sorry, brother, your woman needs you right now. You'll have to leave this one up to us. But we'll do right by you, you've got my word."

Chapter Seventy

Candy

So many questions unanswered. My head is spinning, but there's something that's more important than that right now. Taking care of the man that's my everything.

I follow him into the bedroom and fluff the pillows as he undresses. "Lay down. I'll feed you."

Dozer's grin is quick. "I can get down with that."

He crawls slowly onto the bed and scoots backward until he's propped on the thick stack of pillows. "Will you do it naked?"

I tsk at the nerve. "*No,* I will not. You're covered in cuts and bruises. Me being naked will only do one thing. Cause trouble. You're sidelined, buddy."

That earns me a devilish stare. "Babe, I've got abrasions and bruises. My dick is more than fine."

"Your... penis is attached to all the stuff that's bruised and cut."

As much as I'd love to feel him surrounding me with his heat and strength, and making me forget everything right now, he needs rest. Some TLC. Some cinnamon buns and a quiet night.

"You're as bad as my nurse." With a grumble, he motions me forward with his fingers.

"Worse," I growl back with a shake of my finger, and climb onto the bed until I'm resting on my knees next to him. Fully clothed, despite his bossy request.

When I'm settled, I drag the plate with cinnamon rolls over from the night stand. "Open up."

He licks across his busted lip. "Yes, nurse bossy. I must say you're much cuter than any of those women. Especially if you lose the shirt."

I gently swat his hand away, careful not to hurt his scraped up hands. Finally, he caves and lays back with a heated look in his dark gray eyes.

Oh, the promises they hold. I'm almost scared to admit what I see there. Is forever really possible for us?

Soon, the pressure behind my sternum is almost too much to bear. I shouldn't want to trust this man so easily. I shouldn't put my heart in the hands of another person. But I have.

It's too late.

"Open up, babe," I say when my heart starts to ache so bad it steals my breath.

When I feed him a bite, those penetrating eyes drift closed. He lets out a very satisfied moan. "Fucking amazing. You keep cooking like that, I'm gonna have to increase my runs from four days a week to seven," he murmurs around a mouthful.

As he chews with his eyes closed, I let myself inspect the cuts and purple bruising on his face. A lump grows again in my throat.

Does love always make you feel like this? So helpless to protect the people you care about. So broken when they are hurting...

So vulnerable.

I've been a mess since that call came in during the car chase. Then, when we got to the scene of the chase and his SUV was upside down, smoking, and surrounded by SWAT people dressed from head to toe in black, I almost died.

"What are you thinking about?"

I flinch. The worst thing imaginable.

Softly, he coaxes, "Tell me, sweetheart."

I let my burning lungs exhale. A soft stream of air hisses out and I feel my body trying to relax even though it's impossible for my mind to right now.

"Just how horrified I was when they wouldn't let us near. When I didn't know if you were dead or alive. I swear if Mako hadn't been holding me back, I would have gone crazy on someone."

"I'm glad you didn't see. I was pretty bloody, mostly from my nose and the cut on my forehead."

"I was afraid you were..."

My voice hitches and I have to look away.

His fingers stroke up and down my arm. The touch is whisper-soft and achingly sweet. "I'm hard to kill."

Thank. God.

After a beat, I whisper, "I heard you ran them off the road."

"Damn straight I did. I knew it was my chance to end this bullshit once and for all."

His eyes drop to the icing on my finger. "Now, give me that."

Before I can move, Dozer's got my hand. He tugs it to his mouth, and licks my fingertip. Slowly while he looks right into my eyes.

God.

Instantly, I melt. Inside and out. That ache in my heart flees and my body erupts with heat.

When he's done tracing his tongue over the tip of my finger, in between and up the next, he grins wickedly, "Did you save the extra icing?"

I give him a tight-lipped glare, but I answer, "I did."

"Go get it."

"*No.*"

"Honey, are you really telling me no, that you don't want me to lick icing off your sweet little clit?"

My eyes go wide. Super wide. Maybe wider than ever before. I force myself to blink.

Uh. "When you put it that way, I feel horribly conflicted."

Then, I think better of this crazy idea. That would just be greedy of me. Trying to sound stern, I tug my hand away from his mouth. "You need to be lying down and resting. Doctor's orders."

"I am gonna lie down. You're gonna trot that sweet little ass of yours downstairs, get the icing, smooth it all over your sexy little pussy, and then sit on my face."

Holy. Smoking. Panties. Did he just say sit on his face?

I've never...

Feels so scandalous.

When I gape at him with my face burning, he laughs. The sound makes my skin tingle.

But I see his wince when something hurts.

313

Ignoring the curiosity and heat thrumming in my veins, I scold him. "I saw that. See, I told you, you need to rest."

But Dozer's having none of it. Stubborn man. I bet if I don't go get the icing, he's going to march downstairs and get it himself. Probably naked. I see what the nurse was talking about now. Maybe he should have stayed there.

A throaty growl splits the silence. He tags my wrist and tugs me until our lips are a fraction of an inch apart. Burning gaze locked on mine, he says, "I'll rest tomorrow. Right now. I need to taste you. I need to feel your release on my tongue. I want to hear you scream my name. After that, I need for the woman I love to slide down on my cock and take us both home."

You could knock me over with a feather.

I'm frozen.

Not frozen. I'm burning.

Ooof.

My heart starts to pound. He grabs my ass with his free hand and squeezes hard enough to make me groan. "Get the icing, sweetheart."

I dash out of the bedroom, take the stairs two at a time and grab the bowl of icing.

Beckett howls with laughter when he sees what I've got in my hands. I give him a very unladylike snarl and fly back up the stairs. I'll worry about being embarrassed later.

When I close the door, Dozer's already shoved his pants and briefs down his thighs. His glorious cock is standing up proud and tall.

My mouth goes dry, then starts to water furiously. "Do I get to put icing on you too?"

"That's a *hell* yes. Now get your clothes off before I climb out of this bed and do it myself."

I strip in record time. His eyes on me the entire time.

Clothes fly everywhere as the lust on his face makes my heart stumble.

"God, McKenzie. I still can't believe you're mine."

That. Steals. My. Breath.

I fumble for a reply, but settle on a wobbly smile. Behind the scenes there's a whole fireworks show of emotions going on.

He points a finger at me, then drops it lower and lower until it's pointing right at my burning pussy. "Now, be a good girl and put some icing in all the right places."

"Bossy."

"Always. Especially in bed."

I'm grinning like a lovesick fool as I dip some icing and slather it on my clit. Wow. That's new. Totally arousing too. As if I wasn't already on the verge of coming just from the way Dozer is looking at me.

But this takes it to the next level. The icing is cold and makes my sensitive bud pulse. A little groan slips out of my mouth as I glide my fingers around.

"Christ," he mutters. "Come here."

I step closer to the bed and his fingers slip between my legs, capturing some of the icing. He slowly licks them. "Give me the bowl."

I pass it over and he quickly scoops up two fingers full and slathers it on my nipples. The warmth of his fingers and the chilled icing make my nipples burn with need.

His hand wraps around my waist and he tugs me until I'm on the bed, kneeling over him. That's when he goes crazy on my nipples with his tongue.

Oh, holy wowza. A high-pitched sound takes flight from my throat.

Yes. Heavens. *Yes.*

When he's done there, he scoops up some more icing

and smears it around the head of his straining cock.

"Climb up, sweetie, sit on my face and suck that sugar off of my cock while I eat you for dessert."

Huh, *what? Wait... that's...*

Totally scandalous.

I've read about sixty-nine, and I never got the appeal until now. Now I can't wait.

He chuckles softly. "You should see your face—that dawning recognition is beautiful. I'm gonna have a helluva good time teaching you all the games we can play in bed."

"You're turning me into an eager student."

His fingers move around to my back and slip lower until he's squeezing my butt cheek, teasing his fingers deep into the space between. His voice drops to a growl. "It only gets better. Now climb on, baby, before I pass out from hunger."

The look he gives me evaporates all embarrassment. All unease. I trust him completely. I want him to show me everything we can share.

Hungry for my own taste, I lower my mouth to his cock as he settles between my thighs and starts to lick. His tongue makes me crazy. I'm so electrified, I can hardly lick and suck him.

I'm pretty much panting against the head of his sweet, slick, steel-hard erection.

I'm doing a terrible job.

"I can't—" A moan rips out of me. Then another. Then I'm coming so hard it's like I'm being shot to the moon.

Beneath me, his thighs clench, causing his cock to jolt upward. "Fuck yeah, suck me now, baby."

His body jolts, then his salty release mixes with the lingering taste of icing.

One long shower later we fall into a deep, safe, peaceful sleep. Until banging on our door awakens us.

Chapter Seventy-One

DOZER

"This better be fucking important." I sound more bear-like than human as I fold upright and grab my jogging pants.

Mother fucking hell. I wince as I drag the pants up one leg, then the other. Rolling over five times is a real bitch.

Bang. Bang. Bang!

"I'm gonna break someone's hand," I growl, keeping my voice as low as I can while still showing the menace that whoever's out there is gonna face.

When I jerk the door open, Beckett is standing there with a disarming expression. It's not bad, it's not good. It's almost hopeful.

"I've been trying to get you to answer your phone for an hour. This can't wait any longer."

"What time is it?"

"Zero nine-hundred."

"No effin way." We slept twelve hours at least. Not that I knew exactly what time it was because McKenzie didn't just take us both home, she knocked me out. I don't ever remember sleeping better.

When Beckett picked me up from the hospital and told me that John Rush was in custody alongside his top three men, I knew that the worst was done.

McKenzie was safe. And it was time for us to start creating a life together without a tornado bearing down on us.

I crane my neck to look back at McKenzie. She's wrapped in the sheet, thankfully she's fully covered. My throat tightens at the sight of her hair tossed all over the pillow. My chest hurts as I soak in that angelic little smile on her lips.

She's so fucking mine.

I'm a changed man.

Beckett clears his throat, reminding me he's the asshole that's dragged me from that warm bed. Christ, how did she sleep through all that fucking banging?

"You two need to get your asses in gear. We're going to Nebraska, via Anchorage."

I scrub my hands over my face, hitting both my busted lip and bruised forehead as I go. "Fuck. That's sore."

He gives me a quick once over, followed by a scowl. "Take some Motrin. You're gonna need it."

"*You're* gonna need it if you keep banging on the door like a fucking maniac. What's happening?"

"Something crazy."

Elaborate much? Apparently not. "What's in Anchorage?"

318

He turns to leave, but glances over his shoulder. "The lab we use for DNA."

"Anyone heard of email around here?"

"Get your ass in gear, Dozer. You don't want to put this off. This is some crazy shit. I think that this will best be explained by one of the experts."

He turns, jogs down the hallway, and takes the stairs down toward the first story two at a time.

Something crazy?

I have a feeling when Beckett thinks it's crazy...that's saying something.

Chapter Seventy-Two

Candy

A cloud hangs low over the Anchorage airport as the private Agile Security jet descends. If I had any nails, I'd have chewed them off. That is if Dozer would have let go of my hand.

He's got my fingers locked tight between his, and a grim lock on his jaw. He looks like a professional boxer with all the bruising on his face. If I didn't know him, I'd give him a wide berth.

He's weirdly quiet. So is Beckett. They just hustled our gear out of the house and got us on the Agile plane which had just returned from taking Mako and Marshall to California.

No one wants to talk about what's going on. Can I just

tell you how much I hate being in the dark? We're gonna have a talk about this.

I know they think they're protecting me, but I'm the one that's been flown cross-country, locked up, found out her life was a lie, and fallen in love all while that was happening. I think I can take whatever this is.

Only nothing could ever prepare me for what I was about to find out.

* * *

"Come on in and have a seat," a slender man wearing starched khakis, a sweater, and a lab coat says. His name tag says William Brill. For some reason my mind hangs on the fact that someone probably calls him Bill Brill. Odd thing to fixate on, but my mind is kind of like spaghetti right now, trying to tie itself into some kind of knot that makes sense.

Dozer ushers me to a seat. Beckett and him take the other two.

It's a small conference room with a screen on one wall. Some electronics on the table, and a window that overlooks some kind of science lab. Presumably DNA and other forensics since that's all Beckett would say.

Beckett starts, "Bill, thanks for seeing us in person. I thought maybe you could explain this to Ms. Rush and Mr. Roark better than I could."

The man brightens. This is his thing, that's undeniable. "I'd love to."

After a few keystrokes an image of a DNA helix appears on the screen. He motions to it. "I'm not sure if you know how DNA works, but when we look at the DNA from one person, we can search the database for people who are related."

A picture of a diagram that represents a family tree appears on the screen next. Bill says, "This is just an example, but you can see here, there are uncles, there are children, parents, grandparents." He clicks and zooms in. "We can tell exactly how much DNA they share. See this twenty-five percent sign?"

We all reply yes.

"Okay, now to the reports in question."

He drops his nose to his laptop for a minute, then raises up when something new appears on the screen. "This is the DNA sequence for the man known as John Rush taken from some hairs found in the truck on your property."

He clicks another image. "This is the DNA from the guy the feds have been looking for."

"It's a match," Beckett tells me.

A flood of ice water pours down through my chest even though we were already certain this was the case. "We knew this already."

Bill smiles gently. "This is where things get really interesting."

He brings up another image. "This, my dear, is your DNA."

The lines and bars on the screen mean nothing to me. I vaguely remember something like them in high school science, but it's a foreign language to me. "I know who your parents are," he says gently.

"Parents..."

Beckett lays his hand over mine, "Mac, you've got two parents. Neither of them are our John Rush."

I blink at him. Dozer pulls me closer to his shoulder, tucking me into his strength.

"Oh my god. I've been living with a stranger my whole life?"

Bill clicks on something else and another image pops up on the screen. "Not a stranger. Your father's brother. So, your uncle."

I gasp as tears start to clog my throat. "How?"

The office door swings open and a man in an Alaska State Police uniform walks in. He nods to Beckett and says a quiet, "Hello."

"I'm Trooper Reynolds. Agent Beckett asked me to pull some files together for you."

"My head is spinning here."

Dozer leans in and presses his nose against my ear.

"I've got you."

For a second my eyes drift closed. Thank an angel that he's with me. I need his strength more than ever.

Finally, I gather my composure. "What information do you have?"

He lays a file on the table in front of me. "This is going to be hard to read. We can give you some privacy if you like."

"Please."

The men file out of the room, except Dozer. He slides his chair closer and pulls me into his arms. "Together," he says resolutely.

He brushes my hair back and kisses my forehead. "I need you to know something. No matter what's in there, you need to remember you are my heart now. I'm not letting you go. I'm not letting you suffer alone. I'll do my best to make sure whatever wrongs happened are so far behind us that they will never hurt you again. I'm going to fill your future with love. We're going to fill our home with children. Our hearts with hope."

Tears are raining down my face. With shaking fingers I flip open the file.

Then I dissolve into wracking sobs.

Chapter Seventy-Three

DOZER

Fucking. Hell.

My heart nearly rips out of my chest as I stare at a photocopy of an old newspaper clipping.

Four-year-old child and kidnapper presumed dead after getaway car explodes.

I can't swallow, or breathe as I read the short, heart-breaking article.

A four-year-old girl from Ophelia, Kansas was kidnapped from her home. The last known vehicle she was seen in exploded, leaving no identifiable remains of her or the man who kidnapped her hours earlier.

The parents, John and Amanda Rush, are asking for privacy as they mourn the tragic loss of their precious daughter.

My arms are burning with fury as I lift McKenzie into my lap. She's not crying now. She's limp and that scares the fuck out of me.

I hold her so hard, I have to remind myself not to hurt her.

"It was all a lie," she whispers brokenly.

"He kidnapped you, faked your deaths, then took on your father's identity."

"*All* a lie."

I hold her tighter to me. "This is not a lie. Do you feel me? I love you, McKenzie. There's a family out there that loves you too."

I call for the men to come back into the room. Beckett, the trooper, and the DNA guy step inside as I demand, "We need answers."

William Brill assumes his spot at his computer. "As I was about to tell you, based on the DNA samples, and the analysis we ran with ancestry DNA company databases, you have family beyond the man who presented himself to you as John Rush.

"Who are my real parents?" she asks, hoarsely.

"John Rush. Age fifty. Amanda Rush. Age forty-eight."

The trooper lays a piece of paper from a leather folio on the table. Two photographs, both from driver's licenses are centered on the page.

Beckett says, "You look just like your mother."

McKenzie picks up the paper, staring at the grainy, washed out images as she bites her lip. "I thought my mom left us. That's what Fake John always told me. Oh, my god." Her body tightens and fire starts to burn in her eyes. She pushes out of my arms and quickly off the chair. "I have parents!"

I ask, "Do you have any other pictures?"

"Sorry, I didn't have time to run them before I came over here to meet you."

The room falls quiet as we all digest the information. As I stare at the two IDs, I sift through all the information. "Wait a minute, that article didn't say that an uncle kidnapped the child."

Beckett says, "That's because John Rush never knew he had a brother. Adam Snider."

The trooper says, "We traced your father's birth record, he was a twin. But the other child was given up to an adoption agency. It took a lot of digging, but a guy I know got access to some old records. The documents in the file cited the parents had difficult times, and were financially unable to raise twins."

My anger knows no bounds. "A twin. Fuck. Excuse my language. But that bastard stole their child and assumed his brother's identity. That's fucking harsh. It's a good thing he's behind bars right now because violent is a poor fucking word for how I feel, right now."

"I feel you," Beckett says as he tightens his jaw.

In my arms, McKenzie's fallen quiet, however her breathing is rapid, her color is pale. The emotions are growing too big. She confirms it when she says, "I need some air. I can't breathe."

I stand with her in my arms and pull open the door. "We'll be outside."

Chapter Seventy-Four

DOZER

Ten hours later we're touching down in Kansas. Ophelia isn't near any major airports, but the Agile team pilot lands us on a tiny ass tarmac in the middle of nowhere.

Marshall and Mako are waiting for us. They both look relieved.

"Lovebirds," Mako remarks with a grin as we walk up, holding hands.

"Stuff it."

He chuckles. "Good to see you two. Your face is looking better."

Like I could care, but maybe it is a good thing. I don't want to meet McKenzie's parents looking like I used my face as a battering ram.

She smiles gently up at me. God damn, she's cute as hell wearing my sweatshirt. I lean down and steal a kiss.

"Ready, beautiful?"

Her smile brightens everything, when she says, "So much."

It's been hours since she stared at the two photocopied driver's license photos that the trooper gave her. Beckett was right, she looks just like her mother, and a hint like her father.

Marshall closes the door behind me as I climb in with McKenzie in the back seat. He gives me a nod.

I wasn't sure how all of this was going to go down, but I think McKenzie's about to find out just how much she's loved.

It takes ten minutes to drive to the Rush farm.

The farmhouse is white. It stands large and proud against a bright blue sky. The fields around it are covered in new, spring crops. The grounds are well kept and tidy.

Marshall wastes no time on the long driveway. He slams to a halt in front of the house, next to a wagon that's been turned into a big bed full of flowers.

A woman runs down the stairs, her blonde hair trailing behind her.

McKenzie's in her mother's arms a few seconds later.

Standing on the porch is a man that looks like he's about to shatter.

I tip my chin and he unglues his feet and strides down the steps, crossing the space until he's got his wife and his daughter in his arms.

I choke the fuck up. Like I've never choked up before.

Marshall, Beckett, and Mako move away, letting us deal. I should probably give them some space, but I'm not letting her out of arm's reach.

A jacked-up red Ford truck with the sun flashing off its windshield, comes screaming up the driveway, making my nape rise in warning. Marshall, Beckett, and Mako spread out forming a protective line in front of us.

"They made it!" Amanda Rush shouts with tears of joy streaming down her face. Three young adults burst from the truck. Two young men in military uniforms, one Army, one Navy. Both tall and muscular. The woman, small like McKenzie, is wearing jeans and cowboy boots with a long blond braid over one shoulder.

Before I can blink, I'm swept up into a massive group hug.

The next thing you know, I'm crying. Men do fucking cry. Especially when they know they've just witnessed one of the most beautiful moments that will ever happen.

Of course, I have a feeling I'll cry tears of joy and gratitude so many times in our future.

When she says yes.

When we hold our first child.

Countless other moments that I never thought I'd have. I just feel it. In my heart.

Chapter Seventy-Five

Candy

It's utter chaos in the house. I've never laughed, hugged, and cried so many times. My heart is so full it feels like it will pop all its seams.

But I need to find Dozer. He slipped away an hour ago. That worries me. He'd gotten kind of quiet, but everyone was talking over top of each other.

Amanda catches me looking around. "He's on the back patio, sweetheart," she says with a smile as she carries a bowl of popcorn to the living room where a rowdy discussion about the movie Avatar is going on.

The air is cooling as the sun fades to dusk. Lavender clouds hug the skyline, and the sounds of bugs are beginning to fill the air. I take a breath and slowly descend the steps.

When I find Dozer in one of the lounge chairs, his head is kicked back and his eyes are closed. I walk up behind him and drop a kiss on his head.

When I start to massage his shoulders, the muscles are tense as gnarly tree limbs. "You okay, babe?"

"Yeah. Just thinking..."

"About?"

He presses his mouth closed, but opens his arms. Eager to feel his strength, I curl up on his lap.

"Thinking about my family."

His voice is so somber, that it confirms my suspicion. Something's wrong. Stroking my hand over the silky-soft hair on his forearm, I ask, "Do you feel like talking?"

He's quiet for a beat, so I ask, "Did you know I had two brothers and a sister?"

"I did. But I wanted you to find out here. Beckett told me when we left the lab. They were going to tell you then, but you'd had enough."

"It was a beautiful surprise." I lean against his shoulder, snuggling closer. "Are you close with your siblings?"

"Yeah. We have our differences, but we're close."

"You're the oldest."

"No. I have an older brother. He's a SEAL also. Hard-nosed mother-fucker."

"Kind of like you," I tease.

"It runs in the family."

I open my mouth, then smile, "Mom... god, it feels weird saying that, but anyway. She's got a guest room for us."

"Good. I wouldn't want you to miss a single moment with them, even though I'd like to have you all to myself."

"We can be quiet," I joke as I dance my fingers over the skin at the hollow of his throat.

"Says the woman who likes to scream the roof off when she comes?"

I'm laughing when I hear my brother's voice, "McKenzie! The movie's starting."

"Want to come?"

"I think I'll sit here for a bit longer. I've got a lot on my mind and you need to enjoy them."

I reluctantly climb off his lap but lean down to kiss him. "Promise you'll come in soon?"

"Promise," he replies against my lips.

Just before I walk inside, I turn back to look over the beautiful farm in the falling light of dusk. A feeling of peace settles into my bones. My soul knows this is home. But the sadness in Dozer's energy tells me we've got more skeletons to evict. Because I'm not letting anything come between us and our happiness.

Chapter Seventy-Six

DOZER

The light has completely faded when footsteps snap my awareness up.

"Just me, son."

I rise and shake John Rush's hand. The original one. The loving father.

The emotion in his voice makes my throat sting. "Thanks for bringing my girl home. You've made my life complete. Healed a broken man. Given a woman her heart back."

Even though it is well into night, I can see the emotion shining in his eyes.

"You're welcome. I'd do anything for her."

He motions to the chairs where I was sitting. "Let's talk."

I sit and he pulls a chair close, scraping across the patio tiles.

"What's eating at you, son?"

What? "Why do you think something is eating at me?"

"I've got sons, and heck, *two* daughters now. I know when something's not sitting right. Is it something about our family that puts you at unease?"

"Hell no," I clarify immediately, "Nothing like that. I've..."

Fuck if I know what to say. "I've just got some shit in my head. Forgive my language."

He tilts his head, "You're a SEAL, right?"

"Yes, sir."

"I served. Special Forces. Marine, Force Recon."

The sounds of night close in on us as neither of us say anything.

He shifts in his seat. "You're worried about the things you've done."

Bullseye. I try to hide my flinch. But the bullet bounces around inside of me.

"She doesn't define you by what you did, you know that."

"I know, sir. But *I* define myself by what I've done."

"This is the best time of your life, son. What the fuck is it you're so bound up over?"

I chuckle at his directness. "You'd probably call bullshit if I told you everything that's tangled up in my head."

Like he's in no hurry to go anywhere, he leans back and crosses his ankle over his knee. "Try me."

For some reason, in the dark with this man, I open my mouth and spill my fucking guts.

"I killed before I joined the service. It was an accident, but I shot my best friend while we were hunting. It gutted me. Still does." The pain tears through me as if it was yesterday instead of when I was sixteen years old. When McKenzie told me about her dad, all I could think about was that one moment in time. I'd been locked there, living that nightmare. "Ever since then I always wanted to prove I was something. Something better than I was. That's all I could think about. But ever since, I was half of myself. The other half went into the grave with Paxton."

I drive my hands into my hair. "I saw the way my father looked at me. He thought I was ruined. He knew I was damaged goods. Never said it but I knew he thought I'd never make it into the teams."

A giant fucking lump locks up my throat. But he just sits and waits patiently.

It hurts like hell to tell him this part. "My dad died before he found out I got accepted to BUDS. The very fucking day I got the news he died in a blizzard on our family ranch."

The man lets out a low whistle. "Justin, I'm sorry as hell for that. But let me tell you something about being a father. You hurt for your kids. Your soul bleeds for them. I bet you this farm that he didn't see you as imperfect, he wanted to fix what happened to you and he couldn't. Just like I couldn't fix a fucking thing for Amanda when our baby girl was stolen. All I could do was hold her. But I guarantee you that your father was proud as hell of you. He loved you. He never would have wanted you to feel that you were less than perfect, because you're not. No matter what kind of shit you've got in your head. You're perfect. And I can't say that with enough emphasis."

He swallows, and it's so rough I hear it through the darkness. He leans in close when he speaks to me this time and he sounds like a man that's been to hell and back with a return to the living. "You make my daughter happy. I've seen it with my own fucking eyes. She's been through hell and you've held her, you've been right there to prop her up, to catch her. You're a good man. Your fucking father would be proud of you, because I know I sure as hell am. He might not be around any longer, but you're now my son too. I won't let you forget what a good man you are. Now, get your ass up and get in that house because you've got a new family to celebrate."

My heart is wide fucking open with a beam of something hot and uncontrollable streaming out of it.

He latches onto my arm and tugs me up. His strength surprises me when he locks me in a bear hug and grumbles, "Big motherfucker."

I laugh as we share back slaps. "I was a farm boy too, but don't let my brothers hear me say the word farm. In Montana there are only Ranches."

He socks me in the arm, "Good, when you and McKenzie come to visit, I'm putting your big ass to work."

"Copy that."

He grips my shoulder, pushes me toward the house and falls in step beside me. I feel so much lighter I could fly. I can't imagine how I'll feel when I get McKenzie in my arms when we climb into bed tonight. I'm not sure I'll survive.

Chapter Seventy-Seven

DOZER

"Shhh." I clamp my hand overhear mouth. "Sweetie, I'm not getting shot by your father."

In the darkness, she whispers back, "I wasn't going to do anything."

"Liar. Stop wiggling against me. And definitely stop talking about sex. We are not getting it on in your parents' house."

"I wasn't trying to..."

I tug her back against his chest. "Lies get you spankings."

"I'm going to have to fib to you more often."

I nestle her against my chest, pillow my arm under her head, and rest my chin on her crown. "I love you."

She breathes deeply, then in the softest voice gives wings to my heart. "God, I love you."

Then she goes still. After a long time, she asks, "What changed?"

"Come again?"

"What changed? When I left you on the patio, you were struggling with something."

Oh. That.

"Your dad and I had a man to man."

She goes still and quiet again. "Is everything okay?"

"Better than okay. I think I needed to hear what he had to say far more than I realized."

She softens in my arms and makes a satisfied sound. "I'm so glad. I really hope you'll love them too."

"Sweetheart, I already do. Your brothers and sister are solid. They're great people. I can see so much of them in you."

"It's weird, isn't it? I've never met them and we all seem so much alike."

"Genetics is pretty crazy."

"I feel bad for my father, knowing he had a twin that did this."

I sigh against her hair. "I feel for him too. But he's got his head on right. He loves you, and his whole family with everything. That makes him strong."

It hits me then. Loving McKenzie is also making me stronger than ever before. Strong enough to face what I could never face before.

She's quiet for a while, as her fingers dance over my forearm. I want to lay just like this every night for the rest of my life.

"I can tell he loves all of them so much. It just shows all around this place."

Smiling into the darkness, I tell her, "This is a happy home. They've made something special."

The farmhouse is brimming with photos of the kids, bright colors, mementos from vacations, everything that McKenzie didn't have.

I can't imagine how hard that is for her, but it's also incredibly beautiful that she's now got all of this. During all of this, McKenzie has never seemed to dwell on the past. She jumped right into the now with both feet. A fact she proves when she says, "We'll have a home like this too, won't we?"

Those words.

Gold.

"Yeah, sweetheart, we will."

The backs of my eyes sting. My throat cinches. My chest contracts painfully before my heart starts to gallop. Fuck. I never knew it could be like this. Never saw past the dark shadows in my mind.

The whole world seems like a shiny new playing field now.

Christ, I'm not going to be able to sleep. Hell, it will be a miracle if I don't vibrate off the bed with all the excitement that's building in my chest.

The sooner I get on with that plan, the better. I just need to make some things happen first.

But first things first, I need to show my woman I love her and I need to feel her love, so against my better judgment, I'm gonna make love to McKenzie in her parents' house and do my best to catch those sweet cries with my mouth.

Chapter Seventy-Eight

Candy

The next morning comes fast. The kitchen is more than alive, it's electric. There's so much energy in the room it's almost blinding.

Pancakes are stacked high on plates. My brother, Austin, passes me a giant bowl of fresh fruit. "Eat up. Get what you want before Denver gets a hold of this bowl, he's gonna hog it all."

I take the bowl and scoop out some berries and melon. "Good to know."

"Whatever," Denver says with a mock scowl. "Like you didn't eat fourteen pounds of popcorn last night."

"He does have a point," Mom says as she grins at them.

My sister lifts up her pancake to inspect under it. "Where's the chocolate chips?"

"Honey, I stopped making those years ago when you started getting headaches from chocolate."

Madeline sighs. "Right. I was just hoping."

For some reason that makes me smile really big. Not that she gets headaches, but that we share that trait. "You get headaches from chocolate *too?*"

Dramatically, she rolls her eyes. "It's a curse. I can't even enjoy one of life's most basic pleasures."

Denver feigns an eye roll and flutters his hands over his chest like his heart hurts. In a high pitched voice, he mocks Madeline, "Heaven help me, I just can't live without bon-bons."

His voice drops back low. "Whatever a *damned* bon-bon is."

We all burst out laughing. This goes on and on for the next half hour until we're all fed and happy. I'm floating in the clouds with Dozer sitting next to me, rubbing my back, and my family around the big oak table.

One of the twins is telling about one of his Navy training missions when there's a knock at the door. Bell Bean, the ancient and very pudgy beagle that's been sleeping at my feet yawns and makes a very loud, "Woof."

"I didn't know Bell Bean could bark."

Dad rises from the table. "You should see her when the UPS guy comes. She's all yips and spins."

Dozer also rises. "Let me help with the dishes."

I start to stand too, but he pushes me back down into my seat. "Stay right there, sweetheart. Enjoy the company of your family." He kisses my temple, and leaves me, but I watch as he moves into the kitchen and starts talking with my mom. He's amazing. I'm so blessed to have had a man like him walk into my life. I don't know where I'd be right now without him and his coworkers. Probably in jail still.

That realization sends a shiver down my spine.

When Dad returns, Agent Beckett is on his heels. He's greeted by my mom with a hug. I follow, squeeze him hard as I thank him again for all he's done, and Dozer gives him a handshake. The others welcome him and make room for him at the table.

Mom calls, "Can I fix you a plate?"

"Do I smell pancakes?"

"Yes, sir. I've even got some chocolate chips and whipped cream for the top."

"*What?!?*" screeches Madeline, "You held out on me."

"I protected you from yourself," Mom says with a wink. "You're not gonna drag around with a headache on my watch. We've got things to do."

"Lord, let me guess, scrapbooking?" Madeline asks with mock irritation.

"We're painting McKenzie's old room today. So she's got a nice fresh room, whether she wants to stay, or she wants to come visit again soon. It's gonna be pretty. Whatever color she chooses because I don't know what my baby girl likes now that she's a grown woman."

I don't know how to respond, but I have to turn away because my eyes are pools. Lakes. Oceans. Where is all this water coming from? It's impossible to see as I blink a thousand times.

"Oh, alright," Madeline says and pokes me in the ribs with her elbow. "Hear that, big sister? You get to pick, and you better not copy my room. I'm the only one that gets to have purple. Because you know, I'll always love Barney."

My clogged up throat rumbles with a laugh. "Barney, as in the dinosaur?"

She winks. "Knew that would make you smile." Made-

343

line turns to Beckett, "Now Mr. Gets-all-the-chocolate, what are you doing here today?"

A slow, satisfied grin spreads on his face. "Annoying you, apparently." Then he lays a file folder on the table. "I've got some news for your Pa and Mac."

Madeline leans in and raises her voice. "*Mac?*"

I tug her shirt, pulling her back into her seat. "That's what the guys call me."

Scrunching her nose, she says, "That's a boy nickname."

"I guess it can be either," I reply, but Madeline's not looking at me, she's frowning at Beckett like he's stomped on her toes under the table. That's when I realize it's not about the nickname, it's about Beckett.

He deflects and makes small talk with my dad and brothers and Dozer while he eats, then he gets down to business. "This is sensitive, I'm not sure if you want everyone to stay while I go over the confessions."

My dad sweeps his hand around the room. "This is family, Agent Beckett, we don't hold back from one another. What one of us deals with, we all deal with."

I hold onto the edge of the chair as my heart throbs. Dozer slips into the seat and tightens his arm around my shoulders. "Ready?"

"More than I've ever been."

Chapter Seventy-Nine

Agent Beckett

This is by far the suck part of this job. In this line of work it doesn't pay to get close to people. Hell, you have to brace yourself apart, lest you'll get dragged into some seriously painful shit. But McKenzie and Dozer somehow wore through the shield I carry, and sitting at this table feels like way more than business.

That makes it even harder when I have to tell her and her father about the motivations for her kidnapping.

If I was in Alaska to sit on the interrogations, I'd have been sick. That bastard. It makes me spitting mad every time I read the damned transcript. Which makes me want to protect her from the reasons.

The senseless, selfish ass reasons that a man stole her and kept her as part of a giant ruse.

I open the file and lift the transcript of the confession that John Rush, AKA Adam Snider gave at his interrogation. Turns out Snider is an egotistical asshole and likes to brag about what he's accomplished.

To fool the world for twenty years into thinking he was a single father with PTSD.

A sick feeling washes over me as everyone looks at me. The pancakes I ate went down fine. But now they're cement in my gut. I should have stuck with coffee. *Hell,* I should have fasted.

The cruel things that some people do. I clear my throat and start to read out loud.

"*Interviewer: Mr. Rush, or should I say, Mr. Snider?*

"*Snider: So you finally figured it out, huh? Took you long enough.*

"*Interviewer: Why did you kidnap your brother's child?*

"*Snider: That bastard (Cursing, unintelligible). When I found out I had a twin, I was utterly fucking furious. Saw an article in the Military Times about his military heroics in the Gulf. People that knew him kept telling me how much alike we looked. (Clears throat, spits on floor). When I found him and saw the life he had, I knew that he wouldn't be happy ever again. I'd spend my dying breath making sure that son of a bitch suffered, and I mean suffered.*

"*Interviewer: Why did you have such feelings of hate for your brother?*

"*Snider: I fucking deserved what he had been given, not the life I got. Skid row, drugs, parents that were MIA. You name that shit and it happened to me. One drink short of someone beating me to death. Yeah, real nice life. And John... that motherfucker had it all. Medals, a wife, and a fucking little daughter that looked like a doll. So, I figured. Why not give him a taste of all the pain I had to endure. I take her, he gets to suffer, and I get an obedient servant.*

"**Interviewer:** (Pauses) How did you take John's daughter?

"**Snider:** That was so fucking easy. She was playing with some kids at a petting zoo. Just scooped her up. She was like three or four years old. It was easy to make her believe I was her father. Made my job easy as hell. Never shed a tear. Just did what I said.

"**Interviewer:** So, she just thought you were her father?

"**Snider:** (Snickers) Perfect, huh?

"**Interviewer:** What happened after that?

"**Snider:** I cooked up some fake credentials with a guy in California and moved to Alaska. No one bothers anyone up here. They know how to mind their own fucking business. John never thought to look for someone with his name and identity. Why would he?

"**Interviewer:** So, you just built a life, and then started creating a... new business?

"**Snider:** (Laughs for sixty seconds). Business, yeah, right. An empire. And no one knew I was banking millions. All because I built that shithole shack, which was an excellent cover for me. Especially with the daughter and all. The town people just looked at us with pathetic fucking grimaces. Meantime, I... Well, you know what I do. No use incriminating myself any farther."

"**Interviewer:** You know we have evidence of you selling national secrets.

"**Snider:** That son of a bitch-snitch Laker. He's gonna get a shank in prison.

"**Interviewer:** Are you threatening to kill the man who used to work for you?

*"**Snider:** (Laughs). What do you think?*

*"**Interviewer:** I want to shift gears. Tell me about your time in the Navy.*

*"**Snider:** What about it?*

*"**Interviewer:** What happened in BUDS that resulted in you getting discharged?*

*"**Snider:** You've seen my report.*

*"**Interviewer:** The Navy doesn't look fondly on selling drugs. What does the name Bob Claymore mean to you? And, are you in touch with him now?*

*"**Snider:** (Chuckles). A pawn in a bigger game. He's a douche I knew from the Navy. Indebted for saving him from getting killed in a bar fight. I'm not in touch with him, but conveniently, I hear McKenzie was, once she thought I kicked the bucket. That made it so much easier to get her hooked on murder charges. Nothing screams guilty like jetting out of town.*

*"**Interviewer:** So, you framed her? Why would you do that?*

*"**Snider:** It's a tidy ending. My cover is dead. She's locked up. I can get on with shit I've got in the works. It sucked when you incompetents let her walk away, so we went after her to those woods. Easy enough to fake an accident there. Would've killed her in those woods too, if those guys hadn't been with her. We were outnumbered then, but their time will come too.*

*"**Interviewer:** How are you connected to your neighbor, Mark Forester?*

*"**Snider:** (Chuckles). I love having people owe me shit.*

*"**Interviewer:** So, he lied to your daughter and said you were killed in a hunting accident because he owes you something?*

*"**Snider:** (Chuckles). Everything. He ran off the road*

in a fucking blizzard. I saved his ass. Man was a real pushover. Too bad he had a heart attack and died the day after he visited McKenzie to deliver the sad news. (Laughs).

*"**Interviewer:** That is a shame. (Clears throat, drinks water.) Mr. Snider, I see a theme here, you extort people for your own gain.*

*"**Snider:** Well done again, Officer. You're not as stupid as you look.*

*"**Interviewer:** We're done here. Have a nice long stay behind bars."*

When I raise my eyes from the paper, everyone is frozen. McKenzie's mom is crying silently. The men look like hell's about to be unleashed. Dozer's beyond that. He's nuclear. I'll be surprised if he doesn't rip the door off the house when he goes after the bastard.

McKenzie's sister has fisted hands and a grim slant to her compressed mouth. She's not looking at me any longer, she's looking through me. Right into the soul of a psychopath.

I close the file and shove my hands in my hair. Fucking-motherfucker. Sick bastard. The destruction in his wake may never be healed. When I get a grip on myself much later, I say, "The interviewer and the psychiatrist's notes suggest he's going to have a diagnosis of a serious mental illness. They are going for a life sentence, in isolation in a high security mental facility."

McKenzie blows out a breath as her eyes go to her father. In the softest voice, she says, "I remember confusion, I couldn't understand why things had changed."

Tears start to build on her lashes and every single person in the room holds their breath.

"Dad, did you ever take me on a horse?"

Her father's strangled reply undoes me. "Yeah. We used to ride together. You'd fall asleep on my lap."

Madeline buries her face in a napkin. Denver leans his head against hers and murmurs something we can't hear.

McKenzie rises and goes to her father. He opens his arms and she wraps hers tight around his shoulders. "I remember that," she says brokenly.

I slip out and walk across the yard. Far away. Nothing I can say will help. Time is the only balm, if it even works. Sure hasn't for me. Some damage never eases.

Chapter Eighty

Candy

ATF Agent Beckett is standing outside the Rolly Polly Diner waiting for us. He kind of sticks out like a sore thumb, but an incredibly handsome one.

His smile is warm, and I wonder if it's for me or my sister. She tags my arm and tugs me down the sidewalk like there's a mad possum on our tails.

When we pull up in front of Beckett, she makes an approving sound. "Look at you, all dressed up. What's the occasion?"

He shrugs a shoulder and gives us a little frown. "Just work attire."

Yeah, right. Every time I've seen him before, he's been in an ATF T-shirt, hoodie, or the occasional polo with a logo on it. But today he's in a crisp, freshly pressed, white button down with the sleeves rolled up. He smells damned good too. I don't miss the fact that my sister just did a quick inhale.

Which might explain why she's now vibrating with excitement. Kind of like a puppy that sees a toy.

What am I seeing here... are they *flirting?*

I can't suppress my grin, and Beckett looks at us both suspiciously. "What are you two up to?"

"They're two handfuls," Dozer says from behind me as he loops an arm around my waist. He's finally caught up after parking the car. Small town with a small amount of parking meant that he had to park two blocks away. "Wanna take one of them off my hands?"

A devilish spark lights in Beckett's eyes. I don't know what's going on here, but I've heard a few perplexing exchanges between Beckett and my sister. Some of them made me wonder if they were mad at each other.

"I'd be tempted, but I've got to fly out to L.A. this evening."

Madeline says, "What are the odds? You're kidding."

Beckett holds the door open to the diner, "And why would I kid about that?"

Madeline shrugs and twists her foot, making the metal adornments on her cowboy boot jangle. "I've got a meeting there tomorrow evening. I'm talking with some movie producers about filming my next tour."

Beckett glances around, even cranes his neck so he can see outside the diner. "Speaking of tours, where's your damned security detail?"

Her shoulders jolt back as her mouth drops open revealing the tongue ring she's got. "Why in the world would I need them in Ophelia?"

The instant change in Beckett's eyes has my own brows

shooting up. *Well.* Beckett was always so calm and steady. Now, not so much.

He has to unclench his jaw when he says, "Because crazy people aren't only found in cities, Madeline. You're a highly visible celebrity. Act like you've got a brain cell in that head of yours."

Oh. *Crap. Hang onto your hats.*

I haven't known my sister for long—two days—but I can tell already that if you push the wrong button, you're gonna have a tiny tornado on your hands.

Her eyes go wide. Her nose scrunches up. She makes a shhhh sound, punctuated with squinty eyes, and presses her finger to her lips. "The paper's gonna write about this little conversation, which might upset my momma, so I'd *appreciate it* if you'd drop it. Or at least have the sense not to do this in public."

Too late. This little exchange is going down in the entryway of the local diner in a town the size of a postage stamp. Ears are straining even if eyes are averted.

"Fine with me," Beckett snaps. But the man's leaning over her now, looking down with pure fire in those deep brown eyes of his.

Madeline tightens her jaw and gives him hell. Doesn't matter he's a foot taller than her. "We're gonna talk after we're done here. But get this straight right now. You're not my manager, or my father, so don't think you're gonna tell me what to do." To make her point, she drops a sassy fist onto her hip.

The stare-off intensifies.

Oh, double crap.

Why isn't Dozer intervening? When I glance over my shoulder at him, he's got a smug grin on his face.

Right. He's enjoying this far too much. Before anything

else happens, I jump in and grab Madeline's arm. "Let's eat. I'm starving. This is a *thank you* lunch for Beckett, so be *nice*."

The tension's so thick at the table, I can barely concentrate on ordering. Beckett and Madeline argue over whether tea should have sugar. Whether ketchup or mustard is better, and they even exchange digs over what the forecast is for tonight.

Dozer leans in and kisses my ear. "They'll be in bed before the night is over."

I grin when I turn to face him with wide eyes. "You think?"

He nods. "Wanna bet?"

"What are we betting?"

"How about a handy?"

I'm not even sure what that is, but just the tightness in his voice tells me it's dirty. I put my mouth near his ear, "What's that?"

He chuckles and squeezes my hand. My eyes go wide. "Oh, that."

His lips brush mine. "Yeah, that. So, are we betting?"

"Oh, alright, but what do I get in return if I win?"

His nose dips to my ear and he does the most wicked thing in the world with his tongue.

When he leans back, his smile is downright devilish. I turn back to the table to find the argument has ceased and two pairs of eyes are locked on us. The owners of those eyes are both grinning. Well, at least there's something they agree on.

Chapter Eighty-One

DOZER

"Hey, you doing okay?" I ask when I catch a minute alone with McKenzie. She hit the restroom and I left the festivities and followed her into the house to check in with her.

McKenzie brushes her hair back and rounds her eyes. "Your family is a lot."

"You wanna cut out?"

She looks appalled. "No! Never. I love them."

A knock on the front door distracts me from the kiss I was about to steal.

"More people?"

"Yeah, couple more people are still arriving."

After tagging McKenzie's hand, I head for the door of my brother's house. Drake's on the back patio cutting up with my brothers, so I know he didn't hear the knock.

Through the glass pane on top of the door, I catch sight of a familiar head.

"Beckett." I grin and grab the man in a bear hug.

"Looking more rested," he says as he drags me into a bear hug.

"You too, man."

McKenzie's staring at us with a look of confusion on her face.

"What's going on?"

"Beckett needed some downtime. I told him to come on over and spend some time on the ranch."

She hugs Beckett with a warm smile. "It's good to see you again. Be warned, it's a little crazy out there. They were roping a fake cow a few minutes ago."

Beckett claps his hands together. "Sounds like my kind of party."

McKenzie frowns. "You know how to rope?"

"I know how to hogtie a criminal. Figure my rope skills are good for something."

A cloud of dust suddenly appears on the long gravel road leading into Trident Ranch.

"Who's that?" McKenzie asks as we all turn to watch the vehicle come into sight.

I hide my chuckle when Beckett realizes it's a big black Hummer Limo.

"That's not..."

I say, "Madeline, I'd guess," but I know it's her.

McKenzie jumps down the stairs and takes off across the yard with her hair flying and her smile on megawatt. She whoops, "I didn't know she was coming!"

Beckett grabs the back of my neck, but he's laughing when he says, "You fuck. I might really have to use my rope skills when Madeline sees me. She's gonna go nuclear. You better have a fire extinguisher ready, she's gonna burn this whole place down with those eyes."

I smack him on the back. "Oh, this is gonna be good. You're gonna have to share that story."

"Never," he mutters. "So, is this why you brought me here? So you could play Cupid?"

"Nah. Truth is, it's an important day. I wanted both of you here."

He goes rigid next to me. "How important of a day?"

"You'll see."

When I look at him again, there's a dark emotion in his expression, but his words are kind. "Happy for you, man."

"Me too, brother."

"She loves the house?"

"She's as excited for it to be finished as I am. Another couple weeks and we'll be able to move in. Conveniently, Reagan's going to be traveling for at least a month, so she and I have his place to ourselves. Thank fuck. The last thing I want is my brother listening to us."

Beckett laughs. "Glad I'm staying in Mustang. Nice little town by the way, but I gotta say the bed in that hotel looks like a torture device. I don't know how two people'd ever sleep in it."

In the yard, the women are laughing and hugging. Then McKenzie points toward the porch as she says something, Madeline's body goes ram-rod stiff. Her finger juts out toward Beckett and she bellows, "You!"

"Oh shit, here we go," Beckett grumbles.

Chapter Eighty-Two

Candy

I can't stop laughing as my sister stomps across the grass toward the fake cow that she just tried to rope but managed to get herself tangled instead. "That's freaking hilarious."

Dozer pulls me back against his chest and with a sexy growl he burrows his face in my neck. My skin lights up with tiny goosebumps.

"Huh, what? I was busy looking at your very fine ass."

As he rubs his big body against my back, my face heats to a dangerous level. Any second now that big body is going to be sporting a very big boner. A term I just learned last night, by the way. Justin's just a veritable walking sex education tutor.

"Your family's watching."

"Sweetheart... they know I can't get enough of you. They're happy for us."

"Still. It's *embarrassing*."

"There's no reason to be. They love you. They want us to be romantic."

"Romantic, not erotic." I knew those words already.

He laughs against my neck. "Close to the same. They both end in tic..."

A screech rattles the air. "Oh. My. *GOD!*" Madeline yells as she stomps her very fashionable cowboy boot on the ground. "You're cheating."

Beckett turns and pins her with a glare as he winds up the rope in his hands. The same rope he just used to lasso Fake Jake—a plastic head on a sawhorse.

Agent Becketts's got his calm back, momentarily at least. "How exactly am I cheating?"

"I don't know, but you are definitely up to something. You've never roped anything before and you just did that! You have to be cheating or lying."

He stalks toward her, leans down, and says something only she can hear. I don't have any idea what it is, but her mouth drops open.

Oh, boy. This is getting better and better.

Dozer says, "Got something I want to show you over by the fire-pit."

Not that I'd have a choice. I'm in Dozer's arms a second later. He kisses my temple as he carries me across the lawn. A girl could get used to this. All the snuggling especially.

When we reach the big stone fire-pit, everyone's gathering around, talking, enjoying the beautiful evening. Stars are beginning to show against the periwinkle sky. A light breeze carries the earthy scents across the land and makes the flames dance.

My heart's so full I can hardly stand how good it feels. Kansas felt like home. This feels like heaven.

Dozer is way more peaceful too.

"I love your family. The Wilson's are so nice too."

Alice and William Wilson lost their son in the hunting accident when Dozer was injured. The barrel of Dozer's rifle exploded due to metal failure. The talk with my father helped him open up. It paved the way to having a heart to heart with his mother and the Wilsons about the guilt he had.

I'm so glad. He deserves everything.

Without even breathing hard, he carries me all the way across the yard and deposits me on one of the big logs that's been crafted into a bench by the fire pit. "I'm glad the Wilsons could come. They're my second family."

Dozer's youngest brother sits down near me. He's holding an iPad. "McKenzie, I wanna show you something."

"Sure."

I don't even notice that Dozer disappears, I'm so busy listening to Eli talk about the special homemade sauce he used on the barbecued ribs he made for this evening. I'm expecting him to show me the recipe when Facetime suddenly appears.

I blink at the screen as my brain tries to compute. "Mom!?"

"Hey honey." She leans to the side. "Your dad is here too."

"Hang on," Eli says. He taps the screen a few more times, then my brothers appear.

"What's going on?"

Eli says, "Why don't you ask Justin?"

My heart skips when I see him. He's emotional. Oh my

360

god. *Love.* Pure wide-open love is shining in his beautiful eyes.

This is Justin. The one I see behind closed doors. Not Dozer, not the SEAL. This is the man that holds me gently and tells me about his dreams in the inky blackness of night.

Both of them make the whole, but the man standing before me has his heart on full display. For me.

My heart starts to race and my hands instantly feel clammy. This looks serious...

He drops down to a knee as everyone gathers close. Their chatter drops into an instant hush.

Oh. My. God. This is serious.

"Beautiful, I hope this is okay, I wanted everyone to be here to celebrate tonight with us."

"Oh. God, okay. I'm glad they're here too," I whisper.

He takes my hand in his, then his eyes rise to mine and never leave.

Husky and soft, he says, "I can't imagine life without you."

Gently, he brushes a kiss over my knuckles. He opens his palm to reveal the most incredible engagement ring I've ever seen. Color dances and leaps off of the gigantic round diamond and the two golden stones on the sides.

"You're the sunshine to my dark. The breath to my lungs. The warmth in the dark of night. You're the strongest person I have ever met, and every day you inspire me to be a better version of myself."

He reaches for my cheek and cups it in his palm. "I never thought I could find happiness. Until you..."

The shine in his eyes grows. He swallows roughly and his voice drops as his thumb strokes across my heated skin. "McKenzie, will you be my wife?"

Something bright lights inside of my chest.

Tears sting my eyes, my throat, and blaze across my lashes. "Oh, honey. *Yes!* Yes. Yes."

He slides the ring on my finger. His hand is shaking, but his eyes are steady. So damn steady. Like they always are. This man is my rock. I can't wait to be Mrs. Justin Roark. Can't wait to make our home together.

He wraps me in the fiercest hug ever. Then a dozen arms wrap around us, locking us into a giant circle of love.

I'm laughing, crying, flying.

I was all alone in so many ways. There was no love in my life. Only lies. Only pain.

That's all behind me.

The future's so bright, the glow in my heart bursts into a thousand tiny butterflies with sparkling wings.

I'll never be without family, never be without Justin.

The stars shine overhead like diamonds sprinkling us with their blessings while my fiancé kisses me as our world is filled with cheers.

Chapter 83

Epilogue

Candy

"Babe, there's no way I can see anything with your big paw over my eyes."

"Good. Now, one more step up. We're almost there." Dozer urges me up the final step on the stairs leading into our new house. Since the framing was finished, he hasn't allowed me inside. Sneaky devil.

I've been dying with curiosity and excitement.

"This way." With his big body against my back, his arm around my waist and his hand over my eyes, he guides me inside. The air around us goes quiet as we step into the big, modern farmhouse.

His boots clip on the stained concrete floor as he takes me deeper.

I'm vibrating with excitement. I can't believe we're

finally moving in. "I'm amazed that this is finished. The crew must have worked non-stop for the last few days."

The truth is, I knew they were burning the midnight oil. Trucks coming and going all hours of the day and night. Dozer was right in the thick of it.

I hardly saw him, but when I did, he made sure we made up for lost time.

He says, "They have. We kicked it into high gear. I was hounding the hell out of them. Good thing they know I'll help out on their next job when things run tight. Truth is, everyone was as excited as I am about how the house came together. There's a few more things to be done, but we'll do that together, just you and me."

We suddenly stop. I think we're in the living room based on the direction he's been leading us.

"Keep your eyes closed."

"Yes, master," I tease. I know how he gets off when we play like that.

He growls and the heated rumbly sound makes my body burst to life. "I was planning on making love to you in our new bedroom first, but if you keep that up, we won't make it."

"Oh darn. How terrible," I mutter as I cling to his muscular forearm.

He leans closer, I know this because his breath stirs my hair against my cheek. "Open your eyes, sweetheart."

Before me are two closed French doors with lightly frosted glass. I didn't expect this. Now I'm really curious. "Go ahead," he murmurs softly.

I nearly stumble back when I see what's inside those doors. "A library, for me?" I ask in a choked whisper.

I'm astonished. How did he pull this off without me having any idea?

The large floor to ceiling windows offer soft, diffused light, illuminating shelves upon shelves of books. Dozer built a library. He likes to read too, but this is definitely a room made for a woman to love. It's soft. It's so warm and inviting.

Mahogany bookshelves stretch from floor to ceiling, laden with a dazzling array of spines. Books of every size and color beg to be read. His emotions are palpable as he steps up behind me. "I don't know if you'll like the books I picked, but the space is what mattered most to me. We can replace the books. When I went into your cabin, I knew your reading corner was your haven. I wanted that for you here. A place you can feel safe enough to relax and disappear into an imaginary world."

A sanctuary. Carefully curated just for *me*.

"Oh, sweetheart," I choke out as my eyes tear up, distorting the beautiful view before me. It's a reading corner to die for.

A plush velvet chaise lounge, in a shade of deep midnight, is adorned with a throw blanket and soft pillows. Fuzzy, warm, inviting things. Beautiful things like I've never owned. But the perfectness of the space doesn't overshadow the view, the postcard vantage of the distant mountains. A dreamy place to lose myself in a book while drinking in the views outside. "It's just perfect."

Maybe I'll even get to watch my husband working with the horses out there too.

His arms loop around me as he lets out a slowly exhaled breath. It's so sweet how much he cared. A smile that's coming from my heart warms my cheeks. "I hope you knew I'd love it."

"You've just been through so much. I want this to be a good place for you. Not something that reminds you of..."

I turn in his arms and bury my face into his strong, protective chest. My favorite place on Earth. The only place that matters. "It reminds me how blessed I am to have you."

He ducks and presses a kiss against my temple. "Same, sweetheart."

After a long beat of me soaking up the peace that I find in his arms, I step back and tug his shirt. "Now, let's go see our bedroom."

His eyes dance as a grin slowly grows on his face. "I love you, little sexy kitten, but I want to give you something first."

"Yeah?" I angle my head and wonder what he might be up to. He's given me the world but the smile he's wearing speaks of whole new volumes of special.

He leans over and plucks a book off the shelf. It's wrapped in brown paper.

Hm. "I didn't even see that."

As I take it from him, he leans down and brushes my lips with his. Then he motions for me to unwrap the book.

It's a hardback. Thick and beautifully covered in a vintage floral pattern. *"The Story of Us."*

"It's ours to write."

A lump forms in my throat. *No, this is no ordinary lump, this is a boulder.* The size of the world. Inside the hard binding are pages and pages of journal prompts that will tell the story of our life together. "This is so beautiful."

His arm sweeps across my back and holds me tightly. "It's only going to get better."

I laugh softly through my tears of happiness. "I believe you, love. If there's anyone that makes their promises come true, it's you."

He startles a gasp out of me when he sweeps me up and bounds up the stairs, taking them two at a time. I don't even have time to take in all the beautiful furniture he's used to bring our new home to life.

As we hit the third floor landing, he says, "You pick. Gigantic two person tub, or monster King-sized bed?"

"Both?" I offer on a giggle.

"Damn, woman, I knew I fell in love with the right person."

"Can I see?"

He carries me to the bathroom. Oh. My. God. "Is that tub even real?"

The giant gray porcelain tub is angled across a gorgeous room. The floor is natural stone. Warm, rich, golden wood glows in the morning light. There are tons of plants and even a vase of fresh flowers. I've never been inside a spa before, but this is what they have to look like.

I'm staring like a star-struck kid when he says, "The door rolls up. So when we act like wild animals in here...," he laughs hotly. "We can enjoy the great outdoors at the same time."

I've gotten used to blushing with Dozer, so I'm mostly unaffected. My face at least. But all the right places heat up as I think about acting like a wild thing with him. There's a throbbing heat that's forming between my legs and in my lower tummy right now.

"Honey, we need to hurry."

He pivots so fast my head spins. "We'll come back to that. After I claim my fiancée in *our* bed."

He tosses me on the bed. I bounce, and he pounces.

"Oh my god. This bedroom."

He's already peeling off my clothes. Then his. "Nice, huh? Perfect place for this..."

I squeal when he drops his very hot, very thrilling mouth onto my aching pussy.

Fisting the sheets, I look down. At him. He's a man on a mission. I'm the target. My favorite place to be.

Then I look up at the towering bed posts. Then at the beautiful artwork above the bed—a photo of wild horses running across the Montana landscape.

The pounding of their hooves matches my heartbeat.

There's no way I'm closing my eyes. No way I'm missing a single beautiful thing about the life—the love—that is all around me now.

My orgasm comes in a slow wave, with Dozer's amazing tongue swirling inside of me, his thumb circling over my clit. His other hand holding me tight, pressing flat over my womb. The energy sweeps me up, wrapping me in the brightest, warmest light ever.

Dozer climbs up my body, settling his beautiful weight onto me. Heating me with his radiant energy. "Look at me, sweetheart."

I brush my fingertips along his jaw. "I see you."

He holds my gaze. So much shows in his eyes now. Like he's truly open to me. "I love you more than life."

My voice turns to tatters as I reply, "You are my life."

He makes a throaty sound and drops his mouth to mine, sealing us together as he pushes his stiff cock between my soaking folds.

We kiss hungrily until we need air.

"Together. Nothing comes between us. Ever," he promises.

I hold him the tightest I've held him as his slow, determined pace builds and builds. His eyes stay locked on mine.

"Fuck, sweetheart," he grinds out. "I'm losing my control."

"Let go. I'm ready."

I knew he wasn't talking about his release. Dozer was

talking about the raw thing that's inside of him that needs to crash into me and burn me to the ground. He's been gentle. He's been playful. He's been incredible, but I knew he was holding back.

"You're sure, sweetheart?" he demands as he fists my hair.

I urge him by tightening my thighs around his hips. "More than sure."

His mouth goes to my neck. The bite he gives me is raw, bordering on wild, and drives me instantly into a frenzy.

Then he really starts to fuck me. Hard. Growling. He brutally drives into me, hitting the bottom of my pussy with every stroke.

I love it. Every hard thrust.

I'm so lost in pleasure, all I can do is cling to his arms as I hurtle toward something giant and unknown.

He tugs my head back, exposing my neck further, arching my breasts into the air. His other hand roughly shifts my leg until it's hooked over his arm.

Yes. God.

Yes.

This.

I feel more alive than ever before.

"Mine," he roars as his body pounds against me. "Mine. Fucking mine, McKenzie. I'm never letting you go. Now come for me. I wanna hear you scream my name."

I'm so close.

"Now," he demands, hotly, as his hand moves to my breast. A hot bolt of pleasure lights up my body when he rolls my nipple between his thumb and finger. Hard, but not brutal.

But he never stops driving into me. Dragging his thick head against that place.

Oh. "Yes. I'm—

Rockets explode inside of me.

My body jolts as my voice echoes off of the high ceiling. A screamed chant of "Justin. *Justin!* Justin," comes from somewhere deep inside of me until my voice shatters. Twisting until my love's name becomes one long keening sound that mingles with his roared release.

His body's shaking above me. I'm breathing like I'm sprinting. His smile says it all. God. I'm so in love with this man.

Claimed. Marked. His.

He lowers himself onto me, kisses all over my face. My neck. Murmurs his love in dark, hot whispers.

I get to have this. How I came from where I was to this is a miracle.

Thank you, I whisper to the Universe. Everything was worth it. To have this.

I don't know how much later it is when he carries me to the giant tub and lowers me into the water he's drawn. The massive door is open now, and a light mountain breeze is stirring the steam coming from the water.

We haven't spoken since our earth-shattering orgasms, but there's really no need. We both know. This is it.

Pure. Beautiful love.

He eases me into the water, holding my hand, and slides in behind me. Twisting my hair into a rope, he gently lays it over my shoulder and over his so we can nest together, my back to his chest

"I've been dreaming about this," he murmurs in a lazy voice.

"I've been dreaming about a lot of things." I say as my eyes trace the mountains. "I want to have your babies."

Justin knows I started birth control, so we didn't need

condoms anymore. But I didn't expressly say what my plans were for the future. We've been taking it one day at a time. Haven't even set a date for our wedding yet.

He chuckles softly. "That's not what I expected you to say, but yeah, I've been dreaming about that too. I'd love to build a family here with you."

"Not right now," I add as I trace my fingers over his calf, enjoying the soft scratchiness of his leg hair. "I want to enjoy us first, for a while."

His arms slide around me, pulling me tighter as he presses a kiss to my cheek. "Me too. There are a lot of things I want to do with you."

My grin is instant. "In the bedroom?"

"On the kitchen table. The couch. In the bed of my truck."

"That's quite a list."

"That's nothing, sweetheart."

I'm so happy that my heart feels fuzzy and warm. "When can we get started?"

"I'm ready if you are."

"What happens if we get water on the floor?"

"I had the construction crew put in a drain. Nothing to worry your pretty little head about."

When I turn and climb onto his lap, settling over his already thick cock, he's smiling. "Good. Because I have a feeling this is gonna get beautifully messy."

As he leans up with pleasure softening his gorgeous features, he kisses me and murmurs, "Just like life should be."

+++

Thank you so much for reading Dangerous Secrets. That's the end of the 8 book series.... for now.

Ready to read another off-limits work romance with a

protective military hero? Grab your copy today of Saving Sophia today. There's a sizzling sneak peek on the next page!

P.S. rumor is that Beckett and Madeline are up to something. (Join my newsletter and follow me on Amazon to be notified).

Hot Preview- Saving Sophia

Sophia watches me—her pale blue eyes full of curiosity.

Insanity must be setting in because I set the glass aside and reach for the end of her chestnut brown braid. With a tug, I draw her toward me. When she's close enough for me to feel the warmth coming off her pink cheeks, I pull the elastic band free. Then I start to unwind the braid. With my other hand I do the same to the right braid.

"You should let down your hair more often."

The glow from the Cupid light fixture brightens eyes. Or maybe it's something she sees in me...

"Should I now?"

I nod.

When her hair lays in wavy strands around her shoulders, a hungry groan vibrates my chest. My voice is hoarse. "Beautiful, Sophia." I slide my right hand below the heavy fall of her hair and clasp her head in my palm. When I pull her toward me, she comes easily.

The taste of lemonade is bright on her when I take her mouth. She rises up on tip toes and meets me. Her hand fists the front of my scrub shirt, scraping the skin below.

I'm dying and flying all at once.

I want to eat her alive and breathe her into my every cell.

The kiss is far too hard for politeness.

Fuck being easy. I want her too bad.

When a purr of pleasure vibrates her throat, I know she's just as screwed as me.

Sophia melts against me and my hormones peak at maximum output. All systems are go.

This woman is going to be my ruin.

When I pull back, her lips are swollen from my assault and her cheeks are so flushed they rival Cupid's "I thought about kissing you all night."

The pulse flutters at her throat as she blinks those long lashes at me and lets out a shuddering breath. "You and me both."

I trace a finger over her perfect, smooth cheek. "I pride myself on being a logical person. But nothing about this is rational."

A slow smile turns up her lips. "Not everything in life is logical or rational. Or sane."

I growl and look away from her luminous eyes. When I speak my voice is hard as asphalt and just as dark. "This can't be anything serious."

She whispers, "I know."

"This—"

She yanks my shirt, pulling me flush against her chest. "Oh, shut up, Liam. Just kiss me."

I can't say a word because this time she's stealing my breath.

And the leash that was holding back the ravenous wolf in me snaps.

If I thought I was aroused before, I had no idea what it

could be like to want her.

When I devour her mouth, she rakes her fingers through my hair and I shudder, pushing my hips against her. Every fucking nerve ending in my body lights on fire.

Blood throbs hot and dangerous into my cock. All signals from my neck down are saying go, go, go.

But my brain is trying to put the brakes on.

Until...

Until she climbs me like a damned tree.

I'm growling and laughing as I stumble back against the counter. I clasp her thigh in my big hand as she settles herself against the raging erection that's barely contained by my briefs and scrub pants.

Any doubt I had in my mind about what's about to happen just went up in smoke. She's on the crazy train right along with me.

I whip her around and press her against the counter, tipping her back as I grind into the hot vee of her legs. Fucking delicious. Like a slice of heaven opening up for me.

"Liam," she breathes when we break for a desperate gasp of air.

Our mouths crash back together as she undresses me and I strip her. Our black scrubs fly in all directions.

My fingers find her hot, hot center but just graze it with a tease. Her small fingers clench into my shoulders as I slick my hand over her. I want to touch her everywhere. She shudders as I skim my hands down her body, feeling her curves mold to my hands.

Then I touch her where I've been dying to touch her. Her wet folds are so hot—so soft and delicate that my fingers shake against her.

I have to taste her. Now.

Right fucking now.

Shoving her thighs apart, I drop to my knees in front of her, my hand presses right between her naked breasts, holding her in place on the kitchen counter as I launch myself at her clit.

"Oh god! Liam!"

Her beautiful, slippery pussy tastes like honey. Pure aphrodisiac. I growl against her and swipe my tongue all over her sweet, sweet center.

Sophia shivers, and writhes her legs against me, and moans. I nip and suck her clit, and clasp her thigh hard with my fingers. Her hands wrap around my face, my ears, twine in my hair desperately.

And the more she moves against me, the more I work my tongue over her sweet center.

A keening cry comes out of her. Her skin grows hot beneath my hands. I reach for one nipple, then the other, rolling the tight buds between my fingers. Her body bucks when I tug hard on one of them.

"You're wrecking me," she gasps.

"Not yet, Beautiful, that's still to come." I pull back for a second and drive two fingers into her, seeking her g-spot as I watch the untethered need in her eyes.

I lean close to her clit, turn my eyes to hers, and whisper, "Come undone for me, Sophia."

She groans as I latch onto her most sensitive bundle of nerves.

"I, I'm... Liam!"

With demanding curls of my fingers, I drive her closer to exploding. Her body flames like wildfire against me. Her hot center pulses and grows wetter.

When the first wave of her release hits, I don't stop. I keep driving my fingers into her lush, wet folds. Hitting the perfect spot to make her lose her mind.

Her legs squirm around me. I growl against her and lap at her wetness. She's not done. I know that she's about to explode. The calm before the storm.

Then she goes perfectly still.

"That's it, relax into it."

"Oh... *Ah... I'm gonna...*"

I rise and claim her mouth with mine again. Mixing all the delicious flavors of her together. She gasps and arches against me as my fingers move over that special place. "Let go, Sophia."

"*Yes, yes...*"

Then she screams and her pussy floods my hand with beautiful juices.

God. Help. Me. This unexpected woman is going to be my undoing. Her hair is tumbled around her face, her lashes dark around her shimmering blue eyes awash in pleasure.

Sophia laughs a low laugh and whimpers as she buries her face in my neck.

The thin illusion of control that I have evaporates. I have to be inside of her right now. "You're on the pill. Please tell me you're on the pill or have an implant. Are you okay if I don't use a condom?"

I asked without thinking about my non-existent sperm count. Another dirty remnant of being exposed to BRX713.

But Sophia nods yes. Her voice is so broken I can't even hear her low words. And I shove the thoughts of the toxin out of my head.

I'm alive. And I'm right fucking here.

I grab her hips and press the head of my tree-trunk size erection against her tight entrance.

The urge to drive hilt deep is so strong I have to check myself.

She's small. And so fucking tight. I might tear her wide open.

I close my eyes and tip my head back.

Slow down, Liam. Get a fucking grip on yourself. When I open my lids, Cupid is above me, on the ceiling, staring down with a knowing grin on his face.

Then I start laughing at the insanity of the moment—a deep belly laugh. I grab Sophia up in my arms. "I can't do this with Cupid watching."

Her light laugh tickles against my neck. "I don't care who's watching. Can you make that happen again?"

I toss her onto the big four-poster bed and crawl right the hell up on top of her. "That's nothing, babe."

She adjusts herself beneath me. "If that's nothing, Liam, I'm worried. I almost vaporized in there."

My mouth traces over her neck, my tongue sliding along the long, sexy line of her pulse. I nip at her ear. "Don't worry, I won't let you fly away."

Keep reading Saving Sophia by clicking here. Available on Amazon and FREE with Kindle Unlimited.

Also By Jenna Gunn

The Jenna Gunn Romance Library

Jenna Gunn's books can be found under her name and the pen name Maris Night. Below is a partial list of her books.

Agile Security & Rescue Series
Forgotten Soldier - Cole & Sierra's Story
Dr. Trouble - Scotch & Simona's Story
Off-Limits Protector- Andre & Willow's Story
Forbidden Knight- Wolf & Kate's Story
Clash Landing- Mako & Erika's Story
Lost & Found- Mikail & Gina's Story
Guarding Secrets- Marshall & Danee's Story
Dangerous Secrets- Dozer & Candy's Story

Want a free book?

Guarded by the SEAL- is FREE when you join my newsletter and features the origin story for Agile Security & Rescue.

The Eden Mountain Firefighters Series

<u>Saving Sophia</u> - Liam and Sophia's story
<u>Saving Skye</u> - Larson and Skye's story-
<u>Saving Summer</u> - Carter and Summer's story
<u>Saving Savannah</u> - Caleb & Savannah's story
<u>Saving Valentine's Day</u>- A Novella- Mr. & Mrs. Strong's story

Jenna Gunn Standalone Books
Rocked- Gage, Julian & Winter's story
Dangerous Promise- Kieran & Carra's story

Archer Brother's Series
(Now Under Maris Night Pen Name)
<u>Boss Rules</u>- Bryce and Raven's Story
<u>Faux-Ever Rules</u>- Christian and Maddy's Story
<u>Broken Rules</u>- Brandon and Anya's Story
<u>Do-Over Rules</u>- Bishop and Mia's Story
<u>Friend Rules</u>- Tyson and Abby's Story

Jenna (As Maris Night) Standalone Books

That One Kiss- Brock & Avery's story

Get updates on Jenna Gunn's new releases, book sales, and free books.
Join her newsletter <u>HERE</u>
Jenna's Facebook Group <u>HERE</u>
<u>www.jennagunn.com</u>

Printed in Great Britain
by Amazon

56851386R00215